T0152495

THE DEMON EQUILIBRIUM

CATHY PEGAU

Bywater
BOOKS

Ann Arbor
2021

Bywater Books

Copyright © 2021 Cathy Pegau

All rights reserved. No part of this book may be reproduced, stored in a retrieval system, or transmitted in any form or by any means, without prior permission in writing from the publisher.

ISBN: 978-1-61294-217-9

Bywater Books First Edition: November 2021

Printed in the United States of America on acid-free paper.

Cover designer: Ann McMan, TreeHouse Studio

Bywater Books PO Box 3671
Ann Arbor MI 48106-3671

www.bywaterbooks.com

This is a work of fiction. Names, characters, places, and incidents are the product of the author's imagination, or, in the case of historical persons, are used fictitiously.

With love to S, R, & C.

Always.

catalyst • noun

cat·a·lyst | \ ˈka-tə-ləst \

Definition of *catalyst*

One who provokes significant change or action;
the spark that ignites a blaze.

CHAPTER ONE

Harrington, WY, October 1903

Wide-brimmed hat pulled down to shadow her face, Grace Carter avoided a steaming pile of manure in the middle of the dirt street as she crossed from the Harrington livery stable to the wooden walk fronting stores and establishments. The hardened-mud wheel ruts were from wagons and carriages, not motorcars; she hadn't seen one of those since she'd been in Denver the week before. Ever since she'd left New York, it felt as if years of innovation dropped away for every hundred miles she'd traveled west.

If only it was several years ago, she mused. Things had been a helluva lot easier then. At least she'd thought so at the time.

Now was not the time to be distracted from what had brought her to Wyoming, of all places.

Stopping to flick muck off her trousers and adjust the saddlebags over her shoulder, Grace surreptitiously glanced up and down the street. Was anyone watching her, too interested in her arrival? It was hard to hide newcomers in such a small town. Hard to hide demon activity too, so they should be easier to spot, which was to her advantage.

No one seemed to be paying her much mind. Just folks going about their business. But like demons, the Order of Saint Teresa was also pretty damn good at concealment. She couldn't let her guard down.

Her gaze fixed on the freshly painted Amberly Hotel sign hanging in front of a building separated from its neighbors by narrow alleys on either side.

She's just ahead.

Her pace quickened, the staccato of her boot heels sounding along the walkway.

Impetuous! Impatient! Impudent! Sister Thomasina's description of her rang in her head.

Grace hesitated. Maybe she should slow down, be more cautious.

Impossible. Not if she was this close.

Her heart pattered hard against her sternum as she hurried toward the sign like it was a beacon against the darkest night. If her information was correct, then a nearly yearlong search was about to come to a happy end. Even the pungent bite of horse shit in the autumn air couldn't dampen her mood.

The weary voice in the back of her head did: *What if it's like the last time?*

Grace's step faltered, her hand seeking support against the nearest wall as the patter in her chest became a painful twinge. Her fingers curled into a fist, catching the faded, loose edge of a poster announcing last spring's western tour by President Roosevelt.

Jaws clenched, she took a slow, calming breath. No, this couldn't be like last time, when her contact seemed sure but had been wrong. Disappointment had crashed through Grace, leaving her wrecked. Two days of hard drinking became two weeks of misery, until she'd been contacted by Mrs. Wallace.

And if Mrs. Wallace was wrong? Grace had nowhere else to turn. She would keep trying, some way and somehow, because she'd spend every day until her last seeking her catalyst.

Steady on her feet once again, she shifted her full saddlebags to a more comfortable position and moved forward, focused on the sign. Absentmindedly, Grace tipped her hat to a pair of passing ladies. Some folks were startled to see a woman wearing men's clothing, but Maggie was used to her inclinations, and all that mattered now was Maggie.

She has to be here.

It had been nine months since Grace had woken from a fevered sleep, reaching out to find nothing but sweat-damp sheets. Sister Thomasina had shushed her when she asked about Maggie. Then a man, whose features she couldn't focus upon, had brushed his hand over her face, the calluses of his fingertips rough on her eyelids as Grace fell into dreamless slumber.

When she awoke again, disoriented, aching, and nauseous, something told her not to mention Maggie. Sister Thomasina seemed to be waiting for her to do so, anticipation in her hard gray eyes, but Grace's body prickled with a nameless fear. They hadn't wanted her to talk about Maggie. They hadn't wanted her to remember Maggie at all.

But she did.

In a fog of illness, Grace had escaped the house, later finding herself in a train station in northern Long Island, New York. How she'd arrived there, she couldn't say, but at least she was away from Saint Teresa's. It was no longer a place she could trust. Maybe it never had been.

With no idea of where the Order of Saint Teresa's might have hidden Maggie, Grace went in search of her catalyst, the one person in the world who could help her control and amplify her magic. The one person in the world who truly knew her. Without Maggie, Grace was as lost as a rudderless ship in a storm.

Now here she stood, before the solid door of the Amberly, wood and pale green paint the only things between her and the most important person in her life. She hoped.

Grace let the saddlebags drop to the walk, catching the worn leather between them as they thudded at her feet, catching her breath. She wiped her other hand on the stained canvas of her trousers. Sweat trickled between her breasts despite the cool October day. Her racing heart thrummed in her ears.

Please be here. Please, oh, please, oh please.

She turned the latch and went in. The lobby of the Amberly reminded her of the parlor at the Order's house on Long Island, with its striped upholstery on the padded benches and lace doilies under vases of wildflowers on the tables. Dappled light through filmy curtains warmed the linseed oil-scented room. The aroma of baking bread wafted from the back of the hotel, another reminder of the house back East. She half expected to hear Nan's off-key singing accompanied by clanging pots.

"Good afternoon. May I help you?"

The voice to her right sent a familiar thrill through her. Grace immediately recognized it as Maggie's, the lightness and sweetness of her Irish lilt unmistakable.

She's here. She's really here!

Grace turned, her smile growing and her body tingling as she set eyes on one of the few people who'd been able to see past all the flaws and accept Grace for who she was. Because she was from the same mold herself.

Maggie stood behind a carved mahogany desk, her dark auburn hair pinned up in a bun rather than in the braid or tail she'd sometimes sport, though Grace liked it best when loose about her shoulders. A few tendrils curled around her ears and at the nape of her neck, framing her oval face. Her bright, coffee-brown eyes fixed on Grace, mouth turned up in a slight smile. Her blue floral print dress flared out over voluptuous hips, with long sleeves and a high collar that covered all but her face and hands.

Not the fashionable frock she normally would have worn, or the functional riding skirt and blouse she'd often donned for their hunting sessions, but Maggie could have been wearing a flour sack for all Grace cared.

Grace pushed the door closed, letting the saddlebags drop to the polished hardwood, and swept the hat off her head. "It's me, Mags. I look a sight, I know." Her voice tangled around the emotions that filled her—joy, relief, love—and the rest of her words came out in a rough whisper. "I can't believe I've found you."

Maggie tilted her head, and the smile turned bemused. "I'm sorry. Do I know you?"

4

CHAPTER TWO

Freetown, Long Island, NY, October 1897

Silvered steel whistled past Grace's right ear. Loose hair flipped across her eyes as she ducked to the left. She pivoted on her left foot and brought her weapon around in a low arc. She was quick, but Rémy Le Forte was quicker this time. He blocked her blade before it came anywhere near his unprotected side.

The clang of metal echoed across the brick courtyard. Grace's arm vibrated to the shoulder, and she almost dropped her sword. She danced away to avoid his riposte. Her chest heaved while they sized each other up. The dull sparring edge wouldn't have cut him if she had hit, but it would have hurt. This was a training session, after all, not a blood match. Nonetheless, Grace had plenty of bruises along her sides and thighs to attest to the teaching tool's effectiveness.

"Good," the weapons master grunted. Sweat beaded on his bald head and ran into his muttonchops. The armpits of his muslin shirt were stained with moisture. It had been a long hour, but he showed no sign of the lesson being over.

Grace was similarly disheveled, her shirt half hanging out of her trousers where Rémy had mixed a grappling move with the swordplay. She'd been lucky to get away with only a torn shirttail and a bruised knee when she fell to the ground to escape his hold.

She shoved a handful of damp hair out of her eyes. "Can

we stop now?"

Rémy grinned, but he breathed heavily as well. "Getting tired, *mon minou?*"

Kitten.

Grace's lip curled. Rémy had started calling her that when she was a child. It bothered her, and he knew it. He was baiting her into making a stupid move.

Tired and frustrated, she inhaled a slow breath. Deep in her chest, the flicker of ever-present power flared. She licked her dry lips, tasting salt.

"Ah," Rémy said sharply. "No magic. You know how Sister Thomasina feels."

With effort, Grace forced the magic inside her to subside. A source had the ability to use her power on her own, to a certain degree, but it wasn't a good idea. In Sister Thomasina's opinion, never a good idea for Grace. A potential for disaster was how the prioress had once phrased it.

"You're bigger and stronger than I am," Grace said.

"You are smaller and faster." He held up his bruised left arm. Had her blade been sharp enough, he would have lost his hand just above the wrist. "You have some advantage."

They circled each other as they spoke. Grace knew he was planning another attack. The question was when.

"Why are we training with these anyway? We have magic and silvered bullets for our pistols. No one carries around swords. It's a little obvious."

"*Bof,*" Rémy said, shrugging. "Tradition. Besides, what if you run out of ammunition for your pistol, or you're too exhausted to access your power?" He made an exaggerated expression of concern, thick eyebrows raised. "What then? Maybe you would argue the creature to death, *ma puce?*"

Puce? She searched her limited French vocabulary. Flea.

Grace laughed. She could be as annoying as a flea, especially when lessons went long.

"You are good with the knife." He nodded toward her right leg, where she kept the bone-handled blade he'd given her on her sixteenth birthday in a boot sheath. "But it's best to have a full repertoire of skills."

Cool autumn air chilled the sweat on her skin. Grace expected Rémy to strike while he spoke, catching her off guard. He didn't. The extended pause attested to his weariness. She should exploit his fatigue.

Voices from her right caught her ear. An impossibly warm breeze carried the scent of lilac into the courtyard. She stopped and turned. A barrier of trimmed, fading bushes blocked her view of the path to the house, though there was movement beyond the branches. Who was coming? How could there be such a breeze in mid-October?

Two women came around the hedge. First was Sister Thomasina, prioress of the Order of Saint Teresa, hands clasped before her, gray habit fluttering at her feet.

But it was the other who captured Grace's attention. Sight and sound fixed on that singular figure, Grace found it impossible to move, to breathe. Pale purple edged her vision.

Dressed in a pleated white shirtwaist with a lavender bow at the throat and a long beige skirt, the young woman was a head shorter and curvier than the rangy sister. Her shawl had slipped off her shoulders, secured only by her crossed arms. A few deep red curls escaped the pins that confined her hair at the back of her head.

Across the courtyard, their gazes met and held. The woman pressed a hand to her breast.

A shimmer of heat tickled Grace's skin. The lilac scent increased. Was the intoxicating aroma coming from her? Who was she?

Movement on her left broke through the thrall. Instinct spurred action. Unbidden, magic surged in her chest and flowed through her limbs like a river cresting its banks. Grace made a blocking gesture with her left arm. Her hand slammed into Rémy's descending blade, knocking it away. She straightened her arm and flicked him aside like a gnat.

"Shit!" He flew toward the far hedges.

7

Pain replaced the prickling in her hands as her magic subsided. Her pinky stuck out at an odd angle, and blood ran from a ragged gash along the side of her palm. The swords were dull, but she'd hit the edge of Rémy's weapon hard.

"I said no magic." Rémy leapt to his feet, his face and head a startling shade of red. Hurrying over, he grabbed her wrist, sending a wave of fire along her arm, and dropped his sword, defying his own rules on weapon care. "Why did you do that?"

"I-I didn't mean to," she said, controlling her breathing to mitigate the pain.

Grace raised her head, sparing a glance at the newcomer. Her power sparked. She forced it down, deep within herself so it wouldn't ignite unexpectedly again; that much she could accomplish without a catalyst. Most of the time. The lilac scent diminished, but didn't disappear.

Thomasina's brow furrowed beneath her white wimple, gray eyes narrowed with agitation.

Rémy muttered concern in French too fast for Grace to follow. He pressed a handkerchief to her hand. Grace hissed as pain flared through her palm. "We need to tend to this. Come."

He led her toward the two women, holding Grace's hand up to slow the blood flow. The stranger was about Grace's age, somewhere in her early twenties, but held herself with confidence and maturity. Something Grace lacked, according to Thomasina, particularly the maturity.

"What happened?" Thomasina's outward calm didn't fool her.

Rémy remained silent. Should he try to reply, the sister would only make things worse for Grace. She was old enough to fend for herself, even against the temper of Sister Thomasina. It was up to her to explain. Only she couldn't.

"It was an accident," she said weakly.

"There can be no room for accidents when it comes to power." Thomasina's Glaswegian accent was thicker than usual, a sign she was angry but not furious. When she was furious, Thomasina was damn near incomprehensible. Perhaps she was restraining herself in front of the stranger. She glanced at Grace's bloody hand. "After you get that bandaged, you will spend an hour in the armory cleaning weapons."

Grace's jaw dropped open. "An hour? It was an accident. I didn't mean to—"

Thomasina's eyes darkened. "Would you care to make it two hours?"

Cheeks afire, Grace couldn't bring herself to look directly at the redhead.

Poor control was bad enough, but being treated like a novice in front of a visitor was uncalled for. Though until she was bonded, that was exactly how Grace would be treated by the prioress. Worse, like a child who required strict discipline and punishment. Why was Thomasina always so damn hard on her?

Fuming, Grace continued toward the French doors of the sitting room. She reached for the lever with her right hand and almost sent the blade through the glass panel. Wouldn't that be a fine topper for the afternoon?

Rémy opened the door. "To the kitchen. Mrs. Reynolds has bandages and iodine."

They quickly crossed the sitting room. Grace hoped she didn't drip blood onto the Persian carpet. God knew what punishment Thomasina would mete out then. They hurried down a short hall to the kitchen. The aroma of baking bread and cooking meat met them, and Grace's stomach rumbled. She had eaten little at lunch.

The white tiles of the kitchen gleamed in the late afternoon sun. Mrs. Reynolds and Nan, the cook, chatted at the stove. Mrs. Reynolds, tall and slender in a deep-plum day dress, her black hair in a chignon and smooth brown skin belying her years, turned as Grace and Rémy came in.

Questions lit her dark eyes until they found Grace's hand. "Oh, good Lord. Bring her to the sink."

Nan glanced over her shoulder and shook her head as she continued to stir. Little at Saint Teresa's disturbed Nan unless it affected her food or the meal schedule.

Rémy led Grace to the deep enameled sink. He unwrapped the bloody handkerchief while Mrs. Reynolds ran water.

"Put that thing down, Grace," the older woman said.

Grace bent awkwardly, holding her hand under the water, to lay the sword on the floor with minimal clanging.

Mrs. Reynolds passed Rémy a dish towel from the folded pile under the sink. "Keep pressure on it. I'll get the kit."

Rémy gave her an apologetic look, then gently pressed the towel down on the wound. Pain bloomed in Grace's hand. Tears prickled her eyes.

"Sorry, *minou*. Do you need to sit?"

The endearment was just that, not the teasing tone he'd taken earlier. Maybe the wound was worse than she'd feared. But it wasn't the injury that made Grace feel faint.

"No, I can stand. It's not that bad." A small lie. She moistened dry lips. "Who was that with Thomasina?"

Rémy shrugged. "The new catalyst, I suspect. For Virginia."

Virginia Delacroix, another source at Saint Teresa's. Grace barely remembered Thomasina mentioning that a new catalyst was on the way. After three previous attempts at matching her with a partner, she hardly paid attention when one was brought in.

But there was something about the woman in the courtyard, something she'd never felt before. It wasn't just her physical beauty. There was something about *her*.

"Sister Thomasina believes she and Virginia will form a strong bond," Rémy said. "They're well matched on paper, so now we must see if they can work together effectively."

She knew how the process was *supposed* to work; it just hadn't happened for her.

Mrs. Reynolds returned with the medical kit and held a needle out to Nan. "Sterilize this with the flame from the stove, please."

Grace's stomach twisted. "I don't think I need stitches."

Mrs. Reynolds ignored her. She spoke to Rémy. "Has it stopped bleeding yet?"

He peeked under the towel, which, to Grace's shock, was

more red than white. "*Non.*"

Damn.

"Get the bottle from the cupboard over there." Mrs. Reynolds indicated a row of cabinets across the kitchen. "And a glass."

Rémy let go of Grace's hand and patted her shoulder before he did as he was told. Only Thomasina ever argued with Mrs. Reynolds, upon the rarest of occasions.

Mrs. Reynolds held the towel to Grace's hand, mindless of the blood seeping through the cloth. "A dram or two of whiskey first, to relax you. Rémy, bring a chair too, please."

He returned with a brown bottle and a squat glass, set them on the counter, then dragged a kitchen chair from the butcher's table against the wall. Her hand still over the sink, Grace lowered herself. Maybe sitting was a good idea after all.

"Here." Mrs. Reynolds filled the glass a quarter of the way with amber liquid. "Drink it fast."

Grace complied, shaking her head at the burn scorching her throat and sinuses. She wasn't much of a whiskey drinker; beer was cheaper at the Black Briar pub.

"Another." A second dose was offered.

"Mrs. Reynolds—"

"Drink."

Grace drank. She handed the glass back to Rémy, then rested her forehead on her arm.

"Give it a few minutes. We need to set the finger back in place. Then we'll see if we need to stitch you up." Mrs. Reynolds's voice held no alarm. She was used to residents of Saint Teresa's being battered and bruised.

Grace steadied her breathing. She wasn't usually this undone by the sight of blood, even her own.

Mrs. Reynolds gently maneuvered her pinky in an attempt to set the bone. Pain and nausea lanced through Grace. Cold sweat broke out on her face and chilled her body. She bit down on her right forearm, grunting, refusing to scream.

"Oh, goodness," Mrs. Reynolds said softly. "Well, child, this may hurt a bit."

Another shot of whiskey and thinking about the woman in the courtyard didn't help as much as she'd hoped.

CHAPTER THREE

Harrington, WY, October 1903

Grace stared at Maggie for a few heartbeats, unable to breathe, as if the air had been sucked out of the room. She let out an uneasy bark of a laugh to get her lungs to function, to smother the sob that tried to escape. "That's not funny, Mags."

Maggie had always been a tease. Sharp and deadly accurate with her gibes, but not with Grace. Never with Grace.

She should have been just as anxious about their separation. How could she be joking? Why wasn't she more excited?

Confusion lined Maggie's brow. "I'm not trying to be funny, miss."

Miss.

She wasn't teasing. She had no idea who Grace was.

The elation of finding Maggie after months of continuous travel and clandestine meetings, of disappointment, of constantly looking over her shoulder for Thomasina or the Order or worse, became a thousand-pound weight in Grace's chest that threatened to buckle her knees. Hot tears welled in her eyes as anger undermined joy.

Sister Thomasina and the man from Saint Teresa's. This was all their fault.

"Oh, God, Mags. What did they do to you?"

Frowning, Maggie came around the front of the heavy desk.

"What did who do to me? What are you talking about?" She stopped a few paces from Grace. "Are you all right?"

Grace closed her eyes. No, not even close to all right. The Order had tried to erase Maggie from her mind, but whatever magic they'd attempted hadn't been fully effective. She was hoping Maggie had managed to put up the same resistance.

But she hadn't. Or couldn't.

She doesn't remember.

Grace took a deep breath and slowly released it as she opened her eyes. Maggie stood in the same spot, hands wringing together with nervousness or fear. Grace stifled an exhausted, near-hysterical laugh. Her Maggie had never been nervous or afraid of anything. But this wasn't *her* Maggie. Not at the moment anyway. Surely there was a way to bring her back.

"I'm fine," Grace said. She offered a tight smile. "I must be mistaken. I bet your name isn't even Maggie."

She seemed more at ease now that Grace wasn't falling apart in front of her. "Actually, it is, but it's a common enough name."

Grace swallowed hard. "I reckon it is."

"Do you need a room?" Maggie gestured toward the wooden staircase just beyond the desk. "We have a vacancy and offer clean linens as well as a full bath and meals. Just a dollar a night, fifty cents without the bath and food."

The routine expressions, the cheerful yet indifferent tone, sounded foreign coming from Maggie's mouth. Grace could only nod as she opened the money pouch hanging around her neck and handed over one of her last dollar coins and a few others to cover the fee. What was left jingled pitifully when she replaced the pouch beneath her shirt.

"The room and all that would be nice."

"Lovely," Maggie said. "Please sign the register if you would." She turned with a swoosh of her skirts and led Grace to the desk. She held out a plain black fountain pen. "Your name or mark will do."

Grace took the pen and hesitated, the nib hovering over the half-filled, lined page. Should she use her real name? No one

14

here in Harrington knew her, and no one in the Order knew she was here. Or they shouldn't know. Would it help Maggie to recognize her?

Grace scrawled her name on the line.

Maggie accepted the pen from her with a smile. She squinted down at the fresh ink on the ledger line before rocking the blotter over it. "Nice to meet you, Miss . . . um . . . Canton?"

"Carter. Grace Carter. Sister Thomasina always said my handwriting was atrocious." Grace waited for Maggie to recognize her name, or reference to the sister, but no. Her hopes sank again. "Grace is fine. A pleasure to meet you, too, Miss . . .?"

"Dalton." Maggie straightened and held out her right hand. Grace's rough palm skritched against Maggie's smoother one. Her hand itched, the sensation spreading as it bees danced up her arm. Maggie's eyes widened. She pulled away, clasping her hands together and rubbing her right palm with her left thumb. What had she felt? Maggie gave a nervous laugh of apology. "Shock from the carpet. And it's, um, Mrs. Dalton, actually."

Grace's hand convulsed into a fist, and she looked down. There, as Maggie collected the coins from the desk and locked them in a drawer—a gold ring on her left hand.

Married? *Married?*

She forced her gaze back to Maggie's face, away from the ring. "Mrs. Dalton, then."

Maggie pocketed the drawer key. "You don't seem one to stand on formalities, Grace. I like that. Please, do call me Maggie."

Grace resisted the urge to take her by the shoulders and shake her. *I've always called you Maggie. Or Mags. Don't you remember me? Damn them!*

Deep inside, her magic quivered. Grace took a moment to calm herself.

Maggie turned toward the numbered pigeonhole shelves behind the desk. "Let me get your key and I'll show you to your room." She slid a key out of box number four. "As I said, we have meal service and bathing facilities. You're the only guest at the moment, so if you have any preferences for breakfast just let me know. It'll be chicken tonight."

"I'm not particular."

Maggie smiled demurely as she passed Grace to lead the way to the stairs. Grace caught a whiff of her scent and couldn't help taking a deeper inhalation. Maggie. But not. There was the familiarity of lilac, but the underlying aroma of linseed oil and something spicy was new. Odd.

"My . . . um . . . husband will heat up some water for you if you'd like to freshen up before supper. We don't have running hot water yet, but it's coming one of these days."

Grace opened her eyes, having closed them as she deciphered the strange scent. Maggie stood at the foot of the stairs, one hand on the banister. Grace scooped up her saddlebags and hurried to follow. "A bath, yes. Thank you."

Maggie cocked her head, dark eyes narrowed as she watched Grace approach. Grace's breath caught. There. Lurking far beneath the surface, a spark of recognition? Maggie gave her head a small shake, jostling her curls, and climbed the stairs.

Damn it all. Grace kept her gaze lowered to her feet, avoiding the sway of the blue-covered hips before her.

"Here, to the right," Maggie said when they reached the second floor. "There are just the six rooms, but this one has the nicest view of town. Like I said, you're the only guest staying, but we usually have some others in for supper."

She unlocked the door with a painted number four on it and swung it open. "Supper won't be ready for a bit." She glanced at Grace's dusty bags. "Do you have clothes that need freshening?"

Grace almost laughed. What she wore was pretty much all she owned these days. There was another pair of trousers, a shirt, and a clean chemise in the saddlebags. Her kit was in it as well, far more important than clothing.

"This is it," she said. "I don't have anything else with me, I'm afraid."

Maggie appraised her dusty and stained clothes with a slight pursing of her full mouth and an arched eyebrow. As

16

her gaze traveled up and down Grace's body, Grace's face and neck warmed. Was she looking at the clothing, or at the woman beneath them?

"John likes to have guests dressed for dinner. I think I have something that'll fit. Might be a tad loose, seeing as you're a slender thing." Maggie quickly brought her eyes up to meet Grace's. Her fair cheeks flared to dark pink, but she didn't look away.

Grace moistened her chapped lips. "That would be a kindness. Thank you."

She hadn't agreed to the dress because she particularly cared to follow their rules, but refusing Maggie anything had rarely been within her capacity.

Maggie smiled, and the dimple in her left cheek deepened. Grace's knees wobbled. "I've got a lovely green dress that will bring out the color of your eyes. I'll fetch it and have John heat up some bathwater."

She started toward the stairs, then stopped and turned back. Still grinning, she pressed the room key into Grace's hand. The world tilted. Her magic stirred in the pit of her stomach like a bear awakening from hibernation. It had been many months, and the hungry beast was ready to emerge.

Don't you feel it? Why *don't you feel it?*

"Almost forgot to give you your key. Rest for a spell. It'll take time for the water." She gave Grace's hands a final squeeze and hurried downstairs.

Grace sagged against the door frame as her magic quieted. But it wasn't asleep. This close to her friend, her lover, her catalyst, it wouldn't sleep again.

CHAPTER FOUR

Freetown, Long Island, NY, October 1897

Sister Thomasina escorted Margaret into the sitting room from the courtyard. She held the French door open and Margaret crossed the threshold, her footsteps silenced by the carpet.

"Please, forgive that little episode, Miss Mulvaney." The sister gestured for her to take the chaise closest to the fireplace. She sat, and Thomasina tended the fire. "I'm afraid Grace is still rough around the edges."

Grace. Her name is Grace.

Margaret draped her shawl over the back of the chaise. As soon as she and Sister Thomasina had stepped around the hedge and she locked eyes with Grace, Margaret knew there was something about the girl.

Woman. Grace had to be about her own age. Sweat-stained and bleeding, her blond hair in disarray and her crystalline, sea-green eyes wide with pain, she'd taken Margaret's breath at their first glance. Grace possessed a spirit within her that Margaret had sensed immediately. She wanted to tend to Grace's injury, to comfort her.

You can't, scolded the voice in her head. *That's why you left Dublin. To get away from that very thing.*

What made her think there would be no women in the American facility who might tempt her as Clare had? No, she'd known the risks. Margaret just hadn't expected to be challenged so soon.

"Miss Mulvaney?"

Margaret jumped and pressed her hand against her racing heart. "I'm sorry, Sister. You were saying?"

Thomasina stared at her for a moment. Could she read Margaret's thoughts? The Doyenne in Dublin had hinted at that very thing, but whether it was to tease or to warn, Margaret couldn't be sure. The heat in her cheeks had nothing to do with the roaring blaze in the hearth, and almost everything to do with the woman elsewhere in the house.

The sister stood with her hand on the bell pull near the fireplace. "Would you care for some tea? Dinner will be at half-past seven."

It was just after four according to the mantel clock.

"Tea would be lovely, yes. Thank you." Margaret pushed aside thoughts she shouldn't be having.

"Virginia will return this evening." Thomasina swept her long gray habit under her and sat in the wingback chair on the other side of the low table. She smoothed the heavy material. "I'm anxious for the two of you to meet."

"As am I." Margaret folded her hands in her lap. "I understand she's a very powerful source."

Thomasina nodded. "One of our strongest."

Margaret tilted her head. "But not *the* strongest?"

Not that it mattered. Margaret wanted to make her bond and get on with her calling. It was the best way to put Clare and her past behind her. When she'd left Ireland, she had promised herself she'd perform her duties as a catalyst and take her vows. Nothing but the elimination of demons mattered to one who was gifted, and that required commitment, body and soul. No more and no less than absolute dedication to the Order.

The sister's gray eyes flicked toward the hall leading to the kitchen. Margaret had heard the faint commotion of Grace being tended to. She could have sworn she'd felt a twinge in her own hand. Out of sympathy, certainly.

"No," Thomasina said. The sister met her questioning gaze, but Margaret had the feeling she already knew the answer. "Grace is perhaps the strongest source I've ever encountered in all my years with Saint Teresa's, but she is undisciplined and loses control when her emotions get the better of her."

Margaret couldn't help but smile. "She sounds intriguing."

"Perhaps, but she's not ready to be bonded. Three catalysts have been introduced to her, but none have worked out. One poor young woman was—" She cut herself off, shaking her head, and forced a smile onto her thin lips. "It just didn't work out. I'm sure Grace will find her catalyst when she's ready."

A young woman in a simple black dress and white apron wheeled a cart into the room. She stopped near the table, curtsied, then set a silver tea set and a china plate of small sandwiches on the gleaming wood. She curtsied again and left.

Thomasina bowed her head. Margaret followed suit, hands clasped. The sister blessed the offerings on the table. "Amen."

"Amen." Margaret crossed herself.

The prioress didn't hesitate to play hostess. She handed Margaret a linen napkin that she dutifully opened on her lap. "Milk, Miss Mulvaney?"

"Please," she said. Good, strong, black tea with a touch of milk made everything a little more pleasant. The sister poured out and handed her the cup and saucer. "Tell me more about—" She'd almost said Grace. "About Virginia."

Thomasina began extolling the virtues of the young woman she was to meet, to possibly bond with, in a concerted effort to rid the world of the demon Horde that traveled from their dark realm and caused havoc among humans. It was a vital mission she and her fellow novitiates undertook, one that had saved countless lives in the Order's nine hundred-year history.

Throughout Margaret's girlhood, the Doyenne of the Dublin house had iterated how she and others like her had been touched by Saint Teresa, who claimed to have been visited by Mary Magdalene and entreated to perform her sacred duty, giving certain women extraordinary power. Individually, they were lights among the darkness, but when bonded as a source and catalyst pair, that power could be harnessed to eradicate the demons that walked the Earth. To find such a partner was to be blessed, further reason to dedicate your magic and your life to the cause.

At the moment, all Margaret could think about was the green of Grace Carter's eyes, and the triangle of skin at her throat exposed by the open collar of the man's shirt she'd worn. How a flush had risen to Grace's tanned cheeks. How her own breath had caught with urgency when Rémy lunged and Grace had swept him aside like a bothersome fly. Margaret's power had flared, sending a wave of fire along her limbs and beads of perspiration exploding on her scalp. As quickly as the heat had come, it receded, dissipated in the cool autumn air.

While Thomasina explained the testing procedure of the next several days, Margaret came to a startling realization. Virginia Delacroix would not be the one to bond with her. She would not be the source for Margaret's catalyst talent. That claim would belong to Grace Carter.

The thought of which thrilled Margaret as much as it scared the devil out of her.

CHAPTER FIVE

Harrington, WY, October 1903

Grace lay staring up at the smooth plaster ceiling, mentally wrestling with herself for the past half hour on how she could hint to Maggie about their lives together.

Someone knocked on the door. Grace sat up quickly. Maggie?

Watch what you say. Don't blurt anything out that'll scare her. Be friendly, but don't overdo it.

The knock sounded again. Louder, more impatient. Grace frowned as she rose. That wasn't Maggie. Had the Order finally tracked her down? Would they have knocked?

She reached for the bone-handled knife in her boot sheath and held it ready as she approached the door. "Yes?"

A low, incomprehensible voice rumbled from the other side of the solid wood, the word "water" barely discernible. John Dalton, most likely, telling her the bath was ready.

"Be right down," she said louder.

He knocked again, clearly not satisfied with her response.

Holding the four inches of silvered steel behind her, Grace turned the glass knob with her left hand. Her right tightened around the handle, the weapon fitting perfectly in her fist. There was no reason for her heart to be racing such as it was.

The latch clicked, and Grace cracked the door open. Dalton

stared at her, his black eyes intense beneath coal-colored eyebrows. Dark, slicked-back hair and scruff of beard accentuated his pale face. Narrow shoulders barely filled out his starched shirt and vest. Not the kind of man she would have expected the Order to employ to keep Maggie Mulvaney in check.

Grace took a breath to tell him she'd be right down. The same odd, spicy scent she'd detected on Maggie flooded her senses. Her entire being pulsed with the unquestionable knowledge that John Dalton was *wrong*.

Her magic roared, the surge of power threatening to boil over. Grace grappled for control, her skin feeling as if it was stretched too tight. Few things caused her magic to react like that, and Maggie wasn't near.

He sneered and kicked the door open, hitting Grace. She stumbled back into the room. Controlling the fall, she landed on her left shoulder, then rolled to her feet. Dalton rushed her. Grace swung the blade. He stopped short of having his guts laid open, arcing away like a snake. Lightning fast—faster than a normal man—he closed in on her. He wrapped his fingers around the wrist of her knife hand, squeezing as he twisted. His other hand latched onto her throat, cutting off her breath.

Spots danced before her eyes. Grace tried to tighten her hold on the knife, but it fell from her grip, the clatter on the wood floor lost in the roar in her head. She kneed Dalton in the groin. The snarl on his face immediately changed from contempt to pain. He slammed his forehead into hers, then dropped.

Grace staggered back, bright stars bursting across her vision. She hit the edge of the bed and slid to the floor.

Use your power!

The beast within her turned over, testing its restraints. *Yes!*

No. Without her catalyst, use of her magic after so long might prove disastrous.

Dalton crawled toward her. The spicy scent grew stronger.

Get the knife!

Grace lunged for the glint of silver at the edge of her vision, twisting as she reached out. She landed on her side, reaching toward the handle.

Dalton's weight pinned her legs. His fingers dug into her thighs, her hips, her sides as he crawled up her body.

She stretched further, crying out with frustrated effort. Her hand closed around the smooth bone. She swung blindly. Dalton rolled, taking her with him and throwing off her aim as he forced her onto her back. The tip of the blade sank into the wood floor. He straddled her hips, fingers digging into her arms. Sweat-lank hair hung in his face. The tip of his black tongue flicked over thin lips.

The transformation into his true shape began.

Demon! What the hell is a demon doing here?

Grace bucked, attempting to throw the creature off her. He wrapped his legs and feet around her legs, tight as a tick on a dog, and opened his mouth, exposing short, pointed teeth.

"No!" Panic shot through Grace's body, lending strength to her efforts. But not enough. The demon dodged her attempt to strike his head with hers. He sank his teeth into the juncture of her neck and left shoulder.

Burning pain paralyzed her body as her mind raced. His venom entered the wound. If she didn't get him off, get treated, she'd be dead within the hour.

"Jesus God, John! What are you doing?"

Maggie's shocked voice brought the creature's head up, Grace's blood smeared on its mouth. He hissed, the only vocalization he'd made since forcing his way in.

Dizzy, Grace turned her head toward the doorway. "Run, Maggie!"

Maggie clutched a green dress to her chest, eyes wide as she stared at the thing she knew as her husband. The demon gained its feet and started toward her. She backed away a step, her gaze flicking to Grace, then to the creature again. Why wouldn't she run?

Fear for Maggie gave her strength.

Grace yanked the knife out of the floorboard and heaved herself forward. Venom numbed her left arm, weakening her.

24

She plunged the blade into the creature's calf. It howled and turned as it collapsed, slashing with clawed hands. Its nose had flattened and its eyes blazed purple where there was once white, the irises horizontal yellow slits. The transformation was complete now, no need for pretense.

"Leave her alone." Grace twisted the bone handle, tainting more of the demon's blood and muscle with the silver blade. The creature arched its back and hissed in pain.

It slapped at Grace's hand, though the knife remained in its leg. Bony fingers plucked at the handle, but contact with the magicked weapon caused it to flinch away. This species wasn't the strongest of the Horde's demon clans, thank goodness, but the leg wound alone wouldn't suffice to dispatch it. It crawled toward the window, the closest escape route, alternately mewling and snarling.

Grace tried to sit up. Her left arm hung useless and she shivered uncontrollably. "Maggie, help me."

Maggie stared at the creature, scared perhaps, but not terrified, as a normal young woman would be. Somewhere, beneath the clouding of her mind, the erasure of her identity, did she recognize what it was?

"Maggie! If it gets outside, we're gonna lose it."

Maggie's focus cleared in an instant. She dropped the dress and rushed to Grace. Kneeling, Maggie winced as she reached toward the wound on Grace's neck. "Yer bleedin' bad."

Grace shook her head. "No time. Just point my right arm toward it."

Maggie didn't ask for explanations. She angled Grace's arm toward the demon. The thing dug its claws into the windowsill, trying to pull itself up.

"*Cor unum*, Maggie." It hurt to breathe. "Concentrate on the words. *Cor unum.*"

"*Cor unum?* What is that?"

"*Cor unum, et fortissimi.* One heart, many strong. Say it. Feel it."

They hadn't needed to speak the words after their first few

hunting sessions; the connection had become as automatic as their heartbeats. But it had been nearly a year, and Maggie wasn't Maggie.

"C-cor unum, et fortissimi," Maggie whispered. Then, stronger, "Cor unum, et fortissimi!"

Deep in Grace's gut, her magic sparked. It recognized Maggie, reached out to her as Maggie's magic sought Grace's.

"Yes, yes, that's it."

Her stomach tightened as if she were about to vomit, and Grace gasped. It had been so long since she'd felt her power—their power—so intensely. It pushed out of her, like a dam breaking. Before Grace could wrangle it, Maggie's magic slid alongside her own, though she suspected by instinct rather than with Maggie's full awareness. Maggie stemmed the rush from a flood to a manageable stream that leeched into Grace's chest, her arm, her legs. Icy tendrils wound through her. The stream became a controlled flow, running fast and burning with cold.

Grace's right arm itched and her palm heated. Beside her, Maggie shook. Sweat trailed down the side of her face. Her gaze jumped between Grace's hand and the demon at the window.

"Jesus, Mary, and Joseph," Maggie muttered.

The creature got to its knees and punched through the glass. It straightened its legs, intending to throw itself out the window to escape.

Grinding her teeth together, Grace formed her magic, boosted by Maggie, into a blue and purple swirling ball of cold fire. She launched the ball like a slug from a shotgun. The creature fell back from the window, howling, engulfed in flame.

The backwash of heat swept over them. Maggie ducked her head and cried out, but didn't release Grace's arm, as if she knew it was necessary to maintain the connection.

The thing at the window writhed and burned; the spicy bitter odor filled the room. Grace's eyes watered, her focus on the dying creature until she was sure it wouldn't rise again. When its body stopped twitching and appeared to be little more than a husk, she fell back against Maggie, drained. The magic around the corpse flickered, subsided to a glow outlining the body, but did not completely extinguish itself.

"It's dead," she told Maggie. "You can stop."

Maggie's grip on her arm relaxed. The glow faded, then disappeared.

They sat in silence for a bit, Grace resting against Maggie. The only sound was their harsh, fast breaths. The burnt spice aroma lingered in the air.

"My God, what was that thing?" Maggie asked, disgust in her voice.

Grace shifted. Her left arm and shoulder flared, and she sucked in a painful breath.

"I need my bag," she said, ignoring the question for the moment. She had a few of her own that needed answers.

Maggie carefully eased herself out from under Grace. She found the leather saddlebags beside the bed and dragged them over. Grace tried to raise her arm, but between using her magic after such a long time and the poison coursing through her, her limbs were leaden.

"In the wooden box," she gasped out. "A glass vial of silver nitrate. Hurry."

Maggie dug through the bag, found the kit. She opened it and removed one of the stoppered vials of clear liquid. "This?"

Grace nodded. "Pour it in the wound."

Without hesitation, Maggie tore open Grace's shirt and chemise. She dribbled the contents of the vial over the bite. A new pain seared her skin, burned to the bone. Grace cried out, clutching Maggie's hand. Maggie held hers just as tight.

"Sorry," Maggie said, her voice rough.

"S'okay." Grace's breaths were deep and shaky while the silver nitrate took effect. The pain subsided to a dull ache. She tested the limb. Though slow to respond, her arm and hand moved as they should, and her fingers opened and closed most of the way. If Maggie hadn't been there to administer the antidote, Grace might have died a painful death.

Maggie stoppered the vial and returned it to the box. She

stared down at her hands. Grace waited, letting the last few minutes sort themselves out. Maggie's hands trembled. She lifted her head. Her dark eyes were filled with confusion.

"What was that? It . . . it looked like John, but—" She swallowed hard. "He was my husband," Maggie whispered. "I-we—"

Grace's stomach twisted. Maggie—her Maggie—had lived with the demon, slept with it. Not that she'd known, of course. "It wasn't human," she said, and quickly regretted her words as Maggie paled. "I mean, he was. It was sort of . . . hidden inside him."

True enough. No call to terrify the woman with reality.

"Why did he—it attack you? What's going on here?"

"You aren't Maggie Dalton," Grace said.

She closed her eyes as her body fought the poison in her system. Her magic, though quiet now, was no longer asleep. It rested. Waiting. She looked at her catalyst, at the confusion in her eyes and the tension in her face.

"Your name is Maggie Mulvaney. You're a demon hunter, like me."

CHAPTER SIX

Freetown, Long Island, NY, October 1897

Grace woke in Nan's quarters off the kitchen. The scent of the cook's dusting powder tickled her nose and she sneezed. The pounding in her head, along with the throbbing in her hand, spiked, then settled to merely awful. Gingerly, she sat up to avoid jostling either. The soft glow of the bedside lamp kept the small room mostly in shadows.

She picked up her boots and padded in stocking feet back to the kitchen. Nan and the housemaid, Stella, washed up and wrapped leftovers from dinner. It was pitch dark outside, though probably not past nine.

Nan turned and smiled. "Feelin' better, Grace?"

"A bit, yes." She stopped beside the butcher's table Nan and Stella often used for their own meals and tea. "Dinner over?"

"Yes, but I can fix something for you if you'd like." Nan wiped her hands on her apron and reached for a platter of sliced meat.

Grace's stomach flipped. Bile and sour whiskey bit at the back of her throat. She swallowed it down. "No, thank you. Are the others in the library?"

It was Thomasina's preferred after-dinner gathering place for port and conversation. They would discuss the day's activities, current events, plans for patrols or coordination with other houses, and various topics of interest before everyone turned in.

"They are." Nan gave her wrinkled, sweat-stained attire a quick perusal. "You may want to change, love."

"I was going to go straight to my room and back to sleep," Grace admitted. "Wanted to avoid running into anyone."

Mostly Thomasina or the new catalyst, who was sure to be the center of tonight's attention.

The cook frowned with sympathy. "Sister told me to have you go see her when you woke up."

Damn it all. If Thomasina learned Grace had scurried up the back stairs to avoid her, her punishment would be doubled. "I'll stop by the library on my way. Thanks for letting me use your bed. I don't think I got any muck on it."

Nan waved her off and returned to her cleanup. "No trouble. Go see Sister, then get some rest, child."

The hall between the sitting room, dining room, and library was softly lit with sconce lamps. Feet shushing along the low nap of the hall runner, Grace approached the doors of the library as if expecting a wild beast to burst through.

That would be preferable to Thomasina.

She pressed her ear to the cool wood. The number of voices told her everyone at Saint Teresa's had likely attended dinner but her. As one of only four current novitiates, Grace's absence would be noted. She wondered if Thomasina or Rémy or the redheaded woman had regaled the others with her blunder over lamb and wine.

Grace knocked lightly, assuring herself that it was faint enough not to be heard over the conversation. At least it wouldn't be a complete lie when she told Thomasina she'd stopped by. Mentally accepting the sister's future pursed-lip reaction to her fib, Grace hurried to the stairs.

"Are you all right, Miss Carter?"

The lilting Irish brogue behind her stopped Grace's ascent before she made it to the third step. Injured palm on the balustrade, holding her mucky boots in her good hand, Grace drew a deep breath. No aroma of lilac, only the oil Stella used on the woodwork.

Her cheeks burned as if she'd spent the day in the sun without her hat, a common occurrence. The woman knew Grace's name.

Grace turned around. The newcomer stood in the hall between the library and the stairway, her hands clasped at her waist. She'd changed to a more formal gown of sage green for dinner. Dark red tendrils curled about her ears where her hair had escaped the pins holding the mass of it atop her head.

Her portrait should be in a museum, Grace thought.

Compared to the perfectly groomed figure before her, Grace felt like the dirty waif she'd been when Sister Thomasina had brought her to Saint Teresa's ten years before.

"I'm Margaret," she said while Grace remained spellbound, frozen on the stair. "Margaret Mulvaney." She took a tentative step forward. "Can I help you with your things?"

"No, thank you," Grace said, the words barely audible as her mouth had dried. She worked up a bit of saliva and moistened her lips. "I can manage."

Margaret smiled and a dimple formed in her left cheek. Grace's knees wobbled. "I'm sure you can. How's your hand?"

Grace held up the injured limb. A spot of blood had seeped through the white linen wrap. Her pinky and ring fingers were secured together, a short length of flat wood employed as a splint to keep the injured digit straight as it healed. The last thing Grace remembered before the whiskey took effect was Mrs. Reynolds's soothing tone as she took her needle to the wound.

"Broken finger and a few stitches. It'll be fine, thank you." She lowered her hand and ignored the dull throb of pain that kept time with her thudding heart. "I apologize about earlier, Miss Mulvaney. In the courtyard. My behavior was . . . inexcusable."

That was one of Thomasina's favorite words when it came to Grace.

"Please, call me Margaret," she said. "You have nothing to apologize for. It was a sparring match. In a real-world situation, you would use every advantage at your disposal, wouldn't you?"

31

Grace gave her a wry grin. "You haven't sparred with Rémy. When he says no magic, he means it."

Margaret smiled back. "I'm sure I'll get my chance."

The library door opened and Thomasina stepped into the hall, a small glass of ruby port in hand. Her gaze darted between Margaret and Grace. "How are you feeling, Grace?"

Her concern was genuine, though the false motherly tone made Grace want to laugh. "Better. I knocked, but no one heard, and I decided it was best not to interrupt the evening."

Knowledge of Grace's ruse deepened the brow lines beneath Thomasina's wimple.

"You won't be joining us?" Margaret's mouth turned down slightly with disappointment.

Grace wasn't sure how to take Margaret's reaction. She wanted to visit with Grace? Why? Why wasn't she in there with Virginia?

"Not tonight," Grace said. "I think I'll clean up and get some rest." She turned to Thomasina. "If that's all right?"

"Excellent idea." Thomasina moved forward and touched Margaret's elbow. "Shall we go back inside, Margaret? I'd like to talk to you and Virginia about your trial."

Margaret stared at Grace for another few seconds. "*Codladh sámh*, Grace. Sleep well."

She allowed Thomasina to guide her back toward the library.

Grace had started up the stairs again when the sister called her. She turned. Thomasina stood near the doorway. Margaret was in the library standing between Virginia and Rémy but looking at her. "Yes?"

"You still have an hour in the armory." Her eyebrows met the furrow over her nose. "First thing, yes?"

Grace held still, heat infusing her face. She refused to allow her embarrassment and anger to show. "Of course."

Thomasina nodded with satisfaction. "Good night."

"Good night, Sister."

Grace hurried up the stairs, her stocking feet making soft sounds on the carpet. With everyone in the library, the doors of the four occupied bedrooms on the second floor were closed. Portraits of long-dead members of the Order hung in gilt frames along the walls. Mostly women, though there were a few men. Their eyes seemed to follow her to her room, and she mentally rattled off their names as she passed, a ritual she'd begun as a child. Mary. Camilla. Lupe. Antoin. Bernadette. Another Mary. Genevieve. Ana Sophia. Rafael. Joselyn.

She went into her room, closed the door, and sagged against the solid wood. Thomasina's reminder and heavy-handedness should have made her shake with rage. Instead, Margaret's musical voice echoed soothingly in her head.

Codladh sámh, Grace. Sleep well.

CHAPTER SEVEN

Harrington, WY, October 1903

"Of course I'm Maggie Dalton. I—" She cut off her own protest. Acknowledgment of some kernel of truth lit her eyes. "When I saw that thing attack you, I was scared, but more than that, I wanted to hurt it. Kill it." Maggie leaned forward, hands clenched. "Then you had me hold your arm, and I felt . . . I felt . . ."

Her voice trailed off, grasping for the word that fit.

"Powerful," Grace said.

Maggie was responsible for Grace's magic waking after months of quiescence. Both hers and Maggie's had come to life as the connection was reestablished. It had surprised the hell out of her, like the first time they'd met in New York.

"Yes," Maggie whispered, her dark eyes wide with acknowledgment of the word. "As if I could pick him up with one hand and crush him." Her surety faltered. "But . . . demons? Like in the Bible? You're a demon hunter. And we work together. We're partners?"

She was more than that, but Grace couldn't tell her everything. Not yet. One shock at a time. And depending on how far the Order had gone to erase her memory, maybe not ever.

Maggie stared at her, as if trying to decide who was crazier, Grace for suggesting such a thing as demons and magic, or

Maggie herself for having seen it. The bloody wound on Grace's shoulder and the burned body were enough evidence, Grace thought, but it might take a bit more convincing.

Awkwardly, Grace got to her feet. Maggie rose, keeping the crisped demon out of her direct line of sight.

"Can we go to another room?" Grace asked. "I need to lie down, and I want to explain."

Grace's right arm over her shoulder, Maggie helped her down the stairs to the private living space behind the public rooms of the hotel. The small parlor smelled of lilacs. A closed door likely led to the bedroom.

Grace settled onto an upholstered settee. Maggie took the rocking chair beside it. She folded her hands in her lap and waited, eyes on Grace. She was calm. Too calm to have just witnessed her husband turn into a demon and get burned up by magic. Magic she'd helped generate.

"We work as a team. I'm the source. You're the catalyst. We've been—" Grace swallowed the word she almost used. "We'd been together for over five years before you disappeared."

"I don't remember." Maggie's eyes narrowed. "I don't remember you."

Grace's chest tightened. "I know."

"Why don't I remember?" Emotion thickened her accent, as it always had. "You don't just forget a thing like that, do ye now?"

Grace shifted on the settee, barely able to move. Good lord, she needed to sleep. "The Order of Saint Teresa, the people we work for. Worked for. They did something to you. To us."

Those dark days of confusion and anger had nearly done Grace in. It had been as if she walked through a dream, lost and unsure, not quite knowing who or where she was, barely hanging onto whatever fragment of truth and reality she could grasp. If she'd let it slip that she remembered, would they have tried wiping her memory again? Would they have tried to kill her?

"Why would they want me to forget who I was? If this Order was the one who did this to us, if they're supposedly the force of good against demons, why was one of them here?"

"I don't know, exactly. They wanted us to do something, that much I remember. Whatever they're planning, I don't think it's finished yet. They have to be stopped, but my first priority was finding you. You're all that matters to me, and I couldn't do anything until I knew you were okay, until I—" her voice broke. "Until I saw you again with my own eyes."

Maggie sat back in the rocker, her body stiff. Did she see it? Did Maggie see there was more to Grace's search than merely finding her partner?

"We need to leave," Grace said. "We need to—"

Maggie stood and quickly walked toward the door leading from the parlor. Grace's heart sank. She'd made a mess of it. She should have taken a less straightforward approach, maybe stayed elsewhere. But in her desperation to see Maggie again, she'd shown too much of herself. Magic, demons. The woman who was Maggie Dalton could barely comprehend that. Was the suggestion her relationship to Grace was more than a partnership too much for her?

Maggie turned around at the door, hands fisted at her sides. "Get some rest," she said, her voice rough. "I'll clean up and bring you some tea."

She left in a whirl of blue skirt.

Grace closed her eyes and leaned her head back, letting slow tears of exhaustion and despair trickle down her cheeks unchecked.

CHAPTER EIGHT

Harrington, WY, October 1903

You aren't Maggie Dalton.

Maggie sat in the hotel kitchen, her hands around an untouched cup of tea. Luckily, Jenny, Maggie's morning help, had gone home for the day. The aroma of roasted chicken hung in the air, tinged with the bitter scent wafting from upstairs where that thing had died. Maggie would have to keep Jenny out of room four until the mess was cleaned up. She'd locked the front door and put the closed sign in the window before coming into the kitchen. Her regular diners would have to go elsewhere for supper tonight. Having someone walk in and smell the stench wouldn't do.

The acrid odor seemed to permeate Maggie's every breath. It might not be gone by the time Jenny returned in the morning. She would wonder what was causing such a reek. How would she explain it?

Maggie breathed through her mouth, determined not to be sick from the smell, from what she'd seen and done. Sick from the thought of what she'd lived with these past months. Revulsion shimmered through her, churning in her stomach. Grace said it had been hiding inside John, but Maggie knew she was trying to be kind. She had shared her bed—her body—with that . . . thing.

Her stomach lurched. Maggie forced bile back down, swallowing hard and digging her fingernails into her palms to keep from falling into hysterics. Now was not the time. She had a wounded woman in her parlor and a burned demon in one of her guest rooms. It would all be a laughable, fantastic story if it weren't true.

What was the truth? That she was Maggie Dalton? No. That moniker—this life—had never sat well. Accepted, yes, but she had been nervous and agitated living in Harrington without understanding why. Was it because somewhere inside her she knew she wasn't Maggie Dalton? What about the memories of meeting John? Of their courtship, short as it was in her recollection? Of her life?

What was real?

And what of Grace Carter? There was no denying that together she and Grace had created and controlled the force that had killed the demon. There was no denying the strength she'd felt when she'd held Grace's arm and concentrated on those simple words. There was no denying the connection she felt to Grace.

This is insane.

Maggie stood and dashed the cold remains of her tea into the deep sink. She set the cup on the counter. Bracing her hands on the edge of the sink, she leaned over, suddenly light-headed.

"You all right?"

Grace.

Maggie took a long, slow breath, calming herself before facing the other woman. Grace stood with her right shoulder against the door frame. Her bloody and torn shirt hung off her left shoulder, exposing the red-stained chemise beneath. Her blond hair had loosened from its tail. Bruised-looking flesh beneath her green eyes spoke of the toll the battle had taken.

Maggie had the sudden need to tend her, to keep her safe.

"You shouldn't be up and about." She tried to break eye contact but couldn't. They held each other's gazes across the kitchen.

Grace shrugged her shoulder and winced. She gave Maggie a half smile. "I'm all right. Just needed to let the silver nitrate take effect and get some rest." The smile became a look of concern. "What about you? Everything that's happened must have you reeling."

Maggie returned to the chair beside the table where she and Jenny prepared the hotel's meals. She folded her hands in her lap to keep them from trembling. "There are a lot of things I don't understand."

Grace crossed to her and crouched beside the chair. She reached out as if to lay her hand on Maggie's knee, then drew back. "I know, and I'll explain all I can. I swear." Her intensity seemed to darken her irises from sea to mossy green. "But we need to leave. Now."

Maggie shook her head. "I can't. We can't leave that thing in the room. And I can't leave the hotel unattended. All our money is in the Amberly."

Our money. Mine and John's.

The husband who wasn't her husband. The life that wasn't her life.

Rage and confusion roared in Maggie's head. She had no idea who or what she was anymore. Cold fire flared in her chest, the same sensation she'd had upstairs when she and Grace had fought the demon. Her entire body shook.

Grace fell back, clutching her stomach. "Please, Maggie. I can't—" She waved her right arm as if warding off a bee. The pots and pans hanging from the rack suspended over the stove crashed into the wall. Sweat beaded across Grace's forehead. "Please."

Maggie gulped air, her breath coming too fast to catch. Closing her eyes, she concentrated on calming herself, on stopping the pain that marred Grace's face.

Slowly, her breathing returned to normal, but the ache in her chest remained.

"He was my husband," she said, voice and nerves raw. "I shared his bed, my body, for almost a year." Rage boiled again, but Grace's gasp had her quickly rein it in. Despair joined the anger. She buried her face in her hands. "Why did they do this to me? Why?"

She heard the rustle of Grace's clothes; then her arms encircled Maggie. Maggie leaned her forehead against Grace's right shoulder, taking care to not aggravate the injured side. The scent of Grace's metallic-tinged sweat filled her with an odd sense of comfort as Grace rubbed her back in slow circles.

But nothing would ease the vileness of the truth.

"I've bedded the devil." Maggie straightened and sat back in the chair. Her gaze met Grace's. "I'm unclean. My soul is forfeit."

Horror filled the other woman's eyes. She grabbed Maggie's shoulder and gave a not too gentle shake. "No, don't say that. Don't you ever say that. This is not your doing, Maggie. It's the Order that's unclean and lying with the devil." She rose and took Maggie's hand. "We're leaving. You can forget all about this place."

"I'll never forget." Maggie stood at Grace's insistence, but she didn't move otherwise. Grace faced her, her hot hand still clutching Maggie's.

Anger flashed in Grace's eyes. "Don't you dare give up, Margaret Mulvaney. You have never given in or felt sorry for yourself, and I won't let you start now."

"I'm not Margaret Mulvaney. She's gone."

Tired. She was so tired she could lie down on the floor and never get up again.

Grace held her palms to either side of Maggie's face and brought her own within inches. "No. You're here with me now, and I won't lose you again."

"I can't," Maggie said, closing her eyes.

She touched her forehead to Maggie's. "Please. You have to remember." Her voice broke. "Remember me."

Images formed in Maggie's mind, like buildings solidifying and taking shape as they're approached on a foggy evening.

Maggie sat in front of a vanity in a small bedroom, looking not at herself in the mirror but at Grace as she came up behind the chair. Smiling, Grace laid her hands on Maggie's shoulders. She bent down, her golden hair tickling Maggie's skin as Maggie tilted her head to let Grace kiss her neck.

The image shifted abruptly to the two of them side by side in a filthy city alley, the stench of urine and decay burning Maggie's nostrils. Grace held her hands out, as she had up in the guest room, the blue and purple fireball growing as Grace's power coiled with her own.

Grace made a throwing motion, sending fire down the alley where a pale-skinned being with black eyes and pointed ears stood over two bodies. It hit with a brilliant flare of white light.

The backwash of heat singed her face. Her eyes flew open, and she stumbled back against the kitchen chair. Grace stood in front of her, hands still raised as if cupping Maggie's cheeks.

There was panic in Grace's eyes. Slowly, she lowered her hands. "Please, don't be scared."

"We were—" Maggie choked on the next word, not in horror, but in confusion and disappointment. "I remember an alley," she said, not brave enough to pursue the impressions from the first image. "Fighting a demon."

"Yes."

Blood thrummed in Maggie's head, echoing the rushing beat of her heart. "We met in an old house."

A slow smile curved Grace's mouth. "Sister Thomasina brought you to our chapter of Saint Teresa's to be a catalyst six years ago."

"Catalyst?" The term was vaguely familiar, but not in association with people.

"A catalyst enhances a source's power, makes them both stronger." Grace's expression turned apprehensive. "You know what that power is, don't you?"

Maggie nodded. The word "magic" churned in her brain, but she couldn't quite make it form on her lips. There was no such thing as magic. Then again, there were no such things as demons, or so she'd thought.

"You were supposed to be the catalyst for a different source,"

Grace continued, "but it didn't work out."

"It can't be just any catalyst and source?"

"No," Grace said. "There has to be the right connection. A catalyst and source not only work together, but they have to fit together. Like . . . like . . ."

"A jigsaw puzzle."

"Yes." Grace took a step toward her, then hesitated. "We went through a lot together, Maggie, helped each other, cared for each other's wounds, cared for—" Her face flushed. "Please, we have to go. When the Order learns I've found you, they'll double their efforts in hunting us down."

Maggie glanced upward, toward the room where the dead demon lay. "I can't leave that thing there. We have to get rid of it."

CHAPTER NINE

Freetown, Long Island, NY, October 1897

Perspiration trickled down Margaret's back and between her breasts. The crisp white shirtwaist she'd donned that morning was damp around the armpits, its pleats soft and drooping like overcooked noodles. She had been trying for nearly an hour to connect with Virginia Delacroix. Across the basement testing room, the blonde was in equal dishabille, her hair mussed, catching her breath and drinking a glass of water. Mrs. Reynolds and Rémy seemed to be giving her something of a pep talk.

"Concentrate, Margaret." Thomasina pressed a small towel into her hand. Margaret daubed at the moisture at her throat and beaded on her face. "I realize you and Virginia haven't had much of a chance to get to know each other, but we need to make this bond."

She met Thomasina's desperate gaze. "I don't think this is going to work. She isn't my source."

Thomasina's mouth pinched and her brows furrowed. "You two have all the markers for being bonded. That's why we brought you together."

"I know. I was hopeful too." She wasn't lying; it was just that the truth had changed.

Margaret had been anxious to find her source, to dedicate her life to ridding the world of demons and their feeding on human suffering. On paper, she and Virginia were a perfect match. Both strong in their disciplines, their psychometric examinations, even their birth charts, said they would have a solid pairing.

Then she'd met Grace.

"Try again," Thomasina said.

Before she could reply, to tell the sister it wasn't worth the effort, the door of the chamber opened. Grace stumbled into the room, her face ashen.

"Please," she stammered. "Please stop."

Rémy and Mrs. Reynolds started toward Grace, but she waved them off.

"Grace, what are you doing in here?" Thomasina demanded. "This is a closed session."

"She's not Virginia's," Grace said. She stood straighter, the color returning to her cheeks. "Margaret's meant for me."

Margaret's heart fluttered. *She feels it.*

Of course she did.

Margaret hadn't really connected with Virginia the previous night, not on any level. Truth be told, she didn't particularly care for the other woman. Not that that was a requirement, but it certainly helped to at least get on with your partner.

Grace started toward Margaret, her eyes bright, almost feverish. Margaret's power flickered deep in the pit of her stomach.

"I've been in the armory down the hall, fighting the need to come in here," Grace said. "I felt your power through the wards, and I had to—"

"That's impossible," Virginia said. She stepped forward to cut off Grace's approach. "Magic cannot breach the wards on this room. They were placed by some of the most powerful members of the Order. You're just being difficult. You're jealous that I'm to have a catalyst and you aren't."

Margaret glared at the other woman's back. "No," she said, "*you* aren't."

Grace made an effort to come closer, but Virginia stepped in front of her again. Grace's frown deepened. Margaret's magic surged in response to Grace's irritation. She willed Grace to calm; it wouldn't do to have Grace attack Virginia. Containing Grace's power was like the Little Dutch Boy with his finger in the dike, but there were more leaks than fingers. Grace quieted with her efforts. The leaks slowed.

"Thomasina," Virginia called.

Grace's magic bubbled up again.

"Grace, no." Margaret hurried around Virginia and grabbed Grace's arms, turning her away from the others. "Look at me."

Grace's grim expression softened. "You're not hers," she whispered.

"I know," Margaret said in the same quiet tone. She closed her eyes and swallowed hard. God help her, she'd bond to Grace Carter and no one would stop it. No one could. She focused on Grace again. "I know. But this isn't the way to go about it."

The snake of power in her stomach coiled and settled as she willed Grace to relax. The green eyes holding hers lost some of their intensity.

"Come along, Grace," Thomasina said gruffly. She reached for Grace's arm.

Margaret blocked the sister's hand. Thomasina's cheeks darkened, and beneath her wrinkled skin the muscles along her jaw bulged.

Margaret's heart hammered. She'd dared to touch a sister, the prioress of an Order facility, no less. Oh, she'd done it now. Never in her years with the Order had she defied a sister so blatantly. Being raised in the Church had put the fear of nuns into her right off. Since childhood, she'd been devout and dedicated, obeying every tenet, every rule. Other than seeing Clare, that is.

But she would not allow Sister Thomasina to touch her source in anger.

"I'll take Grace back to her room," Margaret said.

Thomasina's glare didn't waver, though she stiffly stepped back to allow them to pass. Grace glanced between Margaret and the sister, hesitant. As much as she butted heads with

Thomasina, Grace had likely never openly defied any authority figure within the Order either.

"Come on," Margaret said to Grace, grateful the tremble in her hands and stomach weren't evident in her voice. She looped her arm through Grace's and led her out of the silenced trial room to the corridor.

Foolish girl, the Doyenne's words from long ago echoed in her head, as clear as if the old biddy was there beside her.

Foolish, indeed. Although Thomasina might never forgive such a slight, Margaret couldn't allow even someone as important as the prioress to treat her source so poorly.

Her source.

Despite the impending clash that would surely occur between them and Thomasina, Margaret smiled.

Grace grasped Margaret's hand where it lay on her forearm. Margaret covered Grace's hand with her other palm. They climbed the stone stairs together. Grace seemed to gain strength with each step, and Margaret's weariness from the trial with Virginia faded. Could she and Grace be energizing each other now that they were in contact?

Still not exchanging more than a quick glance, they passed the short hall that led to the kitchen, the sound of pots and pans clattering as Nan and her helper cleaned up from breakfast. The aroma of the promised post-trial celebratory apple pie wafted along the paneled hall.

Margaret gestured for Grace to lead the way up the narrow back stairs to the next floor. Grace ascended slowly, her boots thudding on the worn carpet. Perhaps she wasn't as recovered as Margaret thought.

On the second floor, Margaret followed Grace into her room and eased the door closed.

Grace sank down onto the bed. "You probably shouldn't have done that."

Margaret sat beside her. "I'm not keen on her treating you like a misbehaving child."

"Thomasina says I need discipline."

"Discipline in your control, perhaps, but she shouldn't treat you like that. You're a grown woman and an enormously powerful source." Margaret took Grace's hands in her own, taking care with the injured one, feeling the calluses on the palm of the other. Her irritation toward Thomasina ebbed some with their contact. "You need guidance, not punishment."

"She's given me that." Grace pulled her hands from Margaret's and stood, turning her back. "You don't understand."

She was mistaken. Margaret knew all too well how the Order required obedience and discipline. Adhere to your training, follow instructions, and don't question your betters.

Grace's shoulders rose, then slowly sank with a sigh. She faced Margaret again. "I owe her and the Order my life. Truly, Maggie, they saved me and my family."

Margaret hadn't heard how and why Grace had come to Saint Teresa's, why she was so tolerant of Thomasina's abuse. "Tell me, had you been an ordinary girl, would they have cared so much?"

Surprise crossed Grace's face, as if she hadn't considered such a thing. The truth dawned on her and her brow furrowed. She shook her head.

Margaret rose. "Thomasina and the Order saw what you were, what you could become. I'm glad for that." She gathered Grace's hands in her own again. "But don't ever be fooled into thinking *anyone* in the Order is concerned with anything but the mission."

She'd learned that herself a long time ago. Oh, there were those who genuinely cared for the sources and catalysts they trained and tended. Without them, the children brought into the Order would have become mere weapons. And, sadly, some were. The mission always came first: defeat the Horde and protect mankind. The power wielded by a source and catalyst was for that purpose, and that purpose alone.

Grace's gaze dropped to their joined hands. "I know why they brought me here, but that doesn't make me any less grateful. Controlling my magic is critical." She raised her eyes. "I need to do this."

Margaret squeezed her fingers. "You can. *We* can. I've known that since we first saw each other in the courtyard."

Grace brought Margaret's hand up, pressing the palm against her sternum. The heat of Grace's skin came through her shirt. Margaret's hand tingled. Her body hummed.

"Do you feel it?" Grace asked, holding Margaret's wrist with one hand.

Margaret concentrated on the contact between them. There, beneath the sensation of fabric and warmth, beneath the realization that she was touching this beautiful woman. The pulse of Grace's heart and the echo of a second.

"Your power," she whispered.

"*Our* power," Grace corrected. She closed her eyes, a faint smile curving her lips. "It's like waiting on the sidewalk for a parade. You hear the music, feel the vibration of the drums reverberate in your chest, even before you see the band."

She placed her other hand on Margaret's chest, just below her throat. Margaret couldn't help the sharp intake of breath as Grace's thumb brushed the top of her breast.

Surely Grace could feel her heart pounding.

"I feel it. Us," Margaret said.

Grace laughed with delight and opened her eyes. They stared at one another, both grinning. It took all of Margaret's willpower not to lean forward and kiss her.

No. You can't do that.

Grace sobered quickly. Stepping back, she released Margaret's hand and moved hers away. Disappointment tugged at Margaret's heart.

"Thomasina is still going to be upset," Grace said. "She won't easily forgive you for defying her, Maggie."

Maggie. No one had called her that since she was a girl in pigtails, but coming from Grace it was comfortable and right. "It doesn't matter," she said. "Nothing can change what's fated to be."

A slow smile curved Grace's lips once again, and once again

Margaret had to restrain herself from stealing a kiss. She wanted to believe it was their newfound connection that stirred up such feelings; it had been known to happen between source and catalyst. But Margaret knew better. She'd had these stirrings before, with someone who wasn't touched by Teresa and the Magdalene. She had promised herself not to get into a similar predicament here in the States.

Fate may have them become bonded, but it also had her on the path to taking her sacred vows.

Grace stood there for a moment, staring down at the floor. Margaret couldn't see her face. What was she thinking? Was she angry at Margaret for getting them into trouble? Worried about what Sister would say or do?

Slowly, Grace lifted her head and faced Margaret. Her shoulders were back, her chin held high. Neither worry nor fear were in her eyes; determination shone there. "I'm tired of being afraid of who I am. Let's tell her how it is."

CHAPTER TEN

Harrington, WY, October 1903

Nightfall couldn't come soon enough for Grace, but while they waited for the sun to finally sink in the crisp October sky, she and Maggie had cleaning to do. Maggie gathered up the pieces of the broken window that had landed on the walk in front of the hotel, explaining to a concerned neighbor that she'd attempted to kill a spider and misjudged. Grace had stood behind the half-closed door, ready to defend her catalyst from too nosy a neighbor or another demon. It was a relief when the man laughed off the incident and reminded Maggie to have John board the window before it got too cold.

Grace and Maggie patched the window, and then they wrapped the remains of the demon in the sheets from the bed. Neither cared to touch the damned thing; its burnt spice reek seemed to linger on whatever it contacted. Heavy leather work gloves and careful maneuvering of the cloth and remains kept the ashes from their skin. Grace thoroughly cleaned her knife before returning it to her boot sheath.

It took both of them to carry the awkward bundle down the stairs and into the small yard behind the hotel. An old privy provided a suitable location to dump the body.

Maggie held a lantern while Grace pried nails that held the plank door closed. Sweat trickled down Grace's face. Her shoulder ached fiercely. A particularly stubborn nail screeched against the swollen board, refusing to budge any further. Levering the claw hammer with both hands, Grace's grip slipped. Pain seized her wounded shoulder and she cursed.

"Give me that thing before you cause yourself some harm." Maggie yanked the hammer from her hand and shoved the oil lantern toward her.

Grateful for the reprieve, Grace moved aside to let her at it.

"Are you always this damn stubborn?" Maggie asked as she set the claw end to the nail.

"Pretty much. But you gave me a run for my money in that department."

Maggie slanted a look at her that was hard to read. "I've been known to be a mite determined."

"I guess the Order couldn't completely erase everything about you," Grace said. Maggie hesitated, her body stiffening, and Grace immediately sensed her pain. "I'm sorry. I didn't mean to—"

"No, it's all right." She yanked on the nail head, the screech of metal on wood loud in the night. "I'll have to get used to the idea that parts of me are missing."

"We'll get them back," Grace said, though she wasn't completely sure if that was possible. God, she hoped so. If not, they'd have to start over again.

Would the new Maggie want to be with her the way they'd been before?

Grace's stomach turned from more than the stench of the privy. What if she'd found Maggie only to have lost the love of her life?

Maggie grasped the edge of the door and pulled. Rusted hinges barely moved. Grace set the lantern on the ground, and together they wrestled the door open. The reek of decaying shit burned her eyes. They both stepped back.

"At least no one will smell it in there," Maggie said, wiping her sleeve across her forehead. Grace retrieved the lantern and checked the depth. Not as deep as she'd like, but it would do.

They hauled the shrouded demon into the cramped space and dropped the body into the hole. The wet thud sent up a waft of fetid air.

Maggie tugged off the glove on her left hand, quickly followed by the gold band on her ring finger. She looked at it for a few seconds before flinging it down into the dank grave.

Without a word, she pulled the glove back on.

They made quick work of resecuring the door, using the old nails and the same holes, with the head of the hammer covered in rags to muffle the sound.

"Let's get cleaned up and we'll head out," Grace said as she made for the back door of the hotel. "You can leave a note on the door about having a family emergency and being closed for the foreseeable future."

Maggie grabbed her arm. Even through the leather glove, their magic called them together. The familiarity, the longing, brought tears to her eyes. She'd missed Maggie so. What if she never got her back?

"It's getting late," Maggie said. "And your shoulder. We should wait until morning."

"My shoulder will be fine." Grace covered her gloved hand, holding it for a moment longer than necessary, before gently squeezing it and moving it from her arm. Contact was a sort of torture she could neither bear nor resist. "We can't linger. Whoever arranged for the demon to be here will figure out it's dead all too soon and come after us. We can ride to Laramie and get on the train to . . . someplace. West. California, maybe. Wherever we can afford."

The cooperation between the Order and the demons meant they'd be hunted by both now. The concept made Grace's head and heart ache. How could they? How could Saint Teresa's employ demons? What the hell was going on, and what did she and Maggie have to do with it?

She wanted answers, but more than anything Grace wanted to grab Maggie and get as far away as they could from everyone and everything that threatened them.

Maggie opened her mouth, but snapped it shut again. She glanced up at the Amberly. Meeting Grace's gaze, Maggie tugged the gloves off with quick, jerky movements. "Of course. I'll go pack."

She stalked to the back door of the hotel, leather fisted in her hands.

Grace stayed behind for a minute to give Maggie a chance to gather herself. What she really wanted to do was take the woman into her arms and tell her all would be well. They'd get through this, as they always got through tough times. But while the words might be welcome, Grace knew such intimate physical contact could do more harm than good.

At least we're together.

A harsh, humorless laugh escaped her as Grace headed back inside. Together, but still apart. Torture indeed.

CHAPTER ELEVEN

Freetown, Long Island, NY, October 1897

Grace smoothed her blouse and tucked an errant strand of hair back behind her ear. The bun she'd attempted to create was already coming loose, and all she and Maggie had done was walk down the stairs.

"Ready?" Maggie asked quietly, despite the fact that Thomasina wouldn't be able to hear them through the thick library doors. At least Grace didn't think the prioress could hear them. Though she hadn't been in the field for some time, Thomasina's power was impressive. It wouldn't surprise Grace if Thomasina could hear through walls and doors.

"I think so. You?" Grace dried her palms on her hips. A meeting with Thomasina would never not make her nervous. "She's always mad at me, but I think you'll catch the worst of it this time."

Maggie lifted her chin, defiance glinting in her eyes. "She can't change the facts, Grace, and the fact is, we are meant to be together."

The simple—or not so simple—truth of it infused Grace with calm. Like it or not, the sister and the Order of Saint Teresa would have to accept that they were to be paired.

Maggie gave Grace's arm a light squeeze, then knocked on the door. There was certitude and confidence in the knock.

Grace stood straighter, emulating Maggie.

"Come in." Thomasina's voice was muffled by the heavy door, yet clear.

Grace turned the knob and pushed the door open. Maggie preceded her inside, and Grace closed the door behind them. While the entire house knew they'd be meeting with the prioress, the exact exchange wouldn't be shared.

Thomasina sat toward the back of the library, her desk and leather-bound chair in a corner, surrounded by shelves of books and several wood filing cabinets. This was the prioress's public office. She kept a second, more secure desk and cabinets in her personal rooms on the third floor. Her gray habit and brilliant white wimple were always the first things Grace noticed about Thomasina, quickly followed by the iron-gray of her eyes. Had she always been such a sourpuss? Grace could hardly imagine the sister as a young girl or woman, smiling and enjoying life.

Maybe that's what a half century of fighting demons did to you. Stripped you of any sense of joy.

She didn't want to end up like that.

"Have a seat," Thomasina said, gesturing to the two hard chairs before her desk.

Grace and Maggie exchanged glances as they sat. Grace quirked an eyebrow, showing her surprise. It was a rare thing indeed to sit while being reprimanded by the prioress. Both of them sat on the edges of their chairs, knees together and hands folded in their laps.

Thomasina's gaze bored into each of them in turn. It was a technique Grace recognized from her childhood—hell, into her adulthood. The staring and silence often became too much, and the subject of Thomasina's attention would spontaneously burst into babble regarding the incident in question.

Surprisingly, Thomasina spoke first. "How are you feeling, Grace?"

Grace blinked in response, taken aback by the prioress's question. "Fine," she said after a moment. "I feel fine."

Thomasina nodded. "Good. I'd hate to think Margaret's

actions were for naught."

In the other chair, Maggie stiffened. "I was protecting my source."

The prioress's eyes narrowed. "Admirable, though we haven't confirmed that yet. What you thought I'd do to her is beyond me."

"Everyone knows you and Grace have a fractious relationship, Sister. Considering I was supposed to be Virginia's catalyst, you seemed more than a little disturbed that Grace had laid claim to me."

Claimed her. Yes, that was it. Grace and Maggie had claimed each other, hadn't they?

"Grace, you interrupted a closed, protected trial." Thomasina folded her hands on the smooth walnut desk. "Can you explain what happened?"

"I felt Maggie's power through the wards, Sister." It was the truth, but from the arched eyebrow she gave, Thomasina didn't seem to believe her. "I swear, if my own power hadn't reacted to hers, we wouldn't be having this conversation."

Not yet anyway. Grace was sure she and Maggie would have found themselves drawn to each other sooner or late as sources and catalysts were wont to do.

Thomasina shook her head slowly and sat back. "Impossible. The strongest of the Order placed those wards and they're reinforced regularly. You couldn't have sensed any power coming from within."

Grace shrugged matter-of-factly. "I know what I felt."

She wasn't about to deny what had happened, even if Thomasina did.

The prioress pursed her lips, deepening the lines around her mouth and nose.

"You told me Grace was perhaps the strongest source you've ever encountered," Maggie said. Grace startled at that. Thomasina had never said any such thing to her. Ever. "Isn't it possible she has the ability to perceive power where others would not? Particularly power coming from her intended catalyst?"

Thomasina set her hard gray eyes on Maggie. "I suppose so. But that doesn't excuse her barging in or your impudence."

Grace held the edge of the seat, fingers pressed into the wood, to keep from bolting out of her chair. Why was the prioress so damn concerned with obedience rather than what truly mattered? "But it does explain it," she said, trying to remain calm.

The hardness in Thomasina's eyes softened slightly. "Perhaps. We'll still need to test the two of you, to ensure you can make a true bond."

Grace couldn't believe what she was hearing. Thomasina was willing to have them go to trial. She didn't dare to move, half fearing any show of emotion would make the sister take it back.

"I can't see how we wouldn't," Maggie said.

"Grace's power may have reacted to the combination of you and Virginia using your magic, rather than to you in particular," Thomasina said. Maggie opened her mouth, but Thomasina held up a hand, forestalling an argument. "It doesn't happen often, but it does happen. We'll go through standard testing procedures beginning tomorrow."

"Why not today?" Grace asked. Anticipation of feeling Maggie's magic combine with her own made her heart race. She didn't think she'd be able to stand the wait.

"I need to go over your charts to get an idea of where strengths and weaknesses might lie." Thomasina was nothing if not a bastion of preparedness. "Trials are tailored to the participants, not just generic tricks and acts to be performed."

"Tomorrow will be soon enough, Grace," Maggie said. "Besides, I'm a wee tired from this morning."

Grace's face warmed. "Oh. Of course you should rest."

Selfish of her to not consider Maggie. Using power could be draining. Attempting to force its use in a failed trial was exhausting. She should have remembered that from her own fruitless efforts. Her excitement had made her anxious, but she wouldn't burden her catalyst.

Her catalyst.

Grace couldn't stop the wide smile that made her cheeks ache.

Thomasina gave her a disapproving look. "Get some rest. No sneaking in any attempts together. I want you in a protected, controlled environment. Understand?"

"Yes, Sister," Grace and Maggie said in unison.

They exchanged glances again, and Grace stifled a giddy laugh at the glint of excitement in Maggie's eyes. Tomorrow they could officially become source and catalyst.

"Dismissed," the prioress said, waving her hand. She rose and opened one of the file drawers. The one where she kept the Order charts.

Grace and Maggie stood and headed toward the door. Grace's joy was so palpable, it took a bit of willpower for her not to skip through the library. Just before they reached the door, it swung open.

Virginia Delacroix stopped short of bowling them over. Her intense gaze belied the blotchiness of her porcelain complexion.

"How could you?" she demanded. "How could you ruin my bonding?"

Grace shook her head. "You can't ruin what isn't there."

"She's right," Maggie said. "We were never going to bond, Virginia. It was a futile effort. You know that as well as I do."

Whether she'd admit it or not, Virginia was not about to allow a low-born like Grace to upstage her. Though perhaps what really bothered the blonde source was that Grace was the more powerful of the two. Virginia didn't take to being second best at anything.

"Futile or not," Virginia said in a low, controlled tone, "you weren't supposed to be there. I won't forget this, Grace."

She swept around the two of them, skirt swishing across the carpet, and beelined to the prioress.

Grace watched her flounce into one of the chairs, then smiled at Maggie. "Neither will I."

CHAPTER TWELVE

Twenty Miles from Laramie, WY, October 1903

Grace woke up on her right side, feeling the urge to roll over. Her breath fogged before her in the early morning dimness, and her nose was cold. A pinkish glow rose from beyond the mountains.

They had stopped for a few hours of rest after riding out of Harrington well after dark. She hadn't wanted to stop at all, but Maggie had dozed off a couple of times, nearly falling out of the saddle. They'd needed to share a bedroll for warmth, as Grace insisted a fire would risk discovery. Maggie agreed, and both had settled in without complaint. Grace marveled that Maggie had seemed to drop off so quickly and soundly. Her own short stretches of sleep had alternated with wakeful minutes listening for trouble.

Grace rolled onto her back. Her shoulder didn't protest as much as she'd expected. Gingerly, she eased onto her left side. A twinge of pain, nothing she hadn't experienced before.

Looking at her sleeping catalyst, she smiled to herself, still hardly believing they were together. The soft sounds of her sleeping were as familiar as Grace's own breathing.

Maggie muttered something and snuggled closer. Shadows and blankets made it difficult to see her features, but in her mind's eye Grace saw her as she'd slept when they'd shared a bed in the past. Her hair wild about her head, falling into her eyes. Her skin smooth as silk.

She often mumbled in her sleep, sometimes in Gaelic. When the words had sounded harsh, Grace imagined Maggie was dreaming of her parents or the Doyenne at her previous house. Fractious relationships, according to Maggie. When she spoke softly, a slight smile on her face, Grace wondered if she was dreaming of her former lover or of Grace herself. The pang of jealousy had faded long ago, after Maggie assured her she no longer held any desire for Clare, that Grace was her one and only love.

Misery clutched Grace's belly. What if those feelings never returned? She raised her hand, but resisted the urge to caress Maggie's cheek, to smooth back the errant strand of hair covering her eyes.

Maggie mumbled again. "Please, don't."

For a second, Grace thought she was awake, telling Grace to not touch her. The certainty of it was like a kick to the gut, and she stifled a moan, but then Grace realized Maggie was still sleeping.

"Stop. I—"

Maggie whimpered in fear or pain. Was she dreaming about the Order, or demons, maybe John Dalton? Her heart broke for her catalyst, and this time Grace couldn't resist. She draped her right arm over Maggie's shoulder. "Shhh, it's all right," she whispered. "They can't hurt you now."

God, she hoped that was true.

Maggie tucked herself under Grace's chin, perhaps simply drawn to the additional warmth. Perhaps sensing the love and concern coming from her source. Grace closed her eyes and pressed her cheek to the top of Maggie's head. Lilac and sweat and wool scents filled her nose. The Order may have taken some of her memories, but no way in hell could they take Maggie from her heart.

Damn them. Damn them all.

After several glorious minutes of not thinking about why

they were outside on the ground, Maggie stirred as if she was waking. Grace moved her arm away, and Maggie rolled onto her back. Grace quietly mourned the loss of familiar comfort, how Maggie fit against her, as well as her body heat. In the growing dawn, Maggie's dark eyes fluttered open. She blinked up at Grace as if unsure of where she was.

"You okay?" Grace asked.

Maggie rose to her elbows and winced. "Neck's a bit sore."

No mention of the dream she'd had. Perhaps that was a blessing.

Grace sat up. "We'll get a real room when it's safe."

"When might that be?" Maggie asked, flipping the scratchy wool blanket off. Her agitation didn't surprise Grace. Maggie had never been much of a morning person, and a few hours on the cold, hard ground wouldn't improve that disposition. She got to her feet and dusted her skirt. "I suspect the people after you—us—won't give up so easily."

"No." Grace rose. She shook out the blanket and bedroll. "On the bright side, I don't think they want us dead."

"Well, isn't that something to cheer about."

Grace stared at her for a few heartbeats, then started to laugh. Not because what Maggie said was particularly funny, just that it was so . . . Maggie. After a moment, Maggie joined her. Grace missed the sound of her laughter, even if there was a dark reason behind it.

"I'm sorry," Maggie said, getting hold of herself, "but if that's the bright side, I'm sure I don't want to know what the alternative is."

That sobered her up. Considering how the Order had kept Maggie for the past months, Grace knew there was a reason they were still alive. One didn't go through the trouble of taking memories and setting up elaborate living arrangements if there wasn't a reason. But she'd be damned if she'd let the Order and the demons have Maggie back to continue or complete their plan, whatever it was.

Maggie's smile faded as she stared at Grace. "That bad?"

"I'm not sure what they want, but yeah." Grace said. No use whitewashing the truth. Maggie needed to understand how dangerous their journey would be. "No one I've contacted could give me a definite answer. Mrs. Wallace, the member of the Order I met with in Denver, had heard some whispers of funny doings. She's how I eventually found you. Without knowing who is friend or foe, I'm hesitant to have contact with anyone else, on purpose or otherwise."

"Out of the frying pan and into the fire, so to speak." Maggie sighed and took up the corners of the blanket and bedding to help Grace roll them. "We hunted these demons, you said, so perhaps they were trying to punish us?"

Grace took the bedroll and secured it to the saddle, scratching the horse's neck in greeting. "Maybe, but why not just kill us, or even torture us then kill us? They want us alive for some reason."

"Why us?" Maggie asked.

"I don't know."

There had been days during her search for Maggie that Grace had asked what made them targets. Often, in Grace's own mind, the answer was Sister Thomasina's disdain, but would she be that malicious? She'd learned of Grace and Maggie's deeper bond well before Grace woke up to find Maggie gone and the sister pretending she'd never existed. Thomasina wouldn't risk the Order's mission over something so trivial as a personality clash. What could have turned the prioress against them?

"What aren't you telling me, Grace?" Maggie's question pulled her out of a mental rage toward Thomasina. "You know more than you're saying."

Oh, God, if she could only tell Maggie everything. But she couldn't. Not yet. One emotional upheaval at a time.

"I'm telling you all I know about the Order and what might have happened to us." That was true enough.

Maggie quirked an eyebrow at her, clearly understanding that Grace was holding back. Rather than pressing, she shook her head and focused on the horse, petting its soft nose. Maybe she realized she wasn't quite ready for all the answers.

Grace blew out a relieved breath. She cinched the saddle down and untied the reins from the brush. "There should be a creek near that line of trees. We can get a drink and eat a bit of the food I have."

Maggie nodded, but said nothing as she walked beside Grace to the gurgling stream. Their breaths clouded in the cool autumn morning. It felt good to move, to work the stiffness out of her body. The silver nitrate did its job to counter the demon's poison, leaving the muscle and joint achy. She'd recover, and have yet another bluish-silver scar to show for her vocation.

The creek by the trees was no more than a few feet across, feeding the Laramie River from the mountains. The horse nickered and dipped its muzzle to the water. Grace knelt beside him and cupped her hand to capture enough for a drink. Icy cold, just the way she liked it.

Grace splashed some water on her face, wiped off the excess, then dried her hands and face on her shirttail. One of the saddlebags had a packet of dried beef and some hard tack. Not much of a breakfast, but it would tide them over for now.

"I'll be right back," Maggie said, heading toward a thick patch of sage.

Grace didn't envy Maggie having to deal with layers of skirts. She'd appreciate trousers sooner rather than later if they stayed outside more than a night or two. And now that she thought about it, Grace realized she could use a trip behind the bushes herself before they set off.

Their journey to Laramie would take the rest of the morning, at the very least, especially if they stayed off the main roads. Once there, they could find a hotel, a real meal, and get some decent sleep. There was security in having four walls around them, though the trade-off was the potential for being trapped. No scenario—out in the open or hidden behind wood and brick—was perfect.

A scream stopped Grace's heart, then set it racing. She snatched the knife from her boot and bolted to where Maggie had gone. Just as she reached the thick brush, Maggie's magic called to hers. Grace's power flared, making her stumble. Somehow keeping her footing, she dashed between the sages, following the pull of magic. As she came around a bush, Maggie ran at her from the opposite direction. Both tried to stop, nearly crashing into each other. Grace wrapped her arms around Maggie to keep her from falling, her knife held so she wouldn't accidentally impale the other woman. Maggie grabbed Grace as well.

"What is it?" Grace asked. She scanned the area, but neither saw nor sensed any demons.

"S-snake," Maggie said, her breath coming in great gasps. "I was putting myself back together, and there it was." She looked over her shoulder as if the serpent was following her.

Relief washed over Grace. Not a demon. She might have laughed, considering Maggie had fought things worse than snakes, but there were rattlers in the area. Getting bit by one of those was almost as bad as a minor demon bite.

They stood there in the cool, morning light, hearts beating against one another. After a few moments, Maggie shifted. Heat rose on Grace's cheeks. Holding Maggie a touch too long had made her uncomfortable.

Grace lowered her arms and stepped back. "I don't think we're in any danger. Just be careful. This time of year, snakes are pretty slow. You might have disturbed a nest of sleepers."

"Wonderful." Maggie wrapped her arms around herself and searched the ground.

"Go back to the horse and have something to eat. I'll be right there."

Maggie glanced at the knife in her hand. "Going snake hunting?"

Grace laughed and slid the blade back into her boot. "No, gonna go pee."

Maggie started toward the horse. "Watch where you squat. I'll not be sucking venom out of your arse."

Grace's jaw dropped open. Maggie continued walking, but glanced over her shoulder and smiled. That was the Maggie she

64

knew, and Grace couldn't have wiped the smile from her own face if she'd tried.

CHAPTER THIRTEEN

Laramie, WY, October 1903

Eyes closed, Maggie sighed and sank down in the tub until warm water touched her chin.

They may have been on the run from demons and fervent members of a religious order, but that didn't mean they couldn't indulge a little. The Hesse Hotel bathing room was simply appointed with clean white and brass fixtures. Hot and cold running water piped into the clawfoot tub meant Maggie could add more water as she wished. Though her fingers and toes were wrinkled, she wished she could stay there forever.

Tempting, under the circumstances.

Two days on the dusty road was two days too long. Only Grace's patience with her silence as Maggie tried to work through who she was and what was happening made the trip bearable. Riding in front of the blond woman for miles and miles had allowed Maggie to come to terms, more or less, with what was going on, or at least what they knew. The desire to know why they were being sought and what they were up against niggled at Maggie, but getting as far away from those responsible was hard to resist.

Although she wondered if she'd ever learn the answer to the most personal of questions: what had really been between her and Grace?

When Grace had literally run into her yesterday, Maggie had been more than relieved that she was safe from snakes. There was familiarity and comfort beyond mere reassurance.

Earlier that morning, Maggie had woken from a bad dream with Grace's arm over her shoulder, soothing her. That felt right too. If guilt hadn't overtaken her, Maggie would have been happy to stay on the cold, hard ground a little longer. What she remembered from her upbringing, or what she was allowed to remember, was that feeling such things with another woman was wrong.

How could it be wrong to feel safe and comforted? To feel content? To feel . . . love?

Maggie jerked upright, sloshing water over the edge of the tub.

Love? No, that wasn't possible. Gratitude, perhaps, maybe even indebted to her for getting her away from a false life, but she didn't love Grace. Not in *that* way.

Oh, but you did. Once.

No. How?

A knock on the bathing room door interrupted further exploration of the thought.

"Yes?" Maggie called out.

"It's me. Everything okay?" Grace's voice was muffled by the thick wood, but Maggie could imagine her standing outside the door, knife in hand. So protective.

"Yes. Almost done." She couldn't let Grace come in. Not when she was in such a state. "I need to wash my hair."

"I have a couple of things for you," Grace said.

"Just a minute."

Luckily, she had clean clothes to change into. She'd packed a few items and would be presentable while the dress and under-garments she'd worn the last few days were laundered.

Maggie ducked her head under the water and gave her scalp a good scrubbing. Not perfect, but it would do. Rising to the surface, she swiped water from her face and pulled the plug. While the water drained, Maggie squeezed water from her hair and used a towel provided by the hotel to dry off. Her small clothes and dressing gown were draped over the back of a wooden chair. She slipped those on, wrapped her hair in the towel, and opened the door.

Grace had bathed earlier. The men's shirt she wore was unbuttoned at the throat, revealing a tanned triangle of skin. Her hair was slicked back and plaited, the hat nowhere to be seen. Her trousers were darker than the pair she'd been wearing, but with the same black braces. In her strong hands she held a couple of round, flat tins with colorful labels.

"Some tooth powder and deodorizing dust." She tilted her head to read the label. "Contessa Mirabelle's Fragrant Delight." She shrugged and met Maggie's eyes. "It smells nice."

Maggie took the tins from her, smiling. In their rush to leave Harrington, she'd forgotten toiletries. "Lovely, especially the tooth powder. I've been feeling somewhat gummy."

"Yeah, me too. Ran out before I got to you." Grace reached into her back pocket and withdrew a rectangular packet. She unfolded the paper and held it out. Toothbrushes. "Pick one."

Laughing, Maggie plucked one of the bone-handled brushes from her hand and went to the sink. She turned on the faucet to fill a glass.

"I know you like to feel clean from head to toe," Grace said, following her.

Maggie looked up, catching Grace's gaze in the mirror. In her mind's eye, she saw a similar scene to the one she'd envisioned at the Amberly, of Grace coming up behind her while Maggie wore little more than a dressing gown. Of Grace pressing her lips to Maggie's hair, to her temple, to her mouth. The desire to lean into the kiss, to do more, rushed through her.

You loved her, once.

The glass crashed into the porcelain sink.

"Maggie!" Grace darted forward.

"It slipped," she stammered.

Grace stared at her reflection. Maggie couldn't look away, her cheeks flaming.

"You remembered something," Grace said, her voice was

low but sure.

"Yes." There was no denying it, but had Grace seen the same images Maggie had? Felt the same urge?

You loved her.

Maggie backed away from the sink.

Grace set her toothbrush down on the edge and carefully picked up the larger pieces of glass, breaking eye contact within the mirror. "The more we're together, the stronger our connection will become, I think. I hope, because I'm sure we're going to need to use our power again. We should be able to keep it under control. We'll have to be careful, though, until you're more yourself."

What, exactly, would that mean? How would she know when she was truly herself again? Would she feel it when it happened? Would she have to rely upon Grace to tell her? What if it never happened?

The questions ran through her head like a herd of wild horses. "I wouldn't want anyone to get hurt."

Grace turned, shards of glass cupped in her hand. "I'm more concerned about you, Mags. Until you're ready, I don't want to risk you not being prepared for any sudden surges by me. I'll do my best, I swear, to keep you safe."

Maggie took a moment to let her words sink in. "From you. You think I need to be safe from you."

Anguish crossed Grace's fair face. "Yes. I can feel your magic when we're together. It calls to mine. But I can't always control it. That's what you do for me. For us. I got better at controlling my own power after meeting you, and it has been quiet while we've been apart, which is probably a good thing. Now that we're together again, I don't know what might happen if we can't control it. We need to be careful."

"Emotions set it off," Maggie said, recalling how Grace had nearly collapsed in the kitchen of the Amberly when Maggie had been upset. "My emotions."

"Sometimes, yes. Or sometimes proximity to demons." Grace's mouth quirked into a crooked smile. "Let's hope we can avoid those until we're both feeling ourselves."

Maggie tried to smile back, but the enormity of what Grace was saying made it feel like she had fifty-pound sacks of flour strapped to her shoulders. They were on the run from demons, both harboring power they might be unable to control. No matter where they went, no matter how far they traveled, there would be demons sooner or later.

"We'll be all right," Grace said. "We always are when we're—when we work together. Let's finish up here and head on up to the room. A good night's sleep in a real bed will do wonders for us both."

Maggie kept her head down as she prepared the minty tooth powder in a second glass tumbler, unable to meet Grace's eyes for fear another image—a memory?—might race through her head.

Yes, sleep was what she needed. Tomorrow's train to Denver would put more distance between them and the Order and demons, at least for now.

Maybe she'd start to remember who Maggie Mulvaney was and what she could do. But was Margaret Dalton ready for that revelation?

CHAPTER FOURTEEN

Freetown, Long Island, NY, October 1897

Grace paced the corridor outside the testing room, thumb to mouth as she worried at a hangnail, worried about what was to come. Bonding would convince Thomasina that she was capable of moving forward in the Order of Saint Teresa, no longer a novitiate, but a full-fledged hunter. Her reason for being, and for being at Saint Teresa's, would be justified.

The last three trials she'd participated in had ended in failure, and in the case of one poor catalyst, a broken arm. She tried to push those memories aside, with little success. The events were too vivid to completely let her be.

Was she ready this time? What if the same thing that happened before happened today?

I'd never forgive myself!

"Grace, I've been looking all over for you."

Grace stopped pacing and turned to Maggie as she descended the last few steps. Her heart stuttered. *It's the excitement.*

Maggie wore an outfit similar to Grace's plain skirt and shirtwaist, with her hair in a bun, not like the braid Grace had hastily plaited for herself.

"Why didn't you come to breakfast?" Maggie asked.

"I was up early and had some tea and toast in the kitchen with Nan." She'd hardly slept a wink and was grateful when she heard the cook down in the kitchen at five. "I'm sorry I made you worry."

Maggie smiled and took up Grace's hands, her warm fingers reassuring. "I figured you'd be nervous. So am I. But there's nothing to worry about. We know we're supposed to be together."

Elizabeth's cries as she'd hit the far wall of the trial room during their test echoed in her head. "I know, but . . ."

Maggie gripped her hands more firmly and held Grace's gaze. "But nothing. It'll be fine."

There was surety in those deep brown eyes that Grace couldn't bring herself to dispute. She managed a small smile. "Okay."

Clatter on the stairs had them stepping away from each other. Thomasina, Rémy, and Mrs. Reynolds joined them in the narrow hall.

Thomasina moved to the door and withdrew a large iron key from the folds of her habit. "I hope you're both well rested."

"Right as rain, Sister." Maggie spoke to Thomasina, though she was smiling at Grace.

Grace tried to mirror Maggie's expression, but she wasn't quite feeling it. "Ready to do whatever you ask of us."

She *was* ready, other than the nagging fear anyway.

Thomasina turned on the sconces along the walls. They followed her into the room, Rémy and Mrs. Reynolds behind them. The room had recently been wired with electric lights, gas lamps having proved dangerous at times when magic ran out of control. Sister Thomasina locked the door.

Rémy settled into one of the chairs while Sister Thomasina and Mrs. Reynolds circled the room in opposite directions, hands raised. A tickle at the back of Grace's throat worked its way to her chest as the two women whispered words of power to reinforce the wards laid over the years.

"Ready, ladies?" Mrs. Reynolds called to them when she and the sister were done.

Grace and Maggie looked at each other. Maggie touched her arm, smiling, and a light thrill danced along Grace's skin.

The connection was there. All they had to do was show Sister Thomasina and the others. All they had to do was work together, with Grace unleashing her power and Maggie's amplifying it as well as aiding in control.

If you don't hurt her the way you hurt Elizabeth.

A cold, hard knot of doubt gripped her gut.

No, that was over a year ago. Grace had gained a lot of ground since then, working every day to release her power in more measured steps rather than in the massive rush that had overwhelmed Elizabeth.

But what if—

"Grace?"

Grace lifted her head, hardly aware she'd been staring down at her fists.

There was clear concern in Maggie's eyes.

A tendril of doubt tickled at the back of her brain. It was natural to worry about the trial. Nerves, that's all it was. She loosened her fists, spreading her fingers until her knuckles cracked. "I'm ready."

The two of them walked to the front of the room where Sister Thomasina waited.

"Both of you have participated in a trial before," she said, "so I won't bother with the whys and wherefores. You know how critical it is that a source and catalyst have a strong connection and complete confidence and trust in one another."

Grace and Maggie nodded in unison, neither taking their eyes from Thomasina.

"If either of you feels these proceedings are ill-advised, speak now." After waiting a moment and receiving no indication from either of them, she looked to the back of the room. "If anyone feels this bonding test is unwise, speak now."

The opportunity to speak out was mostly a formality. Grace was glad Virginia wasn't in attendance.

When neither Rémy nor Mrs. Reynolds protested the trial, Thomasina stepped back. "Face each other, please, and join hands."

They did as requested. Maggie's hands were cool and a little damp, as were her own, but it didn't bother Grace. Simply touching the other woman made her skin buzz pleasantly.

Thomasina held her right hand over theirs and placed the other over her own heart. She began the Latin prayer invoked before all trials. Grace only half listened, as she'd heard it a few times before. It implored God, Mary Magdalene, and Saint Teresa to guide them and keep them safe.

"Amen," the prioress said, crossing herself. Everyone in the room did so as well. "I want you to slowly bring your magic to command." Thomasina gave Grace a significant look. "Slowly."

Grace nodded, then closed her eyes. With little effort, she called on her power. Deep in her chest, something turned over, as if waking from a night's sleep. A beast that exuded strength and danger. Grace willed it to rise. It came up easily, eagerly, filling her.

At the edge of her consciousness, there was another presence. Something accepting and just as strong.

"Maggie."

"I'm here."

"I know. I feel you."

"I feel you too. Wonderful, isn't it?"

Grace wasn't sure if the words were said aloud or in her head, but she could tell that Maggie was smiling just the same.

"Grace. Margaret." Thomasina's voice was clear, though it sounded further away than right beside them. "I'm holding something. Do you see it?"

Without opening her eyes, Grace "saw" a small globe resting in her hands.

"Yes," she and Maggie said together.

"Excellent. Take it from me."

Grace willed the beast inside her to reach out to the globe. A ropey sensation snaked toward the sister. A second tendril of power ran like an undercurrent in the ocean alongside her own. Maggie. Together they wrapped their power around the globe and tugged.

It didn't move.

"You'll have to try harder than that," Thomasina said, an unseen smirk obvious in her voice. "You're not the only ones with power, you know."

The tendril of Maggie's power coiled around Grace's, lending strength. "This is nothing for us. Together now. *Cor unum, et fortissimi.*"

The motto of Saint Teresa's: One heart, many strong.

A little telekinetic demonstration, even against a source like Thomasina, should be easy. They just had to learn to work together.

Grace focused the power coming from her, the strand now as thick as her forearm. She jerked on the globe. Too much! Grace immediately pulled back, but that didn't stop the laws of physics. The sphere came at them like a bullet.

Her catalyst's magic surged. The globe stopped just short of hitting them, hovering at their sides. Together, they lowered it to the ground.

Maggie's power uncoiled from Grace's, but it still hummed inside her, waiting.

She met Maggie's smile with her own.

For the next half hour, Thomasina had them manipulate a variety of material objects. The exercises demonstrated their ability to work in tandem on the most delicate maneuvers, from balancing multiple items to braiding thin strands of thread. Not everything went perfectly, but they were able to recover most miscues and accomplish the task at hand.

Despite the joy and ease of working with Maggie, Grace found herself perspiring at the end of the session. Maggie blotted her forehead with the back of her hand. Her wide grin made Grace smile.

"Very good," Thomasina said. "Let's take a short break, then try something a little more challenging."

Grace's good feelings all but evaporated. "Like what?"

She'd never gone beyond the attempt at kinetic manipulation. From the questioning look on Maggie's face, neither had her catalyst.

"A bonded pair must be able to accomplish more than moving objects." Thomasina accepted a glass of water from Mrs. Reynolds and sat in one of the chairs. "What you have shown so far is very promising, but for a source and catalyst like you and Margaret, I expect more. You've both studied some basic incantations."

The tickle of doubt, which she'd thought had been thwarted by the last half hour, crawled back into Grace's brain. What would the sister have them do?

Maggie patted her arm. "It'll be fine, Grace. We can do it."

She hoped and prayed that was so.

After the three of them rested, Thomasina had Mrs. Reynolds stand with her at one end of the room while Grace and Maggie stood at the other. Rémy stood near the door. As far as Grace knew, he had no power, so perhaps he was prepared to bolt if things went awry.

"We're going to manifest a small ball of cold fire," Thomasina said. "Nothing dangerous, but if you don't stop it, you'll feel a wee chilled."

The sly grin on her face told Grace there would be more than a "wee" chill.

Grace often forgot that Thomasina and Mrs. Reynolds were bonded, though she'd known for some time. They didn't act like a hunting pair.

"After we're satisfied with your defense skills, you will create attacks against us. These exercises aren't meant to harm, but to help gauge control and potential strength. Ready?"

Maggie took hold of Grace's hand. Power flowed between them. "Ready. Grace?"

She had been in control of her own power earlier, but moving globes and braiding string wasn't applying power against another person. The incident in the yard the other day with Rémy showed Grace's effectiveness there, as well as her lack of control. With Maggie to help her, could she do it?

"Grace," Maggie whispered close to her ear, "I'm right

here with you."

She squeezed Maggie's hand and tried to smile. "I know. Okay, I'm ready."

They brought their power up. Grace imagined a shield expanding in front of them. The sister and Mrs. Reynolds were going to throw a ball, so a shield seemed like a reasonable option.

Thomasina and Mrs. Reynolds raised their hands. Without a word between them, a bluish ball swirled in Thomasina's right palm. When it was no larger than the globe she'd used earlier, the sister hurled it at Grace and Maggie.

For a fleeting moment, Grace considered reforming the shield into a baseball bat, but practicality won out over whimsy and she concentrated instead on maintaining the shield.

The blue ball hit, sending a small shockwave through Grace. Maggie's power melded with her own and the sister's attack dissipated across the surface of the shield. Maggie squeezed her hand, grinning.

"Very good," Thomasina said. "Something a little stronger now."

Grace focused on her power again, and again Maggie's supported and strengthened hers. Thomasina made another throwing motion and held her right palm toward them. An invisible force pushed hard against their shield. Grace grunted with the effort.

"Hold fast," Maggie said.

Thomasina brought up her other hand. The force increased, and the shield wavered.

"You have more in you, Grace, I know you do." The anticipation was clear in Maggie's voice. "Give me more to work with."

Grace had plenty of power in reserve. It roiled inside her, wanting out. But what if it was too much? What if Maggie couldn't contain it?

Thomasina took a step forward, lines deepening across her brow. Mrs. Reynolds hesitated a moment before following. Their combined power pushed against the shield. Its strength wavered.

"More, Grace!"

Grace released more of her power into the shield. The air in front of her and Maggie thickened and hummed. Beside her, Maggie sucked in a surprised breath, but she kept their power contained.

Thomasina nodded. She stepped back, and at the same time the assault on the shield diminished.

Breathing hard, Grace reined in her power. Or tried to. It seemed to evade her attempts to bring it back inside, like a young animal feeling freedom for the first time.

"Maggie."

Immediately, Maggie's power surrounded hers, calming it, containing it. With that assistance, Grace brought her magic to heel.

When it was safely returned to its place, Grace stumbled. Maggie grabbed her shoulders.

"Are you all right?" Concern darkened her eyes.

Grace nodded. "I just need a minute."

"Grace," Mrs. Reynolds said. "What is it?"

"I'm fine. Just a little . . . I'm fine."

She wasn't tired or feeling weakened. Quite the opposite. Her power sat in her chest, quivering with anticipation of release.

Thomasina and Mrs. Reynolds exchanged glances.

"Perhaps we should stop," Thomasina suggested.

"No!" Maggie's forceful response surprised all of them. "Grace, can I talk to you for a minute?"

Before Grace could respond, Maggie guided her to the corner farthest from the other pair.

"Are you all right, really?" Maggie asked in a whisper. "If you aren't, we'll stop, but . . ."

She bit her lower lip, her eyes dancing.

"But you want to continue," Grace said.

"My God, Grace, it's wonderful." Her face lit up with exhilaration. "I've never felt so alive."

Grace understood exactly what she meant. When she used her power alone, it was amazing, like speeding down a hill on a bicycle, on the edge of losing control. But letting it free, relying upon someone else, even Maggie, to keep it from lashing out? That was terrifying. Thrilling, but terrifying, especially since Maggie would likely be the one to get hurt.

"I know, but . . . what if something happens?"

Maggie cocked her head. "Like what? That's what I'm here for. Don't you trust me?"

"Of course I do," Grace insisted. "But I don't trust *me*. I've never been able to regulate my power very well."

"You've never had me with you before, have you?" Maggie's fingers tightened around her arm. "We can do this. I know we can."

She was so sure, so determined. This was exactly what she'd wanted ever since arriving at Saint Teresa's—someone to help her with her power, someone to make her feel complete and useful to the Order. Here she was, standing right in front of Grace, the one person who could make it happen. Her catalyst.

"All right," Grace said. "But if it gets to be too much, we stop."

The smile that curved Maggie's mouth sent a surge of warmth through Grace.

"Of course. Come on." She took Grace's hand and they returned to their place at the end of the room. "We're ready."

Thomasina strode up to them, her face as stern as ever. "Are you sure?" Both of them nodded. "All right. Mrs. Reynolds and I will defend. Give us a moment to get ready."

The two conferred quietly.

"What will we start with?" Maggie asked.

"Cold fire to start, like they did," Grace said. It was an easy use of offensive power she'd been able to handle alone.

"That'll be nothing for them," Maggie said. "What about God's Hammer?"

Grace gaped at the suggestion. God's Hammer was a manifestation she'd read about in one of the library's many tomes, but had never tried, of course. It was not something a lone source would practice, and not a use of power suggested for novices, bonded or otherwise.

Maggie winked. "Just joking, Grace. I'm not insane."

Relief washed through her. "Thank God. I was worried you'd gone over the edge."

"I saw that by the look on your face," Maggie said, grinning. "Thought you were about to faint. How about we start simple and work our way to something more, as we can? Cold fire and the ram."

That sounded reasonable to Grace. She'd manifest several successively larger balls of cold fire. The slow buildup would allow them to adjust accordingly.

"Ready when you are," Sister Thomasina said. She and Mrs. Reynolds held hands. They hadn't needed physical contact for their offensive attacks. Was it an indication of fatigue or the strength of defense they were planning?

A sense of power, like a scent floating on a summer breeze, danced along Grace's spine. Her own power responded, expanding within her like a hot air balloon.

Maggie touched her shoulder. "Easy."

Grace held up her hand and imagined the cold fire ball, useful against most minor demon species according to the Tennent's Demon Index. The blue sphere quickly took shape in her palm. Maggie's power slid alongside hers. The ball glowed with a purplish light around its surface. Their combined magic was more than she would ever try to wield on her own. Grace smiled at the sensation of her catalyst within her.

Bringing to mind the baseball games she'd seen boys play at the schoolyard, Grace wound up and pitched the ball at Thomasina and Mrs. Reynolds. It scattered harmlessly along the surface of the protective shield they'd erected, but the look on Mrs. Reynold's face told her the cold fire was more potent than expected.

"Another," Maggie said. "Stronger."

Grace created a second ball, twice as large as the first. Its interior roiled blue, black, white, and the purple of Maggie's power. Grace's hands trembled as she concentrated on maintaining its form. She hurled it across the room. An audible crackling filled the air, and sparks came from the shield. Thomasina and Mrs. Reynolds jerked back.

"Again. Bigger."

Grace glanced at Maggie. Sweat beaded on her forehead. "Are you sure?"

She nodded, and a thin smile curved her lips. "Very. Bigger, Grace. We can do it."

Positioning her two hands as if holding one of Rémy's medicine balls over her head, Grace brought her power to bear. Not the entire source, but much more than she had ever attempted to release. It rushed through her body, then coalesced in her hands. Cold fire writhed and whorled, blue, black, purple. Her fingers prickled with impending numbness, like when she'd left her mittens at home during a winter walk to town.

She glanced at Maggie. Her catalyst stared across the room, teeth bared in a rictus grin. She was enjoying this.

Grace launched the ball at the other pair. Their shield flared. Loud popping like fireworks erupted. Behind the eddy of color, Thomasina and Mrs. Reynolds stumbled back.

Grace called her power back, reeling it in like a fish on the line. A huge fish that fought every step of the way. "Help me, Maggie."

Maggie's hand on Grace's shoulder tightened, her fingers digging into the muscle. "I'm here."

Together, they returned their power to a quieter state, her body tingling with anticipation of the next exercise.

Maggie wiped the perspiration from her forehead, her smile tempering the great effort they'd both endured. "Brilliant."

"That wasn't as bad as I'd feared," Grace said.

Thomasina and Mrs. Reynolds approached them. The two women were also breathing deeply. Mrs. Reynolds and Rémy poured out glasses of water for each of them.

"Impressive," Thomasina said after she caught her breath. "If that's the level of power you can display now—"

"There's more," Maggie said.

Grace choked on her water. *No! Don't!*

"Grace wasn't letting her entire source out. I could feel more within her." Maggie cast a quick, guilty, glance at Grace, but she didn't stop. "There's more, and we should show you."

"Maggie," Grace started. She swallowed down the denial when she saw the determination in her catalyst's eyes. Maggie wasn't going to let this go. She wanted to show Thomasina and everyone that Grace had more power than anyone at Saint Teresa's. "I don't think that's a good idea."

"You said you'd try the ram," Maggie reminded her.

She had, and she knew Maggie's newfound feeling for power needed to be tested as well. They'd proved to Thomasina and the others that they were to be bonded. Why couldn't it wait?

"We can do more during training," Grace insisted.

"If you and Margaret are up to it," Thomasina said, "I would like to see you attempt the ram. It's a different sort of manifestation, requiring longer sustained focus than cold fire."

The sister wasn't demanding it of them, nor was she showing disapproval of Grace. She was speaking to them—to her—as an instructor, requesting her pupils' demonstration of their abilities. It was the closest thing to being treated as a member of the Order of Saint Teresa as Grace had ever received from the prioress.

This was a chance to prove herself, wasn't it? Hadn't she and Maggie just shown they could work together to control her power? They could do it.

Maggie waited for her to respond, not pushing but clearly hoping they would continue. Saying yes could put her catalyst in danger. Saying no might make Maggie think Grace didn't trust her, didn't think she was strong enough to handle Grace's magic.

"All right, we'll try the ram," Grace said. "But if it's too much, we stop. Seriously, Maggie. It's not worth the risk."

"Cross my heart," Maggie said, making an X over the center of her chest.

Sister Thomasina nodded; then she and Mrs. Reynolds returned to the other side of the room. They consulted quietly, Mrs. Reynolds shaking her head and frowning from time to time. Finally, she agreed to whatever Thomasina had said. They faced Grace and Maggie, held hands, and closed their eyes. After a few moments, the hairs on the back of Grace's neck rose.

Eyes still closed, Thomasina said, "Ready."

Maggie placed her left hand on Grace's shoulder. The heat of her palm sank into Grace's skin, along with the tell-tale sensation of her power. "*Cor unum.*"

The now familiar tingle spread to her chest, pulsing alongside Grace's heart. Grace called up her power. It met Maggie's and swelled, as if rejoicing in the connection. Hands open, palms out, she touched the tips of her forefingers and thumbs together. The spade-shaped opening made by her fingers was positioned right over her heart.

Grace imagined her power—their power—coming out of her body in a solid cylinder through the gap in her fingers. Power curled within her, gaining strength. Maggie's joined hers, weaving itself around the coil. Grace's breathing came faster. Her heart raced, beating hard against her sternum.

"Easy," Maggie whispered. "Let me take some."

Grace carefully relinquished control, like feathering the brakes on a bicycle. Maggie guided the power within her, maintaining its circular course as it built strength.

"More," she encouraged. "Make it stronger. I know you have more than that in you. Much more."

She was right. Grace felt as if she could tap the power of heaven itself, a never-ending source. She could draw enough power to make a ram five times larger than the one she was attempting. A God's Hammer might hardly make her break a sweat.

Though more than likely it would be a chaotic explosion with deadly consequences.

"Don't falter now," Maggie said. "Come on, Grace. Bring it out. Do it."

Grace reached deep within herself. She removed the protective shield inside and let her power free.

Maggie gasped. Her power fought for control as Grace's

flooded out of her, shooting through her chest and between her fingers. The purple light of Maggie's power saturated Grace's blue, but her power wouldn't yield. The blue grew brighter and the bolt of energy slammed into the shield across the room.

Thomasina and Mrs. Reynolds stumbled backward, but kept their feet. Thomasina put her head down, bracing herself against the assault.

Grace's power thrummed through her body, threatening to escape any way it could. Her body shook with the effort of containing it.

Suddenly, the soothing aroma of lilacs filled the room. The purple of Maggie's power engulfed the blue, darkened it.

"I've got you," Maggie said. "Hit their shield again. Harder."

Grace was about to say no, that they shouldn't risk it; then she realized she was no longer shaking with effort. She wasn't completely in control of her power, but it wasn't out of control either. Maggie had taken over.

Grace formed their power into a long, solid indigo column of energy. She sent it toward the women across the way. Their shield sparked and wavered, but held.

"More," Maggie cried. "Harder."

The purple-blue bolt thickened, surging from her chest and hands. An electric crackle filled the air. *Crash!* The women fell back, but the shield held.

"One more. Come on!" Her left hand still on Grace's shoulder, Maggie grasped her wrist with her right hand.

Grace took a deep breath, made the bolt of power as dense as lead, denser. Nearly black, it shot from her chest.

Boom! The ram hit the shield, smashing it to bits. The room shook as if a bomb had exploded. Thomasina and Mrs. Reynolds tumbled, skirt and habit flying. Dust and fragments of stone rained down.

The power in Grace's chest expanded again, building up for another attack.

"No!" Maggie commanded. Her fingers gripped Grace's shoulder, her wrist. "Bring it back. We're done. Bring it back."

Grace trembled, unable to catch hold of her power. "I can't."

"You can."

She wrapped Grace's power in her own purple glow, not smothering it, but calming it. The magic retreated into her chest and settled. Maggie lowered her hands; Grace knew she'd have bruises on her shoulders.

Breathing hard, legs wobbly, and soaked with sweat, Grace turned to her source. Awe and admiration and elation filled her.

"See? I told you we could do it," Maggie said, then collapsed.

CHAPTER FIFTEEN

Laramie, WY, October 1903

After eating breakfast and arranging for their small amount of luggage to be held until they left for the train station later, Grace and Maggie stopped off at the stable. The man there haggled hard, and Grace walked away with one hundred dollars for horse, saddle, and tack. The animal alone was worth nearly that much, but the man wouldn't budge.

Stepping out of the dusty barn, Grace secured the money in the pouch around her neck and slipped it under her shirt. "At least now we have some more traveling money. Wonder if there's a gun and knife shop nearby."

"I can't shoot," Maggie said. A quizzical expression furrowed her brow. "Can I?"

Grace failed to stifle a giggle. "Not at a distance, but with a little more practice you'll be able to defend yourself, if need be. We should carry more than my knife, and I doubt there's a sword shop in Laramie."

Maggie quirked an eyebrow at her. "I'd imagine not."

They had something much better than either conventional weapon, but Grace knew they weren't ready for that yet. Or were they?

Her magic hummed inside her in anticipation.

"We could always find a quiet place to practice our other

option," she suggested. Maggie abruptly stopped, and Grace faced her. "I know we're trying to get away from the Order and all, but if they find us, we're going to need our power. Better to be prepared."

There was worry in her dark eyes, and a hint of fear, but understanding too. She'd seen what a minor demon like the one at the Amberley was capable of doing. There were worse out there.

"We've faced some ugly things together, Maggie. We can do it again."

"But we need to be in step again," she said. "Like dancing."

Grace smiled, recalling one of their first "dances" when they'd trained together. "Yes. Exactly. Do you think you're up for it?"

"I think so. Where can we go?" Both glanced up and down the bustling Laramie street. The town wasn't nearly as large as New York City, but busy enough that privacy wasn't readily available.

"I'd suggest back to the hotel," Grace said, "but if things get out of hand, I don't want anyone hurt."

"There, perhaps?" Maggie gestured toward an expanse of green and trees in the distance that hadn't completely succumbed to the autumn change. They'd passed it on their way into town yesterday. Close enough to walk to, but far enough that on a blustery day such as today it was unlikely to attract casual strollers or nature buffs.

"That might do. Let's find the gunsmith and then take a walk."

Grace asked a passing gentleman if he could direct them to such an establishment. After raising his eyebrows and giving them a once-over, he suggested the Laramie Gun and Knife Shop a couple of blocks away. Grace thanked him, amused by his reaction, and they went in the indicated direction.

The proprietor was more nonchalant about a woman asking for weapons, perhaps because Wyoming had been a leader in women's equality for so long. Or maybe because money knew no gender. Either way, he quickly found two fine, if older, Smith & Wesson revolvers, bullets, and a knife that would suit Grace and Maggie's needs. None were silvered or magicked, of course, but they would do.

"Those .44s pack a bit of a wallop," the man warned them. "I have some smaller models you ladies might find more comfortable."

A Derringer or a .22, more "ladylike" pistols, wouldn't do a damn thing against a demon, other than irritate it. Even a .38 could be dicey without silvered or magicked bullets. They might stand a chance with greater firepower.

Grace raised the gun and sighted it in on a knot in the panel of the far wall. The couple of pounds of metal could tire you out in a prolonged fight, but a .44 slug usually ended a bout right quick if you hit your target. "These'll do."

"Whatever you like, ma'am." He took her assessment in stride and closed the case. "Holsters for both?"

"Please," Grace said.

The man filled the order and Grace handed him nearly fifty dollars. Their longer coats with deep pockets covered the gun belts as well as kept the bullets handy. Grace passed Maggie the second knife they'd purchased.

"Put that someplace you can get to it quickly."

"You ladies headed out to the Territories or something?" the man asked.

Grace glanced back at him as they turned to leave. "Something like that. Thank you."

They buttoned up against the increased wind and hurried toward the open area away from town.

"We'll try a few things," Grace said, holding her hat on her head. "Don't want to be late for the train."

Maggie didn't say anything, just nodded and stayed in step with Grace. It took until they were nearly to the trees before the added weight of the gun settled somewhat comfortably on Grace's hip.

Buildings didn't merely become scarcer, but stopped abruptly at the edge of town, as if some sort of invisible wall had been erected. The neatly maintained street and walkway degraded to an uneven track that led west, back toward Harrington and other small towns.

A path from the road into the heart of the copse meant it was likely frequented by residents. Grace neither heard nor saw anyone, and no one had followed them. They continued farther into the sparse woods, toward the gurgling sound of a creek or stream.

A little practice and a chance to reconnect. Maybe that would help Maggie remember more of who and what she was.

Grace stopped beside the creek. The ground was flat enough to keep their footing and the area open enough to see if anyone approached. It would do nicely for their purposes.

"Ready?" she asked.

Maggie drew her palms down the sides of her coat. "What do we need to do?"

"Just like at the hotel the other day." Grace didn't want to stir up too much of the memory, fresh as it was, but they needed to make that connection again. She drew a deep breath, relaxing her rein on her magic. "*Cor unum.*"

Speaking the words brought a flutter to her gut. The power inside her wanted—needed—out. A few short years ago, she would have had trouble controlling it, but after months apart and Maggie's loss of memory, Grace welcomed her influence, her calming guidance.

Maggie gasped, her eyes wide.

Grace couldn't help smiling. Maggie felt it as well. "It's all right. Let's take it slow." She reached for Maggie's hand but didn't touch her. "Say it with me. *Cor unum.*"

Maggie inched her hand toward Grace's, as if she were about to touch a hot stove or an angry cat. The first contact of her smooth fingers against Grace's made Grace's breath hitch. When Maggie's palm touched hers, Grace's magic beat against her insides. She quickly tamped it down. Overwhelming Maggie now would undo the little progress they'd made.

"It's all right," she repeated in a whisper. "*Cor unum, et fortissimi.*"

"*Cor unum, et fortissimi,*" Maggie said, her voice shaking.

Grace's palm itched. Her hand and arm warmed. "Again."

They said it together. "*Cor unum . . .*"

Before the words left her mouth, Maggie's power pulsed through her along with her own. Their hands instinctively tightened around each other. Grace's magic pushed against her chest, throbbed inside her head. She held it in check, like a massive dog on a taut leash. A shimmer of uncertainty told her Maggie's confidence was wavering.

"Hold on, Mags," she said. "You can do this."

Maggie's jaw clenched as she concentrated. Sweat beaded on her forehead despite the chill in the air. "You're strong."

"So are you." Anxious as she was to release it, Grace kept her power from bursting out of her. "Go ahead. You've done this before, Mags. Feel what we're like together."

The pulse along her arm increased. The beat grew stronger as it reached her shoulder, thrummed up her neck, spread to her chest. There. Maggie's power and her own, beating side-by-side, as if she had two hearts.

Grace's magic flared. The desire to wrap herself around her catalyst, to make them truly one again tested Grace's control. Just as she thought she would overwhelm Maggie, a sensation of calmness soothed Grace, like a cool cloth on a fevered brow.

"I'm here," Maggie said. She licked her lips. "What now?"

Hardly daring to move, Grace glanced around them. She wanted to start with something easy, something basic. "There, that rock by the broken tree. We're going to pick it up."

The rock was about the size and shape of a horse's head.

"That looks heavy."

"We set a demon on fire the other day. Moving that rock will be easy as pie."

Maggie didn't look convinced, but she nodded.

"All right," Grace said, mentally bracing herself to pick up the rock. "Here we go. Slow and easy."

As she had so often in the early days of their training, Grace imagined the rock rising. Her power heaved, as if taking a deep breath.

"*Cor unum*," Maggie whispered.

The pulse inside Grace quickened. Maggie's power slid along her own, melted into it. Every nerve in Grace's body seemed to fire at once. The rock wobbled violently.

Too much!

Grace was about to pull back, afraid one of them might get hurt, when Maggie's magic took control. The rock stopped wobbling. Slowly they lifted it into the air in front of them, hovering several feet off the ground.

"Move it around," Maggie said.

Grace nearly laughed at Maggie's newfound confidence, at the feeling of being one with her catalyst again. She nudged the rock away from them, across the creek and then back. She flipped it around end over end, and had it circle them. The hunk of stone came to a stop, like a dog waiting for its next command.

"You try it," Grace said.

"Me?" Maggie's voice squeaked surprise. The rock wavered, but together they returned it to its steady hover. "You're the magic person, not me."

"We both are, Maggie. We're a team."

Always were, always will be. She quickly pushed aside the deeper needs and desires threatening to spill into this glorious moment. One thing at a time.

"Give it a try. Just move it to the edge of the creek."

Grace eased back on her power, like a locomotive engineer shifting the throttle to reduce speed. Again, the stone wobbled, but Maggie "caught" it with her magic.

"God have mercy, I'm doin' it."

Grace relinquished more control. The stone moved back and forth. It circled the two of them, slowly at first then picking up speed. Grace had to stop trying to watch it and just allowed herself to feel the power move through them. She grasped Maggie's other hand. Facing each other, smiling like children, the rock tumbled through the air as if on an invisible track.

Grace nudged it faster. Something sparked in Maggie's eyes and the speed increased. Soon it was a blur of color at the corner of her vision. Grace concentrated on Maggie, their hands clasped tight. Power and trust and complete harmony filled her.

God, yes! This was what had been missing. She and her catalyst were together at last.

Maggie seized control once again. Grace let her use their power to fling the rock away. It rocketed over the creek, through the thin copse of trees, and hit a young pine. With a sharp crack like rifle fire, the tree shook and split. The top half and the rock crashed to the ground in a rain of needles. Birds, flushed in fear, called.

There was complete silence for several moments while Grace and Maggie stared at the broken tree. Then Maggie giggled.

Grace turned to her. The giggle turned to a laugh, and Grace couldn't contain her own. The two of them snickered and giggled, hands still clasped. It felt so good to be with her like this. Like they'd never been apart.

Maggie tugged her forward, and before Grace realized what was happening, their mouths came together. Maggie kissed her. Hard and deep and perfect. Their tongues twined, and Maggie squeezed Grace's hands.

The double pulse hammered in her chest, throughout her body. Their bodies, for she knew the rush of desire coursed through Maggie as well.

Don't stop. Don't let go. I can't lose you again.

As suddenly as the kiss had happened, Maggie released her hands and stepped back. Eyes wide, she raised her fingers to her lips. Grace reached for her once again, heart sinking.

No no no no no!

"I-I'm sorry," Maggie stammered. "That was ... I'm not sure what that was."

Grace swallowed down a whimper of loss. "Yes, you do."

The hum of their connection waned, and she lowered her hand.

Maggie shook her head, denying what they both knew was the truth. But Grace saw it in her eyes, that she had felt what she'd been feeling. After a moment, Maggie stopped shaking her head and stared at Grace. Fear and confusion and realization all played across her face.

"We were lovers once," Maggie said.

Once. Ever again?

Grace closed her eyes against the twinge of fear of loss brought on by the mere thought. "Not in a biblical sense, because you were going to take your vows to be a novice, but yes."

She looked at Maggie. What more could she say? They both knew the truth of it now.

"A novice? Like a nun?" Maggie's brow wrinkled. "Can't say I can see it myself."

Grace shrugged. Neither could she, but she'd supported her partner's decision.

"How long were we together?" Maggie asked.

"About five years," Grace said. "Nearly from the time we met. Until they took you from me."

"I don't remember everything." Apprehension returned to her face.

"But you remember something." Hope filled Grace. "That's a start."

"Stop saying that." Maggie's brown eyes hardened, and Grace sucked in a breath of pain. Maggie's? Her own? It didn't matter; they were the same. "I remember some, but what does that mean, Grace? Nothing is going to make it like it was, whatever it was."

Hope wilted. Nothing?

"I can't ever go back to being that Maggie, who I was, who you want me to be," Maggie continued. "Things are different. Everything is different. What we had. Who we are. We're different now. *I'm* different. What happened in Harrington—" Her gaze dropped to her clenched hands, her words coming out just as strained. "I need to figure out who I am, and you need to accept whoever that might be."

Silence hung between them for several moments. Grace swallowed down the boulder of emotion caught in her throat. She wanted to reach out, to take Maggie's hands, to hold her. She remained still.

"I'm sorry," she said, the pain of having hurt Maggie bitter and burning. "I didn't mean to—." She swallowed again. "I didn't mean to push you. Take whatever time and space you need, Maggie."

Although Grace couldn't help but pray Maggie would at least want to stay with her in some capacity.

Maggie looked up. "I can't promise things will go back to normal."

Tentatively, she reached for Maggie's hand, half surprised that her catalyst allowed her to take it, and more surprised when Maggie relaxed under her touch. She gave the other woman a small smile. "We'll figure out a new normal."

Maggie drew in a steadying breath, eyes closed.

Grace gently squeezed her fingers. "Come on. Let's—"

The back of her neck prickled uncomfortably, as if someone was drawing a knife along her skin. Her power flared and she spun around, one hand raised to ward off . . . nothing. Nothing was there. Someone could have been behind one of the larger trees. Reaching out with her magic she came away with no indication of anything but birds and insects.

The Order had likely been on her tail since she left the house in New York. Had they finally caught up? Had the Horde? What if someone discovered the body of the demon in the Amberly's outhouse and figured out where they'd gone?

Maggie's boots crunched on dirt and dried foliage as she came up beside her. "What was that?"

"What did you see?"

"Nothing," Maggie said. "It was more of a feeling that someone was there."

How long had that "someone" been there, if there had been someone? Had they seen Grace and Maggie manipulating the rock? Seen them kiss? Or were she and Maggie imagining things? Both of them couldn't have been imagining someone was in the woods, but it was possible one of them did and the other took it as her own.

"Let's head back to the hotel," Grace said. She drew her magic back into herself, but didn't push it as deep down as she had over the last couple of days.

What had they sensed?

CHAPTER SIXTEEN

Freetown, Long Island, NY, October 1897

She felt foolish. There was no other word for it. Simply foolish.

Feet up on the velvet chaise in the parlor, at the insistence of Nan, Maggie sipped her tea. She'd rallied almost immediately after falling to the trial room floor, but that hadn't stopped Rémy from scooping her up and practically running the flight of stairs to the parlor for a comfortable place to deposit her. She had had no time to tell Grace or Thomasina she was fine, just a little drained.

Poor Grace.

Her source hovered somewhere outside the closed door, her agitation as clear through their connection as if she were standing in the room. She was likely pacing, practically wearing a path in the Persian carpet, and biting the ever-present hangnail on her right thumb.

There was no anger coming from Grace, just worry.

The parlor door opened and Sister Thomasina slipped in. Grace peeked over the nun's shoulder. Maggie smiled reassuringly at her source, but Thomasina closed the door before she could catch Grace's reaction. Her anxiety did seem to ease, so that was something.

"How are you feeling, Margaret?"

Setting her cup and saucer down, Maggie stood and

smoothed her skirt, ignoring the slight headache behind her left eye. "Much better, Sister. Can I see Grace now?"

"In a moment." She gestured for Maggie to sit on the chaise once again. Thomasina took the upholstered chair near the foot. "What happened?"

Maggie shrugged. "A bit too much in too short a time. We overdid it. I overdid it."

There was no use saying otherwise. Grace's power had been difficult to control, being their first time and all, but not impossible. They had manifested some forceful attacks and solid defenses. Maggie knew with some time they would mesh effort-lessly. She was capable of working with Grace, and only Grace.

"With more training and practice, we'll manage just fine, Sister," she continued, hoping she sounded confident in herself and her source. "We're good together. You saw that. You saw how strong we could be. You have to allow us to train. You can't—"

Thomasina held up one large, bony hand, stopping Maggie's incessant justifications. Her gray eyes bored into Maggie. "First of all, it's not up to you to determine what I can and what I cannot do. Second of all, no one said anything about not allow-ing you and Grace to continue. Only you or Grace will decide if it's not to be so."

Maggie's shoulders slumped with relief. *Oh, thank goodness.*

Something in the way Sister said that last bit sounded off. "What do you mean, if one of us decides?"

Thomasina shook her head, lips pursed and her brow furrowed beneath the wimple. "Grace. She's in a state because she believes she hurt you."

Anger shot Maggie to her feet. "She did no such thing! Did you tell her I was hurt? That it was her fault?"

She started toward the door, but Thomasina rose and caught her arm.

"I never said anything of the sort, young lady, and I don't appreciate you assuming as much." The sister released her. "A catalyst was injured during one of Grace's earlier trials. Eliza-beth wasn't capable of handling such power." Maggie opened her mouth to protest, but Thomasina raised her hand, stopping her. "I know you are strong enough. Grace knows it too, but she's scared."

"If she knows and I know we're strong enough, how can she think I'd get hurt?" The notion confused Maggie. Didn't Grace believe in her? Trust her?

The lines around Thomasina's mouth softened. "Doubt is a powerful thing, Margaret. Grace can very well believe you belong together, yet still fear for your safety enough to end the partnership."

Maggie's hands were fisted. "I can't let that happen. I *won't* let that happen."

Thomasina stepped aside and gestured toward the parlor doors.

Maggie stalked to the door, shaking. How could she? How could Grace want to end things like this, after all they did to prove to Thomasina they belonged together? She knew they were meant to be partners. It wasn't a choice. They were already bonded.

Damn that girl.

Maggie turned the glass knob and yanked open the door. Grace stood at the far end of the hall, chewing that damn hangnail. Her head came up, eyes wide with surprise and then concern.

"What are you doing up? Shouldn't you be resting?"

"I'm fine," Maggie said, walking up to her. "I'm perfectly fine and don't need to rest. Don't I look fine?" She realized her voice was getting louder and sounding more like the Dubliner she was with each sentence, but it couldn't be helped.

"Yes, but—"

"No 'buts' about it, silly girl. How can you think I wouldn't be able to handle your power?" Maggie snatched Grace's hand up and pressed it to her chest. Soothing warmth seeped through her blouse and into her skin. But it was Grace's wide eyes, so full of shock and worry, that finally cooled Maggie's ire.

"I know you're scared, Grace," she whispered. "I know

what happened with Elizabeth." Grace tried to pull out of her grasp, but Maggie held tight. "She wasn't your catalyst. I *am*. I can't force you to work with me, but we'd both be miserable otherwise."

She released Grace's hand. Grace didn't move. She kept her palm pressed to Maggie's chest. Maggie closed her eyes. There was Grace, not just touching her, but within her, their power pulsing side by side. To lose her would be akin to losing an arm or a leg.

Or heart.

Maggie opened her eyes and looked up at her source. "Please, Grace. Trust *us*."

Slowly, Grace lowered her hand. "I do. I just don't trust me."

Anger flared hot in Maggie's gut and face. Not toward Grace, but toward Thomasina, and anyone else who'd convinced Grace she wasn't capable. "That's the sister talking. I've felt you wield your magic; she hasn't. Get her out of your head."

Thomasina was just inside the library and likely heard that bit. Maggie didn't care.

Grace's gaze dropped to the carpet. With her head down, Maggie couldn't see the emotional cues of her expression. She didn't need to. She sensed the conflict, the concern, the anger.

She touched her palm to Grace's cheek, prompting the other woman to lift her head. When their eyes met, Maggie said, "You are an amazing source, Grace, stronger and more talented than you realize. Don't let anyone ever tell you any different. Together, we'll be unlike any pair Saint Teresa's has ever seen."

Grace covered Maggie's hand with her own. The prickling sensation that traveled across her skin was due to their bonding, she told herself. But when Grace's eyes softened with complete trust, when she gave Maggie the most angelic smile she'd ever seen, something in Maggie's chest hitched. Not her power, but something more primitive and demanding that ached to be released.

Cor unum.

Maggie's throat closed with the effort of swallowing feelings she couldn't have.

Three days after Sister Thomasina officially made them partners, Maggie took in the offerings of the basement armory. Swords, knives, and daggers filled two walls. Long guns and pistols were displayed on another, with crates of bullets stacked in a corner. The blades and bullets were silvered, and those she touched emitted a faint vibration of power.

"I've never used a sword before."

Grace turned from the rack of blunt weapons. "Never? How about a dagger or a pistol?"

Weapons training was standard practice throughout the Order. Should one's power falter or not prove sufficient, a blade or bullet might save your life. Maggie's weapons training in Dublin hadn't progressed terribly far before she had to leave.

"Pistol, but my aim is horrendous."

Grace smiled at her. "Mine too. Silvered bullets don't hold the magic like a silvered blade does, but Rémy says a large enough caliber should slow down most demons either way. Even if we never use swords, practicing with them can help during other engagements." She took a shorter sword off the rack and held it out hilt first. "Let's start with this."

Maggie curled her fingers around the leather-wrapped hilt. The edge was dull, but as she'd observed from Grace's session with Rémy in the courtyard, it could still inflict damage. "Shouldn't we wait for Rémy?"

The weapons master had been sent to town by Thomasina and wouldn't be back for an hour or so. Being one of the longest residents of the house, and therefore spending more time in the armory or practice ring, Grace had become Rémy's de facto assistant.

Grace selected a similar piece from the rack. "We could, if you want." She gave Maggie a crooked smile. "I thought we could work together before Rémy returns and get ahead of the lessons. No attacks, just getting a feel for the weight and used to handling a weapon. More for body awareness and combat

100

technique than actual blade skills."

Maggie grinned and gave the short sword an experimental swing. "All right. What do we do first?"

"First," Grace said, gently removing the weapon from her hand, "we put these aside and warm up. Come stand in the center of the room with me and do what I do."

Maggie followed obediently. They faced each other, far enough apart to avoid interfering with each other but close enough for normal conversation.

"Some stretches to begin with," Grace said, raising her hands over her head. "We don't want to strain muscles."

Maggie mimicked her, staring into Grace's green eyes rather than the way her body moved. "That would be uncomfortable."

Grace took her through the routine that she said Rémy had started her with years ago, slowly at first, then building upon movements as Maggie kept up. Maggie was in good physical health, and was pleased when at the end of the session she had only the slightest sheen of perspiration covering her skin.

"That was fun," she said, wiping sweat off her forehead with her forearm.

"Wait until we really get into it." Grace retrieved the weapons from the bench near the rack. "You may want to think about using the dumbbells to build muscle."

Maggie set her hands on her hips, an eyebrow raised. "Are you saying I'm a weakling, Miss Carter?"

Grace openly appraised Maggie's body, making a silly, squint-eyed expression that had Maggie giggle just as much as it made her body warm a few more degrees. Having chosen a blouse tucked into lightweight trousers and boots, her outfit defined her body more than she was used to. Without a corset to restrain her natural state, Maggie blushed at Grace's scrutiny, good-natured as it was.

"Not at all, Miss Mulvaney. But you'll find that swinging a hunk of metal is taxing before too long." She handed Maggie the sword. "Firm grip, but try not to make the rest of your arm too stiff. You'll need to be able to move."

"I figured as much," she said, grasping the hilt and bending her elbow to point the blade toward the ceiling. She spread her feet to about shoulder width, her left arm slightly away from her body for balance. It was a reasonable weight, for now. "How's this?"

Grace nodded. "Very good. Let's start with some basic moves. Nice and slow."

She swung her sword arm in a low arc, bringing the point over her left shoulder. Maggie followed suit, intent on Grace's movements. The next arc was just above shoulder height, at an opponent's neck if they were of the same height.

"Blows can be adjusted depending on who—and what—you're fighting, but for now just feeling what it's like is important." Grace straightened her arm and lowered it in what could be either a slashing move or a block. Slowly letting her sword point down, she watched Maggie's form. "Not so straight that the elbow locks."

Maggie nodded and bent her arm.

"That's it. Nice and smooth."

Grace pivoted on her left foot, set her right foot forward into a lunge position and jabbed. Holding that position, she looked over her shoulder to watch Maggie.

"Your feet are too far apart and the sword point a little low. Here, let me show you," Grace said. She put her sword down and came up behind Maggie. Hands on Maggie's shoulders, she tapped her back foot. "Bring that one in some and turn your foot forward." Maggie shuffled into position. "Good. Straighten your spine. Good. Shoulders back and raise the sword."

Grace slid her hand along Maggie's sword arm and stepped closer, her chest pressed to Maggie's back, her hips near Maggie's backside. Maggie closed her eyes and tried to steady herself with deep breaths.

Ignore it, she told herself. *Ignore how she feels against you. That part of your life is over. You'll be taking your vows soon.*

The warmth of Grace's skin came through the material of their shirts. She wrapped her hand around Maggie's, the two of them clutching the hilt.

"Relaxed, but ready to move," Grace whispered in her ear. She moved her hand from Maggie's shoulder to her hip. "Like a dance. Follow my lead."

"I've never danced with a partner at my back before." Maggie's voice was low with a husky, breathless quality she couldn't account for. She moistened her parched lips and shuffled her feet forward. The scant quarter inch added to the distance between them did little to help her ignore the feel of Grace's body against hers.

Grace used her hands and hips to guide her through some simple moves. The sword swished up, down, in arcs. The two of them pivoted and slid across the floor. Maggie moved her hips and legs where Grace directed them. She had loved dancing back home.

Grace counted a three-beat rhythm, guiding Maggie through what one day might be a deadly waltz with a demon. She didn't think about that now; she just let her body follow along.

Grace moved her hand from Maggie's hip and slid it along her left arm. She brought both arms up and together, wrapping her in a half hug that woke every nerve ending wherever they touched.

"Grip it with two hands," she said softly. Maggie did as instructed. Grace grasped her forearms, near the elbow. "Slowly swing the sword as we move forward. Ready?"

As one, they circled the room three times. With each step, their bodies rubbed against each other, creating heat. Maggie's breath quickened. Sweat made her hands slick; her shirt stuck to her body. The desire to turn around and—

Maggie lowered her arms and stepped away.

Grace stood with her hands out, as if inviting Maggie to embrace her.

Maggie shook her head, taking another half step back. "I'm sorry. My arms . . . You're a good teacher, though."

Grace smiled. "You're doing well, and you'll get stronger

each day, trust me."

"Thank you." Maggie watched a trickle of sweat travel down Grace's throat, to the triangle of skin between her breasts. Damp material clung to Grace's body, outlining it, more than hinting at the curves beneath. Maggie closed her eyes. *Lord, help me.*

How could one woman affect her so?

"Maggie." Grace grasped her shoulders as Maggie opened her eyes. "Are you going to faint? Do you need to sit down?"

Grace's blue-green eyes darkened with concern.

"No, I—" Maggie licked her lips, tasting salt, like what she guessed the trickle of sweat at Grace's throat must taste like.

Concern changed to something else in those depthless eyes. *She sees it. She feels it.*

Grace stared at Maggie for a moment, the expression on her face reflecting what Maggie was thinking. These feelings went against everything they'd been taught.

And yet . . .

Grace tilted her head. Lips slightly parted, she leaned toward Maggie. Maggie closed her eyes, but didn't move away. She should. God help her, she should . . .

The latch on the heavy door screeched.

Grace jumped back, snatching her hands away from Maggie's shoulders. Both turned to face Rémy as he entered, studiously avoiding looking at each other.

The weapons master tossed his suit coat onto the bench.

"Sorry about the delay, ladies." He glanced up as he unbuttoned his cuffs. "Are you warmed up?"

Maggie's entire body heated several more degrees. "Grace has put me through some exercises."

"I'm sure we'll be able to go further next time," Grace said.

She handed Maggie a sword, giving her a shy grin before retrieving her own weapon and striding to the center of the practice area.

CHAPTER SEVENTEEN

Laramie, WY, October 1903

No one on the street gave them more than a passing glance or courteous nod as they made their way back to the hotel. Servers and patrons in the dining room for an early lunch behaved as expected. What *had* she expected? Grace wasn't really sure. They ordered and ate as quickly as possible, then collected their luggage and walked to the train station.

Grace warily studied almost everyone on the platform. Was the man standing near them reading a newspaper someone Thomasina had sent after her, or something else?

"Relax," Maggie said. "We'll be on the train and away from here soon enough."

Grace nodded but didn't let her guard down. She still hadn't sensed anything when the train whistle sounded in the distance. Around them, people started gathering their bags and saying good-bye to friends and loved ones. The whistle blew again and Grace noticed the puff of black smoke rising against the dark gray sky. The platform vibrated beneath her feet, increasing with the rumbling of the approaching engine.

The Number 3 Union Pacific had slowed well before it reached the station, moving no faster than walking speed until it hit its proper stopping point. The bite of acrid smoke and hot metal washed over the platform. The brakes set, sending a puff of steam boiling out under the engine. Porters and station men opened car doors and lowered stairs for passengers. Men in everything from the rough clothes of a cowboy to the crisp suits and top hats of businessmen stepped down off the train. Women in everyday garb with wide-brimmed hats, some in fancier dresses that probably had never seen so much dust and sage, followed.

Once Laramie-bound passengers had departed and the porters gave the signal, the conductor called for southbound passengers to board. Grace gestured for Maggie to go ahead. A porter held Maggie's hand as she took the first stair step. He held his hand out to Grace, took in her attire, and hesitated. Grace smiled and grasped the rail, getting herself up the steps just fine.

Maggie headed to the nearest available seats in the second-class coach. For so short a journey, they didn't need to spend more than they had to. Once they were in Denver and had a better idea of where they were going, they might need every nickel they could scrape together.

Maggie shoved her carpetbag beneath her seat near the window. Grace automatically sat across from her; that way each of them could watch the ends of the car. It was standard procedure: eyes on the entry points. She pushed her saddlebags and bedroll under her own seat.

Several other passengers joined them in the car—a pair of men with elaborate moustaches dressed in dark suits, a haggard-looking mother gripping the hand of a blond boy who whined about being hungry all the way to his seat, an old-timer who shuffled down the aisle. A few more people took seats as the whistle blew and the conductor made his final call for passengers.

Grace watched each of them, though none gave her and Maggie more than a passing glance. Just folks heading south for whatever reason, minding their own business.

And yet . . .

"I'd like to think I'm just being a nervous Nellie," Maggie

said quietly, "but something's off, isn't it?"

Grace nodded. "Can't put my finger on it."

The back of her neck prickled, though she couldn't pinpoint the exact cause. Was it residual awareness from their session, her power reluctant to go completely quiet now that she and Maggie were reforging their bond?

The train jerked forward and back, then slowly moved along the track. With all the windows up against the chilly October air, the car was comfortable enough, but the hint of dust, leather, and body odor lingered. The train came up to speed, settling into a gentle rocking motion that lulled a couple of passengers to sleep.

Maggie yawned and covered her mouth. "Sorry. I haven't been sleeping all that well I guess."

"It's been a rough couple of days," Grace conceded. "And this morning's practice might have taken a bit out of you. Why don't you try to sleep a little?"

Maggie glanced around the car, her brow furrowed. "I don't know . . ."

Grace nudged her foot with her own. "Go on. It'll be fine."

The other woman didn't look completely convinced, but she nodded, crossed arms, and closed her eyes. Not the position for a decent nap, but any rest was better than none.

Grace settled back with her head where the window and back of the seat met. She allowed herself to relax, to let her mind drift. A man shifting in his seat and coughing drew her attention, but as everyone quieted again, Grace let her eyes close. Not completely lost to oblivion, she heard all that was going on in the car, the cleared throats, the singsong voice of the little boy several rows away, the creak of the wood and leather seats.

A little old nap would feel sooo nice, a voice whispered in her head. Something tickled the backs of her hands, like spiders crawling across her skin.

Grace jolted upright, slapping at her hands. But nothing was there.

Across from her, Maggie was also sitting up, her dark eyes

bright. "What was that?"

"I don't know."

Grace looked around the train car. A number of the passengers had left, gone to the other second-class car, perhaps, but several remained, their heads lolling with the motion of the train.

Except for the young mother and her son several rows away. They were staring at her and Maggie.

"You all right, miss?" the woman asked. Her voice was flat, as was her expression.

"Yes, thanks, just a little—"

The little boy twitched, a tic that jerked his head to the side. He scrunched his face up as if he'd just bitten into a lemon. The tip of his tongue, black as night, darted out between pink lips.

The back of Grace's neck tightened while her power flared in her chest. She was on her feet, palm out to the pair. Maggie stood, holding Grace's other arm, their power melding together.

"What's the matter, ladies?" the boy asked with a lisp. "You look nervous."

The woman and boy vaulted over the seatbacks, high-pitched squeals coming from them.

Grace called up cold fire, the blue and purple ball coalescing in her palm. She threw it, striking the woman who flew back several rows and fell between the seats. The boy kept coming. He stood on one seat and leaped at Grace, arms spread and teeth bared. She gathered another knot of combined power and hit him in his narrow chest. Back he went, his spine cracking against the edge of the seat.

The woman rose from between the seats, her hat and hair askew. Black pits flickered with the depths of hell where her eyes had been. Clawed hands extended, she rushed up the aisle.

Grace put the tips of her thumbs and forefingers together, palms out, and held the opening between her fingers over her chest. The bolt of power she summoned shot out of her and into the demon. Through it. The creature stopped, its red slash of a mouth gaping in disbelief. The clothes it wore smoldered, turned black. It dropped to its knees, then fell face forward.

Maggie jerked away from Grace, taking her power. Grace stumbled, her head swimming. A startled cry from Maggie was cut short. Grace turned. The other demon had its skinny boy-arms around Maggie's throat. It screeched obscenities over her shoulder. Claws dug into Maggie's arms, but the scuffed leather shoes of its disguise prevented it from getting a firm hold. Maggie's mouth was open as she gasped for air. She pulled at the thing's arm, but it was strong.

This close, Grace couldn't attack with her power without Maggie being harmed.

She grabbed the creature's arm and yanked. Maggie made a strangled, gurgling sound. The thing slashed at Grace, slicing into the heavy leather sleeve of her coat. Maggie swung her hand up and hit the demon in the head. It shook itself and howled. A mere slap or punch hadn't stunned the thing; Maggie had hit it with her .44. Iron was almost as effective as silver against demons. The two pounds of metal probably had a little to do with it too.

Grace took hold of the demon again and pulled. Its momentary weakness was enough to get it off Maggie. She flung the thing to the floor and called up her power. As she was about to release a handful of fire, a loud boom filled the car, throwing off her aim.

The fireball launched from her hand, hitting the door that led to the next car. It erupted in flames. Ears ringing, Grace looked at Maggie. She held the .44 in both hands, smoking barrel pointed at the demon on the floor. Or what was left of it. A black, bloody mess was where its head had been.

"Jesus, Maggie."

Maggie blinked at her.

From the corner of her eye, Grace saw the "woman" stagger to her feet. She let out an animalistic screech and clambered over the seats, headed to the door. She ripped it open.

Maggie fired again, the boom and cordite adding to the crackling and acrid bite of burning wood as the demon leapt out of the moving train.

Grace hurried to a window. The demon tumbled down the embankment. Dead? Dying? No way of knowing. She turned back to Maggie.

"We need to get off. Now. Other passengers must have heard the shots and will be here any second."

Flames engulfed the portals between cars, but it wouldn't take long for them to get it under control.

Maggie shoved the gun into the deep pocket of her mackinaw. She glanced down at the sleeping men and frowned. When she looked up again, Grace knew exactly what she was thinking. Those men hadn't slept through a fight like that. They were all dead.

Grace made her way back to their seats and snatched their bags from beneath. She tossed Maggie's bag to her. "Come on, out the back."

The train was slowing, probably at the request of the porter in the other car after hearing the gunshots and having a fire to deal with.

Grace had Maggie precede her to the small metal platform at the rear of the car. Wind grabbed at their clothes and hair. When Maggie was safely outside, Grace turned and hurled another fireball into the center, directly on top of the dead demon. The humans were already dead, and she needed to conceal the demon's body as best as she could. Grace closed the door on the black smoke, squeezing in beside Maggie.

"When the train slows enough, we'll jump," she said over the churning wheels and rush of wind.

Maggie's eyes widened. "Are you insane? We'll break our necks."

"It's that or we explain to the conductor and the sheriff what happened." Grace nudged her toward the metal stairs. "Unhook the safety chain."

Staring at her for just a few moments, Maggie shook her head and removed the chain.

"Try to cushion your head. Remember to roll off your feet as soon as you can."

Maggie squinted against the wind as she looked out at the land whipping past even as the train slowed.

She's not going to do it.

Just as Grace was about to urge her again, Maggie jumped. Her feet hit the gravel embankment, and she immediately rolled to keep from breaking her ankle or leg.

Pride welled in Grace's chest.

"That's my girl," she said, and leaped after her.

CHAPTER EIGHTEEN

Freetown, Long Island, NY, February 1898

Grace slammed the bedroom door behind her, shaking the framed samplers on the wall and not caring a whit should something fall and break. Nothing did. With a grunt of dissatisfaction, she flung her hand out. A slug of magic hit the collection of notes and baubles on her dresser. Paper and ceramic went flying.

"She's impossible."

After four months of training, Thomasina still refused to send them out on a hunt. Why was Sister so reluctant to field test them? She and Maggie were more in sync with each other than some source-catalyst pairs that had years together. If she was looking for perfection, Thomasina would never let any pair go. Mistakes happened, and hopefully they'd be learned from before they killed you. It was the way of the calling.

"It's ridiculous. 'Not ready' my eye. I'm no novice." Kicking a pile of dirty laundry aside, Grace threw herself down on the bed. She buried her face in the worn quilt and drew a breath in preparation to scream.

Be calm, whispered a voice in her head. Surprisingly it wasn't Thomasina's strident order she heard but Maggie's softer, melodious direction. *Don't prove her right.*

Grace sat up.

Was that it? Did Thomasina still see her as practically a

child without discipline?

Stop acting that way and find out.

Were those her own thoughts or Maggie's?

Grace rose and crossed to the door. Just as she reached it, a knock sounded. Maggie stood in the hall.

"I'm not a child," Grace said, a little hurt her catalyst had even suggested it, if she had.

Maggie grinned at her. "You are stubborn and impulsive and contrary. If Sister says black, you say white. If she says the sky's blue, you'd swear on your life it's purple with yellow polka dots."

Grace opened her mouth to protest, but the word "contrary" rang in her head. She laughed when Maggie quirked an eyebrow in a "See what I mean?" manner.

"All right, you have a point," Grace admitted. "But my getting along with Sister shouldn't be a factor. There are plenty of people she doesn't get along with, believe me."

Maggie chuckled and let herself into Grace's room. Grace shut the door, only somewhat embarrassed by the disastrous state of her bedroom. She snatched a sweat-stained shirt off the back of the rarely used vanity chair and tossed it onto the pile of dirty clothes.

"I have no doubt that Sister is at odds with others," Maggie said as she sat on the edge of Grace's bed. "She's just that way. We'll go on a hunt soon. Be patient."

Grace sat beside her, staring at the carpeted floor while she worked the hangnail on her thumb. "Patience is not a virtue I maintain well. That's your forte."

"I still get frustrated," Maggie said. "I just hide it better."

That was true. They had become increasingly aware of each other's emotional states over the last few months, particularly if emotions ran high. Grace found Maggie was much better at controlling herself than she would ever be.

Grace met Maggie's gaze. "I need to do that more, I guess. Hide it, I mean."

Maggie smiled at her. "Expressing your feelings is something that makes you, you. You're very . . ."

"Volatile."

She laughed. "I was going to say passionate."

Grace's face warmed. She knew Maggie didn't mean it in *that* way. They hadn't come close to anything like that since their first session in the armory.

Since then, they'd focused on training. Maggie had seemed, not distant exactly, but careful. When they weren't practicing with weapons, they were coordinating their magic. The rest of their time was filled with study sessions in the library, either continuing their general education or reading one of the hundreds of tomes or papers on demon lore and how to shape their magic. Spells, Grace supposed was the closest word for it, though the more devout authors preferred incantations or invocations.

Maggie was also meeting with those of the Order who were preparing to take their vows. Which was almost everyone but Grace.

"I don't think Thomasina is a fan of passion," Grace said, picking at her ragged nails. "She just hates me."

"Sister counts on your inclination to fight her in order to make excuses to discipline you. And stop chewing on that hangnail."

Grace raised her head and took her thumb away from her mouth. "Excuses for what?"

The amusement was gone from Maggie's eyes. "Thomasina is afraid of you. I suspect she's been afraid of you from the first day you arrived."

The assertion stunned Grace, dropping her lower jaw. Then the absurdity of the idea hit her and she fell back on the bed, laughing. "Oh, that's rich. Thomasina. Afraid of me."

"It's true."

Wiping tears from her eyes, Grace looked up at her catalyst. Maggie wasn't laughing; she wasn't even smiling. "You're serious."

Maggie's brown eyes held hers. "Think about it. Thomasina is not one to show fear. For many the response to fear is anger and an attempt to control. You came here as an ignorant child

114

with more magic potential than anyone the Order has seen in generations. With the right training, the proper catalyst, you could dominate everyone in this house with barely a thought. That scares her."

It made a sort of sense if it were true. Was that why Thomasina never seemed to find the right catalyst for Grace? She would still be unbonded if not for the chance meeting with Maggie.

"Is that what you want?" Grace asked quietly as she sat up. "For us to dominate Thomasina and the others?"

Maggie's mouth curved into a slight smile. "No, I want what you want. To use our magic as we were meant to against evil. But perhaps more than that, I want you to see just how special and important you are."

Heat flooded Grace's neck and face. She turned away, unable to meet Maggie's eyes. "I'm neither of those things."

The coolness of Maggie's palm on her forearm soothed her agitation. Gently, Maggie urged Grace to look at her. "You are all that and more," she said, her voice low. "Especially to me."

"Because I'm your source."

Her hand still on Grace's arm, Maggie smiled. "Because you're Grace Carter."

The source-catalyst bond was strong. They both knew it, felt it.

But there was something more.

Grace leaned in, heart racing.

Impetuous! Impatient! Impudent!

All those Thomasina words rushed through her head as she touched her lips to Maggie's. The sensation that surged from her chest to her limbs was heavenly. Pure joy. She rested one hand on Maggie's shoulder, then slid her other palm to the nape of her neck. Her skin was soft and warm. Loose hair tickled the back of Grace's hand.

Maggie returned the kiss, her tongue flicking gently against Grace's lower lip. Grace couldn't help the whimper-moan she made.

Though no one at Saint Teresa's spoke openly of carnal

relationships, rumors and stories abounded among the novitiates. Some girls had snuck out to meet boys, while others found comfort with each other. Those were the tales that piqued Grace's interest. She often wondered what it would be like if she found that someone.

Now she knew. Kissing Maggie was . . . right. Perfect. And she didn't want it to ever end.

Maggie gasped into her mouth and broke the kiss. She stared at Grace, her brown eyes nearly black, her breath feathering over Grace's cheek.

"I can't." She levered herself off the bed and stood. A pained expression crossed her fair face. "I'm sorry. I'm so sorry."

She started for the door.

Grace hurried after her, afraid she'd completely mucked things up, and grasped Maggie's hand before she could get away. "Please. Don't go. What I did . . . I'm sorry. I—"

Maggie turned. Tears glistened in her eyes. "No, *I'm* sorry, Grace. You didn't do anything wrong. I did. I shouldn't have kissed you. I promised to dedicate myself to the Order and not—" Her voice broke, and her next words were in a near whisper. "And not fall for someone I can't have, to start something I can't continue."

Grace nearly laughed. "But you *can* have me, Mags. I want you to have me, just as I want to have you." The pain in her catalyst's eyes and the comprehension of her words sent a sharp ache into Grace's gut. "You already took your preliminary vows."

Why hadn't she said anything to Grace?

How could she have kept such a thing to herself?

Novices of the Order were encouraged to take a vow of celibacy, as it was believed to increase focus and power. Not all did, as evidenced by Mrs. Reynolds, but for many, the Order was as much a religious vocation as any monastic calling.

"Not officially," Maggie said. "Not yet. But I also made the promise to myself that I wouldn't repeat certain behaviors."

Countless glances and smiles across the dinner table, with Maggie breaking eye contact or making excuses for them not to be alone for long periods of time. It made sense. Painful sense. And now, just when Grace had summoned the courage to act . . . But this was Maggie's personal choice, her personal experience that she had to navigate.

"Repeat certain behaviors?" Unwarranted jealousy prickled around Grace's heart. "You had a lover—a woman—back in Ireland."

Maggie nodded. "The daughter of the new schoolteacher who moved into the tenement next to ours. We saw each other all the time, went to the market together, sat next to each other at church. We became friends." She closed her eyes, gathering her strength. "Then more than friends."

"You loved her."

Maggie opened her eyes. She wrapped her arms around herself, her expression unreadable. "I did. We were together for three months before her father found out about us. He threatened to have me arrested if I came near Clare again. Within a fortnight, she was engaged to the son of one of his colleagues. I went to her one night, begging her to come away with me. She told me she didn't love me, that I'd been no more than a fancy."

Grace frowned. "Did you believe her?"

"I don't know," Maggie said. "It hurt. I cried for a week. Not long afterward, the Doyenne came and spoke to my parents about continuing my education and joining the Order. I was grateful for the distraction."

"You promised yourself you'd never fall in love again."

A small, sad laugh escaped Maggie's throat. "The melodramatic broken heart of a sixteen-year-old."

"It's painful no matter how old you are." The ache inside wasn't just her own. She clenched her jaws, her throat tight to keep tears at bay. "Why are you telling me this, Maggie? To explain your decision to take your vows? You don't have to explain anything to me."

"I focused on my studies and on the teachings of the church and the Order. There were temptations, of course, as would be expected in a convent, but I promised myself not to be deterred from the path I'd chosen." Maggie drew in a deep breath. "Then I came here."

"There was no one else . . . ever?"

"Not until you," she said. "I don't know if it's our magic that drew us together or some other force at work, but from the moment I saw you in the courtyard I knew. No other woman, no other person, has affected me in such a way."

"But you insist on pursuing this vocation." Grace's voice cracked, and a sharp pain sliced through her chest. She knew what was coming and resisted the urge to flee, or to shake Maggie and tell her she was wrong.

"I have to," Maggie whispered, her voice rough with emotion. "I believe in what we're doing, in the power of Saint Teresa and the Magdalene. I believe my pledge will help us with our mission, what we're destined to be, what we've been brought together to do."

At what cost, Grace wondered.

She stared down at their hands, rejoicing in the feel of Maggie's skin against hers, the warmth, the connection. She didn't want to lose that, but she didn't want to put Maggie in a difficult position either.

Grace released her. "I understand."

She said the words, she believed the words, and yet . . . she didn't. But she could not force herself and her personal opinions about such vows upon Maggie, as Thomasina tried to force her will upon Grace. It wasn't right.

Maggie laid her palm on Grace's cheek. Grace lifted her head and gazed into her catalyst's eyes. Maggie touched her lips to Grace's forehead. "I'm sorry," she whispered against Grace's skin.

She turned and left the bedroom, the door softly clicking closed behind her.

Stifling the shimmer of pain that swelled in her chest, Grace snatched up her cap and wool coat. She opened the window, ignoring the blustery night air, and made her way to the roof of the porch. Careful not to make too much noise as she climbed down the trellis and supporting posts, Grace jumped to the cold ground and hurried down the road toward town and the Black Briar Pub.

CHAPTER NINETEEN

Outside Laramie, WY, October 1903

Maggie limped alongside Grace, the new scrapes and bruises on her body protesting each step. They'd been damn lucky they hadn't broken their necks jumping from the train, but the alternative of burning up was far from appealing.

After rolling down the embankment, Maggie and Grace had lain flat against the ground. The train slowed to a stop nearly a quarter mile away. Shouts from men rose on the still air. Maggie hoped that they could contain the fire to the one car, that others weren't endangered by their actions.

May God, Teresa, and the Magdalene protect the souls of those poor people the demons had killed, she prayed, half surprised she'd included anyone but God and unsure what that meant.

The dead had been in the wrong place at the wrong time, caught in the crossfire between herself and Grace and the demons hunting them. Maggie hoped no other innocents would be harmed as she and Grace tried to determine what was going on, but she had the feeling that wouldn't be the case.

Pray the damage is minimal.

Once they'd determined the two of them were in one piece, Grace had suggested they head to the next town, so they started walking.

"Do you think there are more demons?" Maggie asked. If

there were two on the train, who could say there wouldn't be more? And how would they know until it was nearly too late?

"I hope to hell not," Grace said with weary honesty. "They do tend to congregate in larger cities, but whether those two were particularly assigned to follow us or happened to be on the same train is tough to tell."

"I don't tend to believe in coincidences," Maggie said. "Not anymore."

The disheveled blonde gave her a crooked grin. "We'll probably live longer that way."

It was nightfall before they made it to the small town of Parkford, circling away from the railroad tracks as far as they could manage. Coming in from a different direction might make it less likely to connect them with the railcar fire once news spread, Grace had suggested. And news would spread.

The hotel and saloon they found was a deteriorating old home that offered cheap rooms and cheaper whiskey. The owner looked askance at them when they entered bone-weary and dirty, but didn't ask questions. Just the sort of place they needed.

"Only got rooms with one bed, yanno," the man said, his eyes flicking between the two of them.

"We're sisters," Grace answered smoothly. "Shared a bed on the farm for years. She hogs the blankets."

The man gave a guffawing laugh. "Yeah, I did that to my brothers."

Exchanging half a dollar for a brass key, Maggie and Grace trudged up the creaking stairs. In the parlor-turned-tavern, piano music and the hum of voices sounded so normal. Did those people know anything about the evil among them? Any sort of hint or suspicion that perhaps the man next to them making his bet might not be what he seemed? That the woman serving their drinks or tempting them might just as soon kill them as bed them?

Shouldn't someone tell them? Warn them?

Maggie gave herself a mental shake to dislodge the thoughts. She couldn't assume everyone was a demon.

"Do you feel something?"

Grace's question pulled Maggie back to the present, to the dingy hall in front of a scratched-up door with the number six painted on it. A burst of laughter came up the stairs.

"Do they know anything?" she asked.

The gas lamp in the hall half illuminated Grace's smudged face. She glanced toward the stairs, then back to Maggie. There was a sadness of sorts in her eyes.

"No." Grace shrugged. "I don't know. Some might, but most people? No. They'd panic at the thought, do stupid things like accuse their neighbors or someone they didn't like of being demons. It's happened before."

The obvious came to Maggie's mind. "The witch trials?"

Grace nodded, turning to fit the key into the lock. "The people tried and executed were innocent. The irony being there *were* demons in Salem and elsewhere. They fed off the fear and panic for years, even instigated a few investigations of human victims to feed off their experiences. Sister Thomasina has an account in her library. One of the Long Island Order's source-catalyst pairs nearly got caught up in that mess."

She pushed open the door. The lamp from the hall illuminated a room that was barely large enough to fit the bed and a small table. Maggie and Grace hesitated in the doorway. They'd been told there was only the one bed, and it did appear large enough to fit the two of them, barely. More room than the bedroll they'd shared on the way to Laramie at any rate.

Casting a sideways glance at Maggie, Grace sighed and strode into the room. She tossed her bag onto the floor on the side of the bed closest to the door, then struck a match to light the kerosene lamp on the table.

"It'll do for the night." She took off her hat and hung it on a hook driven into the wall.

Maggie went in and shut the door behind her. She skirted around the end of the bed to set her bag down. "Cozy."

Grace gave her a tired grin. "Sure, let's call it that. The water closet is down the hall. At the risk of sounding paranoid, I

122

suggest we go together. Just in case."

It was unlikely any demons would have followed them to this establishment, but Grace had the right idea not to take chances. Maggie searched her bag for her toiletries.

"Whenever you're ready."

They made their way back down the hall to the cramped water closet. Grace stood watch first while Maggie cleaned up as best she could. As she brushed her teeth and washed her face, she sensed Grace on the other side of the door. Not just her magic, which the two of them had brought to the ready, but an awareness of the woman herself, her concern, her weariness, her care for Maggie.

Maggie tried to probe those feelings a bit further. The care Grace felt for her was a warm, soft blanket. Understandable, considering their partnership, but there was more. As soon as Maggie tried to see beyond the veneer of friendship, there was resistance. Caution. An anxiousness that made her think Grace was hiding something.

Not hiding, she decided. Protecting herself and Maggie.

She doesn't want to scare you.

The memories Maggie had regained were confusing, and the feelings that surfaced when she had kissed Grace didn't help. Or, maybe they did. As they had walked to this little town, Maggie's mind had wandered. Now and again, flashes of their lives together ran through her brain. It wasn't all there, she knew, but enough to tell her what had gone on between them.

They were pleasant recollections, despite the uncertainty of her feelings toward Grace. Pleasant until the face of John Dalton intruded, reminding her of what she'd lived with.

Maggie shuddered, revulsion slithering up her spine.

Unclean.

She put the thought out of her head the best she could, replacing it with Grace's words. It wasn't her fault that the demon had been inside John. It wasn't her fault she'd believed him to be her husband.

But did it matter who was to blame? She'd been touched by

123

that unholy thing. Wasn't that all that mattered?

She was too tired, too confused to think about it.

Pushing all thoughts of John Dalton aside, Maggie finished her ablutions and traded places with Grace. As they passed each other in the doorway, their gazes caught. Grace's cheeks flushed and she quickly looked away, hurrying to close the door behind her. Had she detected Maggie's attempt to read her? Probably.

Standing in the hall, Maggie let Grace be, focusing instead on the few patrons who climbed the stairs to their neighboring rooms. The conversation and laughter from the lower floor were quieter now, indicating others were leaving the establishment or going to bed.

Grace came out of the water closet and the two of them returned to their room. Grace locked the door.

"I didn't detect anything, did you?" she asked as she unbuttoned her shirt.

Maggie watched for a moment, then turned her back. "No."

She unbuttoned her bodice and skirt and slid them off, then removed her soft corset. She took a deep, heady breath.

"I don't understand how you wear those things," Grace said.

Startled, Maggie turned around. "You don't?"

Grace stood on the other side of the bed in her thin shift, her trousers and shirt hanging on the hook in the wall, her coat draped over her bag on the floor. Her gaze traveled over Maggie's body, bringing Maggie into full awareness of her own state of undress.

Maggie sat, her back to Grace, causing the bed to creak, and trying not to think about the form of the other woman beneath the cotton shift. She worked at the laces on her boots. "I guess you don't. They aren't so bad, really,"

The opposite side of the bed sagged and creaked with Grace's weight. "Judging from how you moved when we were attacked, your clothes don't encumber you. That's good."

"You prefer trousers," Maggie said, setting her boots aside. "Do you ever wear skirts?"

Behind her, Grace rustled the bedclothes, springs squeaking

as Maggie imagined her getting comfortable under the covers. "Not if I can help it. Used to, when Thomasina made me. But nowadays? No."

Gooseflesh rose on Maggie's arms. The chill of the room prompted her to hurry under the blankets. She took care not to touch Grace, no easy task in the narrow bed. From the corner of her eye, Maggie noticed Grace lying stiffly, staring up at the ceiling. But on the inside, there was something different from the calm exterior Grace projected. She thrummed with awareness of Maggie; their quiet connection vibrated between them.

"Are you ready for me to turn down the light?" Grace asked, her voice with just a hint of quiver in it.

"Yes." Maybe it would be easier once the light was out.

The bed creaked as Grace leaned over to douse the lantern. As her eyes adjusted to the near blackness of the room, the only light coming from the small window over the bed, Maggie listened to Grace's breathing. That seemed normal enough, yet she could feel Grace's heart beating alongside her own, fast, as if they'd just finished running.

Calm yourself, girl. Just go to sleep.

"Good night, Maggie."

Maggie closed her eyes. "Good night, Grace. *Codladh sámh.*" Grace startled hard enough to make the bed tremble. She opened her eyes and turned to look at the other woman. "What? What's wrong?"

"Nothing." Grace turned onto her side, her back to Maggie. "It's nothing. Good night."

Some sort of curtain came down between them, bringing a sudden pang of heavy sadness to Maggie's chest. What had happened?

It's been a long day. She's just tired. We both are.

Maggie listened for a long while, gauging Grace's breathing before she was certain Grace had fallen asleep.

CHAPTER TWENTY

Brooklyn, NY, April 1898

Stepping off the train, Grace breathed in the damp, acrid air along with the pleasant scent of lilacs that meant Maggie had come up behind her.

Sister Thomasina had finally deemed Grace and Maggie ready for their first hunt.

A pair from Brooklyn met them at a Flatbush Avenue station near Prospect Park, a quieter section of the metropolitan area as far as demon activity was concerned. Nervous anticipation danced along Grace's limbs. It was a cool, spring evening—not dark yet, but the sun was headed down over New York Bay.

Roberta Simmons and Cora Edelman greeted them on the platform. In their thirties, easygoing with friendly smiles, Roberta's touch of rouge and lip color set off her lovely brown skin, while Cora's dark eyes and hair accentuated her fair, freckled complexion. Like Grace and Maggie, the two women wore serviceable skirts with narrow belts, pleated blouses, heavy shawls thrown over their shoulders, and hats pinned to upswept hair. All four also wielded umbrellas whose handles concealed thin, silvered blades. Nothing too fancy, of course. They needed to blend in with almost any neighborhood, outside of the most prestigious or impoverished.

Grace would have preferred her shirt and trousers for their

first outing to easily access the knife in her boot and avoid her skirt getting in the way, but Thomasina insisted she wear appropriate clothing when out in public.

"We'll start out slow and easy," Cora assured them. "This way."

Cora linked her arm through Roberta's and turned down Flatbush Avenue. While Grace often saw lady friends stroll arm in arm, she wasn't sure how Maggie would respond to such a gesture. They'd managed to keep physical contact to a minimum since the kiss in her room, and there had been no other awkwardness. At least nothing noticeable. Grace hoped like hell Maggie hadn't been able to see what she had stashed deep in her heart.

As they walked with the other women, making small talk, Grace wanted to tell them that she and Maggie were ready for something more than "slow and easy," but held her tongue. This was their first hunt, after all, and she didn't want to appear too cocky. Maybe after a few minor demons were dispatched they could seek a greater challenge.

The cool evening had brought out couples and small groups strolling down the streets, laughing and carrying on. Storefronts and gas streetlights added a warm glow to the darkening avenues. Someone played a tune on a piano inside a music store. Two men stood in front of a stationery and printer's shop, chatting while one swept the walk.

"We don't mind something more than slow and easy," Grace said.

Cora gave her a knowing look, as if she'd heard that plenty of times. "There are higher-level activities, but we aren't going for those."

"The Legion," Maggie said.

When going for thrill kills, as with the prostitutes or other street people, demons tended to prey upon those who wouldn't be missed or mourned. The more insidious hell spawn were the kind known as the Legion. They sought victims they could emotionally torment for a sustained period, feeding off their misery for months. Those demons were also more difficult to hunt, as they managed to blend into the populace, creating deeper relationships with their targets. Specially trained hunters pursued those, playing a delicate game of intrigue, sometimes for years.

"Correct," Roberta replied, gesturing that they'd be turning down a side street where there was less foot traffic. "We're interested in more immediate results."

"With less risk," Cora added. "At least for now."

"Have you ever done anything longer, more involved?" Grace asked.

Cora and Roberta went quiet and tension crackled in the air.

"Yes, several years ago," Cora said. She and Roberta lost their carefree air. "It was . . . difficult."

Grace hadn't meant to dredge up anything painful for them. "I'm sorry."

"It's all right." Roberta seemed to shake off whatever emotion had surfaced. "We were successful in getting the bastard. That's what matters."

Cora drew Roberta a little closer. "Sometimes you don't realize what you have in you, what you're willing to do to survive, until you're in the thick of it."

Roberta patted the other woman's hand. Grace heard one of them cough, as if trying to cover some other expression.

The four walked a bit further in silence. They spoke no more of what had happened, and Grace didn't want to pry. If events or lessons learned were pertinent to fighting demons, she was sure Cora and Roberta would share their knowledge. Their personal journey was not for public consumption.

Some scars you get will not be the kind to show off to friends, Rémy had once said. *Some are not scars at all, but wounds that remain open and sensitive for quite some time.*

"This way," Roberta said, guiding them down a dark, narrow street.

Brick buildings stained with grime and smoke seemed to lean toward each other. The stench of sour beer and urine burned

128

Grace's eyes and nostrils.

"There's a pub and a few dope dens here." Cora's voice was low, her gaze sweeping along the street and doorways. "Easy pickings for demons. Mostly young, low-level sorts."

"Where you find the prey, you find the predators," Maggie said with a hint of sadness in her voice. People may have chosen alcohol and other things to ease their pain, or whatever their reason, but none considered what else might be waiting for them in the dark and shadows.

"We'll start here," Roberta said, securing her umbrella through her belt. The others followed suit. "Let's see how it goes."

Now that she and Maggie were on a real hunt, after real demons, a thread of nervousness weaved itself through her anticipation.

Maggie's support came through even before her catalyst took her hand. A sense of strength and comfort moved up her arm and into her chest. She sent the same back to Maggie.

A door opened, and the raucous notes of a bawdy song Grace had often heard at the Black Briar filtered onto the street. A man stumbled out, his arm over the shoulders of a woman who had her arm around his waist. Both laughed as he slipped on God knew what, nearly taking them to the ground.

"There, I think," Cora said just loud enough for them to hear. "Careful about getting too close."

They let the couple get a little ahead of them, then followed. Treading the same path, something irritated Grace's nostrils, something that wafted over the stench of urine and rot and alcohol, a spicy bite. She rubbed her nose against a sneeze, but the tang seemed to be printed on her brain.

Cora and Roberta reminded them to remain calm but attentive. Losing the couple wouldn't end their night—there were plenty of demons to be had—but it was good practice to stay on target.

"Try to be aware of spotters and such." Roberta pointed out shadowed doorways and low roofs. "Sometimes they work in pairs or trios, waiting for their accomplice to select and isolate a victim."

"Understood." Grace followed her lead and searched the area as they continued behind the laughing, stumbling pair. She called up her magic and sent out a thin tendril, seeking any hint of other demons. Nothing but the couple before them.

Him or her? From the distance they maintained, it was difficult to be sure.

"What do you think?" Maggie asked, her voice low, barely brushing Grace's ear. Their magic was one, their perceptions the same.

"Can we get closer?" Grace asked Cora and Roberta.

"We will once we get around this corner." Cora indicated an alley. "She won't get far with him."

"I don't think it's her," Grace said.

Cora and Roberta glanced at her, then each other.

"Generally, they prey upon drunks and drug addicts," Roberta said. "He's the inebriated one, by far."

Grace swallowed hard and exchanged a look with Maggie. Her catalyst nodded once, encouraging her confidence. "I know," she said, "but there's something about *him*."

They stopped at the corner, allowing the drunk man and the woman to get ahead.

"Likely headed to the blind alley just down that way," Cora said. She turned to Grace. "You two take the lead. We'll be right behind you."

"You're sure about the man?" Roberta didn't sound convinced.

Doubt crept into Grace's thoughts. Was she?

"She's sure," Maggie said. Grace nodded. "Let's go."

She slid her hand into Grace's and they headed down the alley.

Staying in the shadows, they caught a glimpse of their quarry turning down the only gap between the buildings. The dead-end Cora had mentioned.

Maggie squeezed her hand. "*Cor unum, et fortissimi.*"

She barely finished the first part of the phrase when their

respective powers rose and met. The sensation of rushing blood and energy took her breath for a moment, it happened so swiftly. Almost immediately, Maggie was there to mitigate their combined magic.

They were ready.

They peered around the corner of the narrow alley. It opened on a small cul-de-sac that was barely lit by a single light over the rear door of one of the three buildings that enclosed the space. The man and the woman stood to the right, in the shadows of where two of the buildings met. The man pawed awkwardly at the woman's breast, his face pressed to her neck. She didn't reciprocate, hardly moving at all and not seeming to say anything.

Was she wrong? Was the woman the inhuman creature after all, waiting for the right moment to strike?

Grace and Maggie eased forward, circling the perimeter of the dead-end. The spicy scent grew stronger as they approached.

The man said something too low to understand.

The woman cried out softly, "Please. Stop."

His hand went under her skirt. "You want this. You want to do this. To *be* this."

"No." The word came out in a sob. "Not that."

"Slut," he growled. "Whore" echoed off the bricks. Grace's stomach tightened. Every word he spoke had to make the woman hurt more, and he was lapping up every drop of her pain. "All you're good for is the streets. You know it's so. Say it."

A wordless sob from the woman.

That was enough. Grace's anger spiked with her magic. Maggie met Grace's power with her own. Grace formed fiery blue darts within her palm, something small and controllable with the demon in such close proximity to its human prey.

She threw the darts at the man. *Take that, you bastard.*

He howled when the phantom projectiles pierced his coat and trousers and smoldered against flesh. He shoved the woman aside and turned to face the assault.

"Bitch! Whore!" His voice resonated with an inhuman undertone. He started toward Grace and Maggie, his eyes orange-red bright spots in the darkness.

"You need a better vocabulary." Grace threw another handful of darts at his face.

The demon squealed and stumbled, trying to wipe away the magic.

"Finish him," Maggie said.

Grace drew on their power, forming a bluish-purple fireball, and lobbed it at the demon. It hit him square in the chest with a satisfying *thwump*, igniting his clothing. The spicy scent that hung in the air turned bitter as he burned. The high-pitched scream he emitted set dogs to barking two streets over.

From the corner of her eye Grace saw movement. Another demon? A helper they hadn't detected? She started to generate another fireball, but it was Roberta going toward the woman who huddled against the wall.

"Stand down," Cora said from behind her and Maggie.

They withdrew their magic from each other. Power seeped back into Grace, quieted for now. She breathed hard, not from exertion but from the excitement, the adrenaline, that still coursed through her.

Maggie's hand on her arm drew her attention. Her catalyst smiled, dark eyes dancing in the poor light. "Brilliant."

"Roberta will escort the woman back to a safe place." Cora urged them to retreat toward the main alley. "Come on. We'll meet her a few blocks from here. There's a tea shop that stays open late."

Leaving the demon smoldering on the cobbles, they followed Cora back the way they came. After several turns, each bringing them to more populated streets, they stood on Flatbush Avenue once again. Grace marveled at how everyday people knew nothing of demons, had no awareness of what had just happened a few blocks away. Or if they heard or saw anything, how the idea of demons and magic wouldn't occur to them.

"What will Roberta tell the woman?" Maggie asked.

It took a moment for Cora to respond; she seemed lost in her own thoughts, walking stiffly, with purpose. She stared at

Maggie, her brow creased, as if seeing her for the first time.

"She'll weave some sort of tale," Cora said. "She's good at convincing people they didn't see what they thought they saw."

"Useful skill to have." Grace wondered if it was a natural talent or something the Order had taught Roberta.

"Quite." After several steps, Cora stopped in the middle of the walk. Grace and Maggie stopped as well. "How did you know?" she asked, a mix of wonder and confusion on her face.

"Know what?" Grace couldn't think of what she meant.

"How did you know it was the man and not the woman?" She didn't say the word demon, for too many people populated the street where they stood. "You shouldn't have been able to tell which was which until we were closer. How did you know?"

How *did* she know? She looked at Maggie, who had the same bemused expression Grace knew she herself wore. Grace turned to Cora again. "I-I don't know. I just did. There was some sort of odd scent in the air . . ."

Maggie nodded. She had smelled it as well.

Cora shook her head, assessing Grace and Maggie as if from a different angle. She had no idea what Grace was talking about. "Roberta will be along soon and we'll go after another."

Cora walked off, fists opening and closing at her sides.

Maggie slipped her arm through Grace's and they hurried to catch up. When she looked at her catalyst, Grace noticed Maggie was grinning.

"What are you smiling about?"

Maggie hugged her arm tighter. "Cora knows you're somethin' else, just as I always said."

Grace smiled back. Suddenly, she was aware of Maggie's warmth, the press of her breast against Grace's arm. She wanted to kiss her catalyst, her partner, and never stop.

It's the magic, she reminded herself. *The rush of shared power, of defeating evil.*

No, it was more than that. Far more than that.

Maggie's smile shifted into not a frown exactly, more like her own realization of what was happening. She knew what

Grace was feeling. Moreover, she felt the same.

Grace knew that was so from the pit of her stomach to the bottom of her heart, from the tingle of her toes to the sudden dryness of her throat.

Eyes locked on Maggie's, Grace tilted her head. Maggie's lips parted as she leaned forward, but in anticipation or protest? Grace couldn't sort out all the impressions she was getting from her catalyst.

A sudden burst of laughter from a group of young dandies approaching from up the street shot through the evening air. Maggie jerked back, going so far as to pull her arm away and separate herself from Grace.

Grace frowned with disappointment and irritation. Maggie's guilt also bled through. Or was it her own?

"We should catch up to Cora." Maggie barely touched Grace's arm to encourage her to start after the other hunter.

At the café, the three settled at a lace-covered table in a quiet corner. Cora ordered a pot of strong black tea. They were the only patrons, other than a couple who shared a pastry.

While they waited for Roberta, Grace couldn't get the terrified face of the woman they had just saved out of her mind. How many more like her were hurt every day, every year? If the people around them only knew what really happened to some who were less fortunate, would they care? Did the group of dandies have any clue that there could be demons among them? Though perhaps their sort were victims as well, succumbing to their own desires and foibles.

Grace glanced at Maggie as she spoke quietly with Cora about the mundane things young women in a tea shop spoke about. Yes, she knew a thing or two about desires and foibles.

CHAPTER TWENTY-ONE

Freetown, Long Island, NY, September 1898

Maggie stepped into the overly warm front room of the Black Briar. A wave of stale beer, stale bodies, and cigar smoke nearly had her step back out into the cool late-summer night. Resolve overcame revulsion and she entered, shutting the heavy wooden door behind her. None of the patrons sitting at the bar gave her more than a glance, despite the fact she was obviously female and unescorted, a violation of pub rules.

"Someone's in for a heap o' trouble," one of the men said.

You're damn right about that, Maggie thought as she scanned the room. A faint whiff of magic caught her attention.

There, at a table in the corner, Grace sat with her back to the wall, facing the entrance, her cap and coat on despite her proximity to the fireplace. The cap held her hair up, and the coat was bulky enough to conceal her figure. They didn't fool Maggie, of course, and wouldn't have fooled any of the men there, but the hint of magic Grace used completed the illusion well enough for her to pass.

Grace focused on the spread of cards in her hand, flicking the one on the end with her thumbnail. The four men sitting with her were chatting, drinking their beers.

Maggie strode up to the table. A pile of coins sat in the middle of the scarred wooden planks, and the players had varying amounts of cash at their elbows. Not a rich man's game, for certain, seeing as there were mostly pennies and nickels.

One of the men glanced up and winked. "We'll deal you in next time, sweetheart."

Grace's gaze shifted from her cards to the man who spoke to Maggie. Her fair cheeks paled. "Shit."

All of the men turned to Maggie.

One guffawed. "Uh oh, Johnny. Looks like you been caught."

Grace shot the man a glare. "She ain't my mother." She looked up at Maggie. "You don't belong here. Go home."

"You don't belong here either," Maggie said.

"Mostly cuz he stinks at poker," one of the men said.

The others laughed.

"Better 'an you," Grace challenged, pointing at his smaller pile of coins.

Maggie crossed her arms. "That's neither here nor there."

"Aw, what's the big deal?" the man nearest Maggie asked. He snaked his arm around her waist and drew her onto his lap. "Stick around, sis. We'll show you a good time."

Grace's power spiked. Maggie dampened it as best she could while elbowing the man none too gently in his gut. He "oofed" and released her. Maggie gained her feet as Grace rose, her hands clenched, and her face red as she glared at the man.

"Touch her again and I'll—"

"I'm fine," Maggie said. She patted the offender on the shoulder, pleased he was wincing and rubbing his stomach. Luckily, the other men teased him into laughing about the incident. "No harm done, eh?"

"Nah," he said. His indifferent expression hinted that he knew he'd deserved what he'd gotten. "You in or out, Johnny? We got a game to finish."

Grace pushed her chair in and gathered her small pile of coins. "Out. But I'll beat the pants off you next time."

Amid the friendly taunts of the players, Grace took Maggie's arm and escorted her to the door.

"See you 'round, Johnny," the bartender called. "Maybe next

time bring your girl in and she won't be so stirred up when you don't come home on time."

Grace rudely waved off the laughter that followed them out the door.

"Yes," Maggie said, extracting her arm from Grace's hold. "Maybe I'd like a drink or two with you and your friends."

"Pretty sure you wouldn't." Grace shoved her hands deep into her coat pockets.

"You can drop the magic disguise. No one'll be looking too closely at you on the way back."

It was late enough, and chilly enough, that the streets of Freetown were all but deserted. The mile walk to the house would be only somewhat uncomfortable, as long as the weather didn't change much.

Though Maggie saw no difference in Grace's appearance, the light sheen of power surrounding her source faded and disappeared.

"You shouldn't have come out," Grace said. "It can be dangerous."

"Dangerous for me, but not for you?" Maggie snorted a laugh to keep her ire in check. "Spare me your chivalrous platitudes, Johnny."

Grace glared at her. "Don't call me that."

"Why not? Isn't that who you are when you sneak out and hide at the Black Briar?"

Grace stopped under the last light post before the road to the house became little more than a dark path. Her eyes were wide, her expression one of offense. "That's not true. I'm not hiding at the Briar. You found me well enough." Her fists clenched, and the wave of her anger caught Maggie by surprise. "I'll own up to the drinking and gambling," she said hotly. "Being Johnny for them makes it easier to do something I enjoy and just forget about life for a bit. I don't even know why we're having this conversation. It's none of your business what I do when we aren't hunting."

She started off again, arms swinging stiffly, as if she was

keeping herself from punching someone.

Maggie crossed her arms, peeved to have stopped and lost the heat of walking, but the heat of her own confused irritation would suffice.

It took a few moments for the hurt under Grace's words to register.

"Is that all we are now, Grace? We just hunt together when an assignment comes up? Living separate lives, like Mrs. Reynolds and Sister Thomasina?"

Grace stopped just outside of the soft yellow light of the lamp post, her back to Maggie. But Maggie saw her shoulders heaving, the pain and turmoil from her source palpable. How long had Grace hidden such emotions?

No, they weren't merely hunting partners, but Maggie had pushed Grace away. What had she expected to happen?

Slowly, Grace turned around. Her jaw was set, and tears ran down her reddened cheeks. "I try, Maggie. I honest to God try to do as you wish. But you can't have it both ways. You can't tell me we shouldn't act on our feelings and then tell me how to keep myself from thinking about you every damn minute of every damn day. It's not fair."

Realization hit Maggie like a fist in the gut.

She drove Grace to the Black Briar, to drinking and playing cards as a way to distract herself. Just as Maggie distracted herself with her studies preparing for her final vows.

"This is my fault," Maggie said, her voice nearly strangled by guilt. "I misled you, kissed you when I should have controlled myself."

Grace shook her head. "I won't lay blame on you. We kissed each other. We're partners, and we will figure this out, but for now—" Her voice caught and she closed her eyes. When she opened them again, her pain shimmered in unshed tears. "For now, we need to stay away from each other unless we're training or hunting."

Maggie stared at her source, jaws clenched to hold back her own tears. She had made a mistake. A huge mistake. All the time spent in the library, avoiding Grace. It had been the easy way out of a difficult situation. Easier for her, but not for the most important person in her world.

"I'm sorry, Grace." Her throat locked. It took her two hard swallows to find her voice again. "I never meant to hurt you. Never."

The sad, broken smile Grace gave her nearly brought Maggie to her knees. "I know you didn't."

She turned around and disappeared down the lane, her footfalls rapidly fading.

Maggie stood at the side of the road, allowing Grace time to get back to the house, and allowing herself time to collect her thoughts. Shivering, she purposely kept her steps slow when she finally started walking. In a way, perhaps, she was punishing herself for being so foolish. She rubbed her arms, teeth chattering. She couldn't go back on her commitment to the Order, but she couldn't continue hurting her source either.

By the time she returned to the house, her cheeks were numb and her legs felt leaden beneath her skirts. On the second floor, Maggie went to her room. Hand on the knob, she glanced at Grace's door. No telltale band of light leaked from beneath it, but she heard a thud and a curse from within.

Maggie's heart fluttered. Grace was still awake.

She doesn't want to talk to you.

No, but Maggie knew she wouldn't sleep as long as this turmoil was between them. It hurt twice as much knowing she'd caused it.

Maggie moved to Grace's door and knocked. There was no reply, but Grace's emotions jumped, as if pinched. She knocked again.

Within seconds, the door opened. Grace was still dressed, her shirt half open, her suspenders off her shoulders and hanging past her hips. Her blond hair was out of the braid that had been tucked under the cap she'd worn to the Black Briar. A small lamp burned on the bedside table behind her.

She stared at Maggie with the same hurt in her eyes that

had been there since they'd stopped at the corner. Since they'd kissed months ago and Maggie had pulled away.

"I need—" No, enough of what *she* needed. "Can we talk, please?"

Grace didn't move for a few seconds, and truth be told, Maggie wouldn't have been surprised if she had shut the door in her face. But she didn't. Grace stepped aside and let Maggie into her room. She quietly closed the door, then leaned against it, arms crossed.

Another nervous flutter tickled Maggie's gut. She couldn't let it stop her. She couldn't keep hurting her source like this.

"I'm sorry," Maggie said, feeling Grace's pain, her wariness. "You're the most important person in the world to me."

"If I'm so important to you, why are you pushing me away?"

"Because I'm an idiot."

Grace's snort of a laugh helped ease the ache a little. She wiped her eyes with her sleeve. "That's the truth."

Maggie choked out a chuckle of agreement, but grew sober again. "Because I didn't want to get hurt again. Because I knew Thomasina and the Doyenne would be angry if I were to forsake my vows, even if they weren't officially taken." She stepped closer to Grace and laid her hand on her source's arm. The heat of her seeped through the cotton. Her love wrapped around Maggie's soul. She returned that warmth, the feelings she'd denied for too long. "Because I don't *want* to forsake my vows, but I can't deny that I have feelings for you."

Grace unfolded her arms and grasped Maggie's hands. "That's what made it hurt so much."

Maggie nodded, relieved that Grace understood, but that didn't solve their problem. "What now? We can't just ignore this any longer."

"And I don't want you to go against your promise," Grace said.

Maggie felt the tinge of disappointment in her source, but the support for Maggie's decision was stronger. "Can we do everything but . . . *that*?" She knew her emphasis on the word told Grace exactly what *that* was. "Can we have feelings, be together, and not cross that line? Or is it too much to ask?"

Grace stared down at their hands. Her churning emotions were the same as Maggie. After several moments, Grace met her gaze again.

"What sort of being together?"

Celibacy was part of the Order's vows. What wouldn't violate that promise?

"Hugging. Holding hands." Maggie could see in Grace's eyes that she was hoping for more. "Some kissing."

Knowing herself, she didn't dare propose more.

Grace swallowed and nodded. "All right. I'd rather have that much than lose you altogether. I couldn't bear that."

"Me neither." Maggie drew her in, wrapping her arms around Grace's waist. Grace rested her chin on Maggie's shoulder. "Thank you for understanding."

"Anything for you, Mags." She nuzzled Maggie's neck. "Anything."

CHAPTER TWENTY-TWO

Outside Parkland, WY, October 1903

The sun was brilliant in a bright blue sky, the autumn air fresh and crisp. Maggie and Grace walked to the Parkford train station, a small building barely more than a shack on the side of the road, to purchase new tickets to Denver. Fellow travelers seemed friendly enough, though Grace found herself scanning the few standing there for signs of trouble. Yesterday's attack might have been opportunistic, but they had to assume the Order and the demon clans knew about Maggie escaping their purview. Better to be alert than complacent.

There was a great deal of conversation around them regarding the fire on the previous day's train. No one understood how the car could have gone up in flames to begin with. One of the bodies found was so completely burned as to be unidentifiable, barely recognized as human, according to accounts.

"Thank goodness for small favors," Maggie said quietly as they sat on a wooden bench listening to two gentlemen discuss the event.

Grace spoke with her lips close to Maggie's ear. "Lucky for us demons burn fast and furious."

The train announced its arrival with a loud blast of its whistle and the bluster of dust and steam. Few got off any of the cars, making it easier and faster for the waiting passengers to board. Grace and Maggie found a seat in the last row—for ease of watching the other passengers as well as potential need for a quick escape. Again.

The train whistle blew twice more, and with a shout of "all aboard" from the conductor, their second attempt at going south began. Grace felt Maggie within her, equally on alert as they picked up speed. There wasn't another scheduled stop for nearly two hours. If a demon had boarded, it had a small window of opportunity to attack, as had its brethren the day before.

Grace didn't think there would be another attempt on them so soon, and not in the same manner. Demons were adamant, but they weren't stupid. Repeating an attack method would draw more attention to them than they were willing to withstand. That was an advantage the Order had over the evil bastards. Despite their desire to inflict harm on the human race, there seemed to be too much competition among themselves for demons to organize enough to overwhelm a prepared and attentive enemy.

"I think we're okay for now," Grace said, allowing herself to relax some. She sure as hell wouldn't fall asleep on a train ever again.

"For now," Maggie repeated. There was a hint of defeat in her voice, but she offered a small grin to counter it. "It'll be nice when we don't have to live our lives 'for now.'"

Grace couldn't agree more, but for the likes of them, there was a different level of normal. The plan to disappear out west with Maggie was starting to look less feasible. What made her think they could just walk away?

Anger gurgled in her stomach. Damn the Order and damn the Horde. She was sick and tired of them both.

"I don't think we'll get to do that," Grace said with a frustrated sigh. "Not any time soon, at least. We need to put an end to this before we can hope for anything approaching normal."

Maggie cocked her head. "What do you suggest?"

"Let's visit Mrs. Wallace. She might have some advice, maybe even some answers for us now that we have a little more information."

"She's with the Order." Maggie sounded skeptical, and with good reason.

Grace considered the older woman she had met with a month ago. "She helped me find you."

"To help *us* or to help *them*?"

It wasn't an unreasonable question.

"My gut says to help us, but we'll be careful." She gave Maggie a grim smile. "We don't have much in the way of choices."

Maggie nodded absently and stared out the window at the browns and greens of the land they travelled. Two small worry lines dimpled the skin between her eyebrows. Grace wanted to smooth out those lines, to tell her all would be well. She had hoped that once she'd found Maggie, that would be the truth, that they would be together and start new lives elsewhere, far from the Order.

A thump and clatter near the door between cars caught Grace's attention. Maggie's power came up alongside her own as they both focused on the end of the car. The door opened and the conductor came through. Not a demon, just a man doing his job.

Grace and Maggie exchanged glances as their magic subsided.

Someday they'd live normal lives. Today was not that day.

Denver, CO, October 1903

"Are you sure we can trust her?" Maggie asked.

They stood on the rain-damp street at the edge of Denver city limits outside a three-story home painted a pretty blue with purple and white trim. The lawn was neatly cropped, and autumn flowers along the slate path to the porch had somehow managed to survive the chilly nights. Horses' hooves clopped down the street as the carriage they'd hired to carry them from

144

the train station to Mrs. Wallace's address made its way back to the heart of the city.

Whether Mrs. Wallace's involvement was to their benefit remained to be seen in Maggie's opinion. At the moment, she trusted no one but Grace.

"It'll be fine," her source said, starting up the walk.

Her source. The idea of their partnership, their connection, had become normal. That had to be a good thing.

"That isn't an answer." Maggie didn't move to follow.

Grace turned around, frowning. "I don't have the answer you want."

She was frustrated; they both were. And scared. For each other, for their situation. Of course, there were no sureties. Grace had taken risks to locate Maggie and learned to put at least a little faith in the people who had helped her. Maggie hadn't gotten that far yet.

"I know. Sorry. I'm just . . ." She started forward, but Grace stopped her with a hand to the shoulder.

"I know," Grace said softly, understanding in her green eyes. "But she's all we've got at the moment."

They had each other, but they'd need more than that to truly escape the Order.

Maggie nodded, and together they walked the path and climbed the wide stairs of the porch. Grace rapped on the dark purple door with the scrolled brass knocker.

After a few moments, a young woman in servant's black answered. She was about Grace and Maggie's age, with dark hair and pale skin, as if she never went outdoors. Suspicious near-black eyes darted between Grace and Maggie.

"Yes?"

Something twitched inside Maggie, a sense of familiarity. Had she met this woman before? Beside her, Grace startled, as if waking suddenly. Their power flickered and warmed Maggie's belly.

"Good morning," Grace said. "Is Mrs. Wallace available? My name is Grace Carter. She knows me."

The maid or housekeeper or whatever she was opened the door wider. "If you'll wait here in the foyer, I'll get her."

They stepped inside and the young woman shut the door behind them. The foyer was brightly lit and gaily decorated with paintings of landscapes hanging on the walls of the hall and stairway. Bric-a-brac and figures stood on shelves and side tables. The cool air smelled of cinnamon and coffee.

Without another word, the young woman headed down the hall. She passed an open doorway on the left, then turned right down another hall and disappeared.

"It's quiet in here," Maggie whispered. She shifted on her feet, her bag feeling cumbersome in her hand.

There were no voices, no clatter of dishes or kitchen noises. Wherever the servant had disappeared to, it seemed to be deeper into the house than the next room.

Grace peered up the dimly lit stairway. "Mrs. Wallace didn't strike me as a particularly loud person when we met."

"It's a little unnerving." Maggie craned her neck to follow Grace's gaze. "A house this size should have—"

"Mrs. Wallace will be out shortly."

Grace and Maggie both jumped. The maid was right beside them. How had she approached without making a sound?

The young woman gestured toward the open door on the left. "She asked if you'd have a seat in the parlor."

Heart almost back to its normal rhythm, Maggie led the way into the room. The back of her neck prickled as she passed the maid.

Just nerves, she told herself. *You're in a strange house with a woman who may or may not be trustworthy. Take a breath and relax.*

The fire was crackling in the fireplace, and a tea service was arranged on a side table within the cozy room. Again, it was as if Mrs. Wallace knew they'd be arriving.

"She'll be right in." The maid backed out of the room and turned toward the same hall she'd disappeared down before.

Grace set her bag down by the chair that allowed her to see the entirety of the room. The divan and other chairs afforded a less advantageous view. Maggie took the seat on the divan closest to Grace. The tea service was on the table near her. Maggie held her palm to the plump silver pot. Thankfully, it was cool to the touch.

"Did you expect it to be hot?" Grace asked.

Maggie was only marginally embarrassed to have been caught in that very thought. "If it had been, I'd have been halfway to the door already."

A smile curved Grace's mouth. "I'd have been right behind you."

"I hope I don't scare you that much," an amused, musical voice said from the doorway.

Once again, Maggie jumped, and their magic flared. The two of them came to their feet, half ready to fight or defend themselves, half in acknowledgment of their hostess.

"Please, relax, ladies," Mrs. Wallace said. "I have no intention of harming you."

The lady of the house wore a high-collared russet day dress that nearly matched the color of her eyes. Her graying black hair was fashionably coiffed, up off her neck in an elaborate coil. Delicate lines on her oval face showed an indeterminate age. Older than Grace and herself, but younger than Sister Thomasina, as Maggie remembered her.

Smiling, Mrs. Wallace strode up to Grace, her right hand extended. "Grace, so nice to see you again," she said as she took Grace's hand. Releasing Grace, she turned to Maggie. "I see my information was helpful. I'm very happy you're safe."

Maggie reluctantly allowed the woman to shake her hand. The contact was completely normal. Why was she so jittery?

"Please, have a seat." Mrs. Wallace gestured toward their places. She glanced back toward the door where her maid stood. "Beatrix, be a dear and bring the tea in. And those little almond cookies."

Beatrix hesitated, her dark eyes jumping to each of them before she departed to do her mistress's bidding. Something was off about Mrs. Wallace's servant, but Maggie couldn't put her finger on it.

Mrs. Wallace moved the silver tea service from the side table to the table in front of the divan and the other chairs. She sat in the chair with her back to the door. "I read about the strange fire on the train out of Laramie last night. Seems that several passengers are unaccounted for."

She continued to arrange cups and saucers, neither asking if Grace and Maggie were involved nor making any sort of eye contact. Yet Maggie got the impression she knew the truth.

"An unfortunate incident," Maggie said.

Mrs. Wallace looked at her, her eyes sparkling. "What a lovely accent. I spent six months in Waterford early in my training. I hope to go back someday."

Beatrix returned, bearing a tray with a floral china teapot and matching cups. She set them on the table before them, and Maggie leaned away from her. There was something about the servant that set her on edge. Her too-quiet arrivals? Her piercing black eyes?

Beatrix removed the silver service and put it back on the side table where it had resided.

"We should use the silver for guests," Mrs. Wallace admonished.

"I just polished it," the other woman said. "I'm not going to do it again so soon."

Maggie blinked at the curious exchange. She glanced at Grace. Her source's eyebrows were arched, but otherwise she seemed undisturbed by how mistress and servant spoke to one another.

Beatrix stepped away from the seating area, yet remained in the room. Mrs. Wallace poured out the tea, ignoring the maid's insubordination.

"I'm glad you were able to accomplish your goal, Grace," she said. "Are you here to return the favor?"

Trepidation tickled the base of Maggie's spine. What had Grace promised in return for the information this woman had given her? She hadn't mentioned any of that. What price was she willing to pay to have found Maggie?

Grace moistened her lips as she accepted a cup and saucer. "Not quite yet. We have more questions and need more information."

Mrs. Wallace gave her a knowing smile. "Surprise surprise."

Trepidation became annoyance. "You know more about what happened to us than you're letting on," Maggie said.

"No, no." Mrs. Wallace held up a beringed hand. "At the time, I knew only what I'd told Grace. This I swear."

Grace narrowed her gaze. "But you know more now."

"Not as much as I'd like, I assure you." The older woman drew a deep breath, glancing between the two of them. "My God, you really do fill a room, don't you? You may want to work on that." Without explaining what she meant, Mrs. Wallace looked to Beatrix. "Come here, please."

The servant hesitated, but then did as she was bade. She sat on the far end of the divan, close to Mrs. Wallace's seat, hands clenched. "Don't."

Mrs. Wallace shook her head slightly, a sad, resigned expression on her face. "They'll figure it out soon enough, and they need to understand."

She closed her eyes and raised one hand, palm out, glowing a dull green. Beatrix shivered, her fists shaking.

All at once, a spicy scent filled Maggie's nostrils and the uncertainty about the maid blossomed into fear and anger. She and Grace shot to their feet, shoulder to shoulder, power tinging their hands purple and blue, respectively.

A roiling ball of fire coalesced in Grace's hand. "Demon!"

CHAPTER TWENTY-THREE

New York City, June 1901

Arm in arm, Grace and Maggie strolled down the brightly lit boulevard, music and laughter from clubs and dance halls filling the hot summer night. Maggie's cornflower blue dress and flowing silk wrap hid the bulge of the pistol accessible through a secret pocket. She cooled herself with a lace fan in her free hand. Grace's knife was strapped to her thigh, easily reachable through a similar slit in her skirt. She was sweating in the unaccustomed clothing, even though she wore as little under her gown as she could get away with.

They had just finished dinner with Cora and Roberta, mixing the business of coordinating their hunts with the pleasure of catching up on personal lives. After coffee, the other women had headed in the opposite direction in search of their own quarry. Demon activity had jumped in the last few weeks, and several teams from the Order were working in the area.

"*Cor unum*," Maggie whispered, more out of nearly three years of habit than any actual need to create a connection. Their magic sparked before the phrase was fully spoken.

"A little farther, I think," Grace said, indicating an alley a few more blocks away. "That's where the pair of doxies was found."

Maggie released Grace's arm and secured the wrap around her shoulders with a loose knot. She'd toss it aside, if necessary, to avoid getting tangled.

Maggie's power trickled through Grace as her catalyst prepared for battle. There was no guarantee a demon or two would be about in any particular neighborhood, but sweltering summer days made humans hot and cranky. Short tempers were like candy to the Horde.

Her own magic slid alongside Maggie's, the two tendrils twisting around each other. With each step, each breath, their power strengthened, filled her. Filled them both. Was this what dope fiends experienced, this rush of adrenaline? This heady sensation of being invincible? No wonder they succumbed to their addictions.

She knew they weren't invincible, and had a few scars to show for it, but there was no denying the fact that together she and Maggie were a force to be reckoned with.

A dank odor wafted on the air. Not the typical stink of garbage or urine or unwashed bodies. There were those too, but roiling within the stench of human waste was a now-familiar spicy bite: demon.

"They're close," Grace said, her voice no more than a whisper.

She surveyed the dimly lit avenue, aware that there weren't just fewer people on the street; she and Maggie were alone. Their footsteps echoed back from brick buildings. The sound of music, of safety, faded in the distance.

"To the left," Maggie said, nodding toward an alley.

They stopped at the corner of the building and peered down the narrow lane. Light bled into the darkness from the streetlamps, just enough to show two figures along the opposite wall. From their motions and the sound of heavy breathing, it seemed they were engaged in carnal activities Grace didn't want to consider. Not with a demon. The question was, which one was their quarry?

Maggie tugged on her arm, drawing Grace back. She put her mouth close to Grace's ear. Demons had excellent hearing. It probably knew the two of them were there, but hopefully not who and what they were.

"We'll come around the corner, angry that this chippy's

151

invading our territory," Maggie said.

That could work, considering the area. Just passing some of the ladies garnered looks that burned, as they tussled over territory all the time. Even if this block *were* hers, a trumped-up dispute would not be unusual.

"Sounds good," Grace said. She increased the flow of power to her hands, but not so much that they glowed the tell-tale blue of full readiness.

Maggie did the same, her hands faintly purple, their deep connection sending a thrill through Grace. "All right. Let's go."

They strode around the corner as if they belonged there, as if they owned the street. The magic flowing through Grace hummed agreement. Yes, she and Maggie were the greater power here, in charge.

The alley dead-ended at a low wall, the light from windows on the other side lending weak illumination.

"Hey," Maggie called to the couple against the wall. "What the hell do ye think yer doin'?" Her accent had taken on a less refined note. "Yer in our fecking alley. Get out."

The man stopped thrusting against the woman. Both turned their heads, but neither moved otherwise. Shadows played across their faces, the light coming from behind, making it difficult to discern features. The odor of urine and garbage mixed with the aroma of demon. Until she and Maggie were closer, they wouldn't be able to determine their target.

"I'll get to you two next," the man growled. "Keep your knickers on."

"That's not how it works," Grace said. She inhaled. The spicy scent was more pronounced. Damn it, which one?

He stepped away from the woman, fussing with the front of his trousers while she smoothed down her skirt.

"I know exactly how this works, bitch." He gestured, and the first needle-sharp effects of his attack hit Grace. Beside her, Maggie grunted as she absorbed the same before their shield was fully up.

At least they knew which one was the demon.

Grace made a fist and punched the air in front of her. The demon reeled, arms windmilling. He didn't fall, but stood swaying, head hanging.

The woman raised her hands. "My turn."

Shit.

"I've got her," Maggie said, and hurled a purple fireball at the creature.

The hum of their power vibrated through Grace. The demons they'd encountered were often unpleasantly surprised to find the "weaker" member of the team was anything but. Maggie was a force to be reckoned with in her own right.

"And I've got him," Grace said, drawing on her magic. Blue claws extended from the tips of her fingers.

The demon advanced, head bowed and arms out, ready to grapple with her.

Hold your ground. Grace trembled with anticipation, fighting the urge to run at him. Her split skirt made maneuvering easier, but going toward him could put her closer to Maggie's fireball.

The demon leapt at her from ten feet away, mouth open to reveal long, pointed teeth.

Grace struck as he descended, raking eldritch claws across his chest. Magic burned slashes through his waistcoat and shirt, into his skin. The stench of scorched flesh rose with his howl of pain. The force of her power threw him into the brick wall of the building.

He lay there, stunned. Grace went after him, trusting Maggie had her target well in hand. He raised his arm as she slashed at him again, cutting to the bone. He scuttled back, along the wall, through the filth and garbage.

"Not so tough after all," Grace said, avoiding the kicks to her legs he attempted as she moved forward. "I'll end you quickly, as a mercy."

"Do it," a rumbling voice called from ahead, deeper in the alley. "Then it'll be our turn."

Grace's head snapped up. Two more demons stood on the low wall. They were larger than the male and female, with broad

153

shoulders and thick necks and legs.

A flash of purple to her right and a scream of agony told Grace that Maggie had dispatched the female. Grace thrust her arm forward and impaled the male through the chest with her claws. His high-pitched keening was shortened by a swipe that decapitated him. His head rolled to the middle of the alley. Black blood oozed out of his neck.

Eyes on the two large demons, Grace withdrew the claws and stepped back. Maggie joined her. Her catalyst breathed a little fast, but was none the worse for wear. Maggie touched Grace's shoulder. Grace's power flared and she held her hands out, one facing each demon. Blue bolts shot from her palms, directly toward their chests. They dove into the alley, somersaulting then coming to their feet as the bolts passed harmlessly over their heads and hit a far wall.

"Damn it." Grace drew on her magic again, boosted by Maggie so the attack would be ready faster.

"Nice try, sweetheart," one of the demons growled.

"Let's eat," the other said, and rushed Grace and Maggie.

Grace threw a blue and purple fireball at the first demon. Simultaneously, Maggie launched a dozen small bluish-purple missiles in succession at the other. Both demons staggered, their skin sizzling, but they kept coming.

"Again!"

They launched another attack just before the demons came within reach. But the bastards were ready this time, and struck as they were hit by the pair's magic.

The demon backhanded Grace across the face. She hit the ground with a grunt, her head ringing. Across the alley, the other demon had Maggie against the wall, his hand around her throat, her feet off the ground.

Grace scrambled to her feet. Her instinct to assist her catalyst was tempered by the sensation of Maggie drawing on their power. She'd have to hold her own for now. Grace focused on her opponent. The demon grabbed for her. Grace pivoted. As she swung her arm, she infused it with magic. Hard as steel, sharp as a razor. Ducking under his outstretched arm, she hit the demon's side. Magic cut into him. He roared with pain and anger. Bringing a granite fist attack to bear, Grace punched him with the other hand. He staggered back and fell.

Thank God Rémy insisted on grappling as well as weapons training.

Across the alley, Maggie had escaped her foe. A large hole through his middle spoke of a damaging attack, but the demon wasn't down. He threw a ham-like fist at Maggie's head. Maggie dodged, but not fast enough. The blow caught her on the side of the face. She spun and fell to her knees.

"Maggie!" Grace started forward, but something snagged her foot. She fell, breaking her fall by twisting to land on her shoulder, and rolling. As she turned, she threw a stinger at the demon on the ground.

The creature's claw tightened painfully around her ankle as her magic hit him square in the face. He released her and swiped at what would have felt like the attack of one thousand bees.

Grace scrambled to her feet and threw another volley at the demon near Maggie that was pounding on the purple shimmering shield she had erected. The blow she'd received may have prevented her from calling up an offensive attack, but thankfully Maggie had had the wherewithal to defend herself.

The demon turned to Grace and snarled, shaking its left arm where her attack had landed. It lowered its head and sprinted toward her.

Grace called up the fastest manifestation of her power she could access. Her entire being shimmered with blue flames. As the demon hit her and drove her to the ground, she wrapped her arms around it. Her magic seared into the creature. She held on even as her back hit the cobbles and her teeth nipped her tongue.

Head rattling, the metallic bite of blood in her mouth, Grace strained to intensify her power. The demon roared, reared back, breaking her hold, and raised a clawed hand.

Suddenly, it was flying off of her, hurtling sideways to the grimy ground.

Grace looked over to see Maggie standing a few feet away, arms extended forward. Her hair was a loose and wild cloud of auburn around her head, her dark eyes nearly black as she stared at the lifeless demon.

After a moment, Maggie lowered her arms and came to Grace to help her up. While they stood there together to catch their breath, Grace noticed blood trickling from a small gash on Maggie's cheek.

"Here." She dug into her discarded purse for a handkerchief. She touched the cloth to her catalyst's cheek, fighting the urge to stroke her skin to sooth the injury. Grace passed the handkerchief to her. "Was that from a claw? Do we need the silver nitrate?"

Maggie dabbed at the cut, wincing slightly. Grace could already see it was going to leave a spectacular bruise under her eye. "No, not a claw. Just from his hand." She surveyed the bodies in the ally. "Better get rid of these before someone stumbles on them."

They hauled the demons to a place they could rapidly incinerate them. Not many would question the rank odor that rose from the alley, and she and Maggie would be long gone before anyone happened by.

"We should get cleaned up," Grace said, leading her source toward the main street. "Cora mentioned an uptick in activity on the west side."

Maggie took her arm and grinned. "Brilliant. Let's go get some more."

CHAPTER TWENTY-FOUR

Denver, CO, October 1903

Beatrix's eyes widened, yet she didn't move, perhaps frozen with fear at being identified.

Mrs. Wallace quickly put herself in front of the offensive creature, a shimmering shield of green raised before them. "Stop. She's mine."

Stunned by the proclamation, Maggie could only stare at the woman, a mix of anger and repulsion churning in her gut. She hardly dared to breathe, unwilling to take in more of the tainted scent. John. She—it—was just like John.

"What the hell's going on here?" Grace growled.

"Let me explain." Mrs. Wallace lowered her hands, but they remained outlined by the green tint of her power at the ready. "Please."

Maggie felt Grace tamp down her magic, though she didn't suppress it completely. Maggie's power pulsed in her chest in time with her heart, accompanying her ragged breathing. A demon. There was a demon standing less than five feet from her. In the home of a member of the Order.

"Maggie," Grace said softly. "I won't let her hurt you."

A different sensation came through their connection, of Grace's care and concern. Maggie accepted it now, but didn't—couldn't—stand down. "We need to leave."

Flee or fight. The desire to destroy the demon produced a metallic bite along the roof of her mouth and at the back of her throat, a quiver of barely controlled rage in her voice. She'd spent most of a year under the guard of such a being with some terrible purpose in mind. She wasn't about to truck with one now.

Grace pivoted, half blocking Maggie's view of Mrs. Wallace and the demon. She leaned in, her lips close to Maggie's ear. Her voice was rough with the effort of countering Maggie's power, of containing her instinct to destroy the demon before them. "I know you don't want to be here with her, and we'll leave as soon as we can, I promise. But we need to know what Mrs. Wallace knows." She lifted her head to meet Maggie's eyes. "Please."

Maggie clamped her jaws together, breathing hard through her nose. She reached out to Grace, meeting her source's hand. They grasped each other's fingers. That sensation of comfort and understanding enveloped her, decreased the trembles of rage and fear. Maggie withdrew her power, reeling it back into her chest, as her breathing returned to normal.

Grace nodded, a small, appreciative smile on her lips. She faced Mrs. Wallace, her hand still clutching Maggie's, the smile gone. "Talk."

Mrs. Wallace sized them up for a moment, then withdrew her power, at least so far that her hands no longer glowed green. She returned to her seat, giving Beatrix a reassuring touch on her shoulder before sitting.

"Seven years ago," she said, "we were on a hunt, one of the last I'd undertake with Mr. Wallace."

All the pairs Maggie vaguely remembered encountering were females. "I thought only women were hunters in the Order."

"There have been some men," Grace said. "They're usually not as strong as women, but there are the occasional male sources. There are some portraits hanging on the wall at the Long Island house."

"There aren't many men directly involved with Saint Teresa's," Mrs. Wallace said. "Those who have the ability to use magic were gifted through their mothers."

"Most are not able to wield power," Grace added. "They somehow become associated with a house in other roles. Like Rémy."

Mrs. Wallace nodded. "Charles was my catalyst. His power was decent enough, but our relationship was the true bond. As I was saying, we were on a hunt and came upon a pair of demons we thought were attacking a mother and child."

Demons fed on human misery. Most savored the intensity of fear and imminent death. Stronger ones could mark an unfortunate human and feed off their suffering for months or years.

What had the demon who'd pretended to be John Dalton gotten from her?

Maggie shuddered at the thought and forced it out of her head.

"What happened?" Grace asked.

Mrs. Wallace gestured for them to sit again. Maggie and Grace remained where they were. She seemed disappointed by that, but Maggie didn't care.

"As we made our plan of attack, Charles and I realized the two larger demons weren't hunting humans, but training a third by using the smaller one." Pain wrinkled her brow. Beside her, Beatrix sat in stoic silence. "We dispatched the three older demons and were about to put the youngster out of her misery."

Her expression softened as she looked to Beatrix.

"My God," Maggie said, disbelief keeping her voice to a whisper. "You saved her." She gaped at Beatrix. "You kept her."

"She was cold and dreadfully hurt. A defenseless little thing." Mrs. Wallace met Maggie's incredulous gaze. "We couldn't leave her. Oh, she fought at first, scared as she was."

"A demon," Grace added. "She was born to fight you, to kill you. Kill *us*."

At that, Beatrix's stoic mask fell. She winced as if struck. "I wouldn't."

Mrs. Wallace reached out to lay a reassuring hand on Beatrix's knee. "We helped her, and she swore her loyalty."

Near-hysteria came out as a sob from Maggie's throat as

159

memories of her "husband" flashed through her mind. This conversation was ludicrous. "And you believed her?"

The older woman directed her gaze at Maggie, eyes hard. "Yes. I trust her with my life."

"They tried to kill me," Beatrix said. "Mister and Missus saved me. I swore I'd be good." She held up her right hand. A long pink and black line crossed the pale palm. "I swore it."

Mrs. Wallace showed her palm as well. A similar scar neatly blended with the natural creases. "Blood oath. Completely binding."

"Until you die," Maggie ventured, guessing what it entailed. "After that, Beatrix returns to the realm to share what she's learned here."

Grace squeezed her hand gently. "A blood oath links their lives. When one dies, so does the other."

"Charles offered to take the oath," Mrs. Wallace said. She and Beatrix exchanged a sad expression of fondness for the late Mr. Wallace. "I had a stronger bond with Beatrix even before we decided to do it." She looked at Maggie and Grace again. "I don't necessarily expect you to understand, but I thought it important that you learn who we were rather than discovering it in the course of our visit."

Grace tilted her head. "You had a ward up around her."

Mrs. Wallace's words came back to Maggie. "You said we fill the room. Our power. You figured it was a matter of time before your ward was revealed to us."

The woman inclined her head, a small smile curving her lips. "Exactly. To be honest, I'm rather surprised you didn't pick up on it sooner."

"We're a little tired," Grace said by way of explanation. "You know about the attack on the train. What else do you know? Anything about what happened in New York?"

Maggie could appreciate Grace keeping the events in Harrington close to her chest. Did Mrs. Wallace know the reason behind the Order's attempts to wipe their memories?

"Please, sit down," Mrs. Wallace said. When they did, she

smoothed her dress and settled back into her seat with her cup and saucer in hand. "I'm afraid I don't know much more than when we first met, Grace. You were understandably sparse with information about your circumstances at the time. I discreetly contacted a few friends, quite trustworthy souls, I assure you." She sipped, a thoughtful expression lining her brow. "They either knew nothing or feigned ignorance. Except for one."

"Who?" Maggie asked. She doubted she'd recognize the name of anyone Mrs. Wallace mentioned, but Grace might.

"I'd rather not say. Sources of information can be touchy about revealing themselves." Mrs. Wallace set her cup and saucer on the table. "Tell me, what happened in New York last year? What did that shrew do?"

"Shrew?"

"Thomasina," Grace supplied.

"Who else?" Mrs. Wallace asked with a grim smile.

"Thomasina was somehow responsible for our separation." Grace shifted in her seat, and her anxiety shimmered through Maggie. Their fingers tightened around each other. "She and some man, I don't know who, wanted us apart but kept alive."

Mrs. Wallace nodded. "They managed to spirit Maggie away to Wyoming, but my question, and yours, I presume, is why? Tell me about this man. What did he do?"

"I don't remember a man," Maggie said.

Grace swallowed, then moistened her lips. "He's the one who tried to take my memories of you. The one who took yours, I'd reckon."

Across the seating area, Mrs. Wallace narrowed her gaze at them. "What did he look like?"

Maggie looked to Grace as well. She recalled nothing of that. Her last memory of the time before Wyoming was returning from a hunt with Grace.

"Large, broad-shouldered," Grace said. She closed her eyes, brow furrowed with the effort of remembering, or the pain of it. "Black eyes that seem to see into your very soul. Bald, no, sparse hair at the back of his head."

As Grace described the man, Mrs. Wallace grew pale, stricken as if she'd suffered some sort of terrible fright. "Silas March," she whispered.

Grace's eyes flew open. "You know him."

"I know of him," the other woman corrected. "You claim he tampered with your memories?"

"Not claim," Grace said. "He did it. He must have. And put Maggie under the guard of a—" She stopped herself from using what was likely an expletive when she caught Beatrix's eye. "A demon."

"A demon?" Mrs. Wallace's eyes widened, clearly shocked at the idea. "Tell me."

Grace glanced at Maggie. Though she had no desire to relive that last day in Harrington, she nodded, giving Grace permission to explain. Grace gave Mrs. Wallace a brief account.

"You poor dear," the older woman said with real sympathy.

"Who is this March person?" Maggie asked to steer the conversation away from herself, from the memories.

"March is in charge of a branch of the Order that most are unaware of, or pretend doesn't exist." Mrs. Wallace shifted in her chair, clearly uncomfortable at the mere thought of the man. "If he was involved in your situation, it's not good. Not good at all. What do you recall of meeting him?"

Grace shook her head. "Nothing else, just vague impressions."

"I don't even recall that much," Maggie added. She hated being so ignorant of her own situation. How could she help if she couldn't remember what had happened?

"March is the key," Mrs. Wallace said. "He's an unusually strong male source who lost his catalyst ages ago, from what I hear. Now he's the Order's training specialist. Or more precisely, retraining specialist. He is charged with making sure anyone who questions the Order's mission is reminded of their duty. What did you do that required him to get involved?"

Grace worried at a hangnail on her thumb. "Not something they wanted us to remember, but not something worth killing us over."

"Small comfort, that," Mrs. Wallace said. "Whatever it is, the Order of Saint Teresa won't just let you disappear." She shifted uncomfortably. "They've put out word, quietly, but it's circulating."

Tension prickled at the nape of Maggie's neck.

"They're looking for you. It's only a matter of time before they catch up, especially if you encounter any more demons and reveal your whereabouts. But I don't think they want to make a big production of it."

Grace closed her eyes and rubbed her temples. "I don't know why they're doing this."

"I believe you do." Mrs. Wallace looked at Beatrix, who shook her head in response to some sort of unspoken communication from her mistress. The older woman sighed. "I don't think there's much choice."

"What are you talking about?" Maggie asked. "Choice in what?"

"If you want to figure out what happened, and why, you'll need to have your memories restored."

Grace sat up straighter. "Do you know how to do that?"

Mrs. Wallace and Beatrix exchanged glances again. Beatrix's frown deepened. Whatever the procedure was, the demon thought it was a poor idea. As much as Maggie distrusted her, there was something to be said of that. Something not good.

"I do," Mrs. Wallace said. "Or rather, we do."

"Missus . . ." Beatrix shook her head again. "It's not safe for you. What if they find out?"

Mrs. Wallace grasped her hand. "The Order won't find out. We're safe here. I know it's difficult, dear, but you've helped me before. This is even more important."

"Before?" Maggie couldn't imagine this March person had enacted such a terrible thing prior to her and Grace, but perhaps he had. A shudder ran through her.

"An old friend who had trouble recalling her family," Mrs. Wallace said. "She didn't even recognize her own children. Hers wasn't a magical cause, but I think the same technique might work here."

Fear burst within Maggie and she shot to her feet. Grace gasped, as affected by the sudden jolt of emotion as Maggie had been. "No. I'll not have some demon pick through my brain."

Grace recovered and stood with her. She took up Maggie's hand again. "I know you went through a lot this last year."

Maggie yanked her hand from Grace, anger mixing with the fear that threatened to overtake her. "You don't know. I lived with him, Grace. Being with that . . . that thing day in and day out, knowing now what he was, that he touched me."

Her stomach flipped. Being with Grace these last few days had helped her to start putting that life aside, but what they were suggesting was too much.

"No." Maggie shook her head, not caring who saw the look of disgust on her face. "No. We fight them. Kill them. I'll not submit myself to one willingly. I can't."

She ran from the parlor, through the foyer, and out into the cool evening.

CHAPTER TWENTY-FIVE

Freetown, Long Island, NY, June 1902

The cab stopped at the gate, jolting the carriage and waking Grace from the doze she'd managed to slip into when they'd left the train station half an hour before. The horse snorted and jangled his tack with impatience.

Grace gently shook Maggie's shoulder. "We're home."

Maggie came awake, blinking and rubbing sleep from her eyes. She climbed down from the carriage and waited in the light of the lantern at the gate while Grace paid the driver. He tipped his hat, clucked his tongue, and gently flicked the horse's rump with the reins. If he had any thoughts on the two young women he'd picked up at the train station being as disheveled and bruised as they were, he'd kept it to himself. The horse started off, hooves clomping on the hard-packed road.

Maggie found her gate key in her purse. The well-used hinges made hardly a sound as they opened and closed the magicked iron. The house was dark, as expected at that hour, though Thomasina or Mrs. Reynolds often stayed up until everyone was home safe. Grace and Maggie had trod the path from gate to door so often they didn't need any light other than the half moon.

"I can't wait to get to bed," Maggie said, covering a yawn.

They were both tired, aching from their battles, physically and mentally drained. Demon activity was in higher gear than usual, and even the minor sorts had been cockier of late. Until

165

she and Maggie riddled them with magic bolts anyway.

Still, there was an air of purpose about the last few demons they'd encountered, an intensity she hadn't noted before. Not that demons gave up so easily, but recent battles had a different feel and flavor. It was something to discuss with the others over dinner or port in the library.

For now, Grace could hardly pick up her feet. "I'm not sure I can make it up the stairs."

Maggie hooked her arm around Grace's. "Come on, we can make it."

Together, they rounded the corner of the house, making for the magicked and locked side door. Grace caught a flash of light from the corner of her eye. She turned her head. The carriage house that Thomasina used to give herself a bit of solitude sat across the manicured lawn. The prioress often stayed there in quiet meditation or fasting while the rest of the denizens carried on their duties and lives. A house full of mostly young women, even those dedicated to as serious a cause as eliminating demons, had a frenetic atmosphere at times.

The windows of the carriage house were dark. Or were they?

Grace allowed Maggie to guide her to the door while she watched the windows. There. Another flash of light.

"What's she doing in there so late?"

"Who?" Maggie asked, stopping to see what Grace was looking at. "Thomasina? She's probably on one of her fasts again and can't sleep."

"Didn't she just have one a few weeks ago?"

The sister had been particularly short-tempered recently. Grace had chalked it up to Thomasina being Thomasina, but when the prioress hadn't attended two consecutive days of meals at the house, Grace figured she was fasting.

"Did she? I don't keep track." Maggie tugged her arm. "We need to sleep."

With a final glance at the carriage house, Grace worked the spell to allow them entry and then followed her catalyst inside. Despite tired, dragging feet, they moved along the rooms, stairs, and corridors with relative silence. They stood at Maggie's door, indulging in nothing more carnal than a kiss good night, testament to their mutual weariness.

"*Codladh sámh*, love," Maggie whispered, her palm cupping Grace's cheek.

Grace held her hand still and turned to press her lips to Maggie's palm. "Good night."

She watched Maggie retreat into her room, a final tired smile curving her lips as she waved and closed the door behind her. Grace rubbed her eyes and turned toward her own room. A glint of light through the French doors that led to the small balcony across from her room caught her attention. The carriage house.

Just Thomasina with hunger-induced insomnia.

Grace went into her room, not bothering to turn on the light. She stripped off her clothing and boots, leaving everything in a pile, crawled into bed, and closed her eyes. The night's events replayed in her head. Mistakes they'd made that would need to be remedied before the next hunt, attacks they'd enacted to successfully take on three demons, two of whom were particularly strong.

Grace used relaxation techniques Rémy had taught her to put the excitement and worry out of her mind and settle in to sleep. As she drifted off, her brain turned to something else that was bothering her.

What was going on at the carriage house?

CHAPTER TWENTY-SIX

Outside Denver, CO, October 1903

Grace gauged the reaction of Mrs. Wallace and Beatrix to Maggie's hasty, emotional departure. Beatrix stared down at her entwined hands. If a demon's feelings could be hurt, Grace supposed Beatrix was as upset as Maggie. Mrs. Wallace put her arm around her ward's shoulders and caught Grace's eye. She seemed to understand Maggie's reticence, but Beatrix was her main concern.

And Maggie was Grace's.

Grace rose. "Excuse me."

She followed Maggie out, the rawness of her catalyst's emotions getting stronger with every step. To keep them both on an even keel, Grace responded with her own projection of comfort. It wasn't much, but it should help. She knew Maggie sensed her approach as well as heard her footfalls on the hardwood.

On the porch, Maggie stood with her back to the door, leaning on the wooden rail and staring across the lawn toward the city. Insects buzzed about and birds chattered in the golden- and red-hued trees nearby. The blue sky over the snow-capped mountains made the scenery look unreal. Idyllic. Except that inside a woman consoled a demon, and an arm's length from her Grace's catalyst was trying desperately to hold herself together.

Grace came up beside her and put her arm around Maggie's shoulder. Maggie stiffened for a moment, then relaxed against her. They stood that way for a bit, sharing strength and listening to the birds.

"I can't do it," Maggie whispered.

Grace leaned her head against Maggie's. "I know," she said just as softly. "I'm sorry we came here. I didn't know what else to do."

Maggie shook her head. "No, we needed to come here. Mrs. Wallace is the closest thing we have to an ally. You said that yourself."

It was true, and they needed all the help they could get, but if coming to Denver only hurt her catalyst, they would find another way to keep themselves safe.

"We can still head west, like we'd planned," Grace suggested. "Get as far from the Order as possible." She tightened her hold on Maggie. "California or Canada or Alaska even."

Maggie chuckled softly. "Alaska? And what would we do there?"

"I dunno. Live among the gold miners and natives." The idea wasn't half bad, inviting even. "We can open a little hotel or boardinghouse somewhere. You greet the customers and look pretty, and I'll chop wood and scare off the polar bears."

Maggie laughed for real this time. The amusement lighting her eyes was heartening, for the few seconds it lasted. "You've never chopped wood or dealt with bears in your life, I'd wager."

Grace shrugged. "So I'll learn." She gave Maggie a gentle jostle. "Come on. We'll leave right away. Tonight, if we can."

"We can't, and you know it, Grace Carter." Maggie tilted her head to look Grace in the eyes. "They won't rest until they've found us, no matter where we go. But I appreciate the fact you're willing to hare off to Alaska, just the same."

"I'd do anything for you, Mags." She resisted the urge to cup Maggie's cheek, to stroke her skin with the pad of her thumb. "Whatever it takes to keep you safe."

Maggie smiled, though her dark eyes held some uncertainty.

She shook her head and gently eased out from under Grace's arm. Grace hoped she hid her disappointment well enough.

"We can't keep running," Maggie said.

The truth of it was plain to both of them. Whatever the Order wanted from Grace and Maggie, they'd been willing to play an awfully long game so far. That sort of planning wasn't shelved so easily. Eventually, the Order or the Horde would find them.

"No, we can't," Grace admitted, "but no one will make you go through anything you're set against. I promise that."

Maggie stared at her for a moment, realization dawning, showing as fear in her brown eyes. "You're gonna submit to the demon, let her search your mind for the memories, aren't you?"

There was no choice really, not if they wanted to get to the bottom of what the Order had done to them. They both knew that, too.

"It'll be fine," Grace said, hoping she projected confidence. "You'll be there to keep me safe."

Anger joined the fear on Maggie's face, in her life force that was a low hum beneath her own skin. "You can't do this. That thing will get into your head and then what? I'm not strong enough to protect you by myself."

Grace set her hands on Maggie's shoulders, holding her still and staring into her eyes. At the same time, she exuded all her love for and confidence in her catalyst, her partner, even if Maggie couldn't return it. "I know it's scary, that you aren't so sure of your power right now, but you can do it. You have to if we're to figure this out."

The emotional turmoil within Maggie churned like a stormy sea. Grace did what she could to calm her, recalling that, at the beginning of their partnership, it had been Maggie who was often called upon to settle Grace's soul.

"You're too damn stubborn to just walk away, aren't you?" Maggie asked, acknowledgment of the answer in the resigned tone of her question.

"There's something going on here, and I think it's something bigger and badder than we suspect." Grace thought about what had happened to them, what they knew about anyway, and frowned. "I'd much rather go spend the rest of our lives in Alaska, but since that won't keep them off our backs, we might as well figure this out. I want to know everything they did to us and why. Knowledge is power, and we need every advantage we can get our hands on. Even if it's painful."

Maggie nodded. "I just wish there was a better way."

"Trust me," Grace said with a humorless laugh, "I don't relish the idea of someone poking around in my brain either, demon or not. But like Rémy always said, you're never out of options until you're dead."

"Let's avoid that, shall we?"

"Agreed." Grace slipped an arm around Maggie's shoulder again and guided her back to the front door. "Come on. We'll let Beatrix into my head and then go find a saloon. I think we'll both need a drink afterward."

Mrs. Wallace had Grace get comfortable on the divan in the parlor while she quietly spoke to Beatrix in the far corner. Maggie sat beside her, fingers nervously fiddling with the material of her skirt, watching them. Grace covered Maggie's fidgeting hand with her own and gave a gentle squeeze.

"Sorry," Maggie said quietly. "I just wish this was over and we were on our way."

"Me too," Grace admitted, pushing down the gurgle of apprehension that churned in her gut. If Maggie became aware of her anxiousness, she'd insist they stop before the session even began. "But we can't be on our way until we know what we're dealing with."

"I already know what we're dealing with." Maggie stared hard at the young demon as she and Mrs. Wallace concluded their conversation.

Grace gave her catalyst another reassuring squeeze of her hand as the others came to them.

"Beatrix and I will sit together on one side of you, Grace," Mrs. Wallace said. "Physical contact is preferred for a cleaner connection." Then she spoke to Maggie. "You'll want to have similar contact on the other side, I'd wager. You won't be directly affected, but you'll be able to feel and see everything we're doing."

"And stop you if you do anything harmful," Maggie said in a voice that was both soft and cold with absolute certainty. There was no doubt in Grace's mind that Maggie would hurt or even try to kill both Beatrix and Mrs. Wallace should the need arise. Grace would do the same.

Mrs. Wallace recognized the promise as well. She nodded once. "Understood, but you have nothing to fear. We want to help."

Beatrix didn't seem as enthusiastic as her mistress, but she didn't openly protest either.

"March and Thomasina are up to something," the older woman continued. "It would behoove us all to find out what. Are we ready to begin?"

Anxiety flared again, and Maggie reacted with her own spike of fear. Grace quickly suppressed the nervousness and stroked Maggie's hand. "Ready."

Beatrix shyly sat beside Grace on the divan. Despite the close quarters of the seating, the demon managed to not touch Grace. Mrs. Wallace moved the wingback chair closer, smoothed her skirts, and took her seat. On Grace's other side, Maggie watched the two women as if they were poised to attack.

"Beatrix," Mrs. Wallace said, "put your hand on Grace's, please."

Beatrix's trembling hand covered Grace's where it rested on the seat. Her skin was rough and dry.

"Close your eyes, Grace. Relax. Clear your mind of the turmoil of the last few days, the last few weeks and months." Mrs. Wallace's voice was soothing, like a mother urging her child to sleep. Grace closed her eyes. "Good. You're safe here. No harm will come to you under my care. This I swear, by the love and guidance of Saint Teresa and the Magdalene."

Maggie gripped Grace's fingers. Her catalyst would make sure of that as well.

"Do you feel Beatrix?"

Mrs. Wallace didn't mean the physical contact between Grace and Beatrix. The demon's cool fingers covered her hand, no longer trembling. No, Mrs. Wallace wanted to know if Grace felt Beatrix in her mind. Swallowing down her uncertainty, Grace allowed a small fissure in the mental wall she'd fashioned. Gray and amber smoke swirled in through the opening. It hovered at the edge of her mind, waiting.

"I feel her," Grace said.

"Good." Mrs. Wallace sounded almost relieved. Had she been concerned that it wouldn't work? That Grace would offer too much resistance? "I want you to think back to the last time you were at the Long Island house, when you and Maggie were with the Order."

Grace concentrated on the images she'd been able to maintain. The attempt to erase Maggie from her memory hadn't succeeded, but events leading up to the time she woke months ago were hazy. Every time she tried to recall them, they slipped away like an eel.

"I can't . . ."

"You can," Mrs. Wallace said gently yet firmly. "Think about walking through the corridors, into your room."

Eyes closed tight, Grace tried to concentrate, but the memories she came up with were earlier. Training with Maggie, studying incantations in dusty tomes, their first kiss . . .

"Wintertime. Our last hunt," Maggie said beside her. Her voice was soft, as if she were half asleep. "We came back from the city and saw lights in the carriage house. It wasn't the first time."

"The carriage house," Grace repeated, seeing the cedar-shingled building as if from the second floor of the main house. "We sat in the window seat, in the dark, and watched the house as a couple of carriages arrived."

"Thomasina's sanctuary," Mrs. Wallace confirmed. "What else?"

Hazy images of the house, of the interior lights flickering as people entered, passing by lanterns. No sound save that of Maggie's quiet breath and the creaking of the main house or an occasional cough from one of the other hunters sleeping in a nearby room.

"It was late," Grace said. "Well after midnight. No one should have been about."

"We should have been in bed," Maggie added.

Was she remembering as well? Using Grace's memories?

"Who was there?" Mrs. Wallace asked.

Grace tried to discern the figures as they alighted from their carriages or passed the windows of the carriage house, but to no avail. "Can't tell. I'm going to look."

In her mind, both past and present Maggie said, "No, wait."

Grace didn't heed either of them.

CHAPTER TWENTY-SEVEN

Freetown, Long Island, NY, December 1902

"Grace, wait."

Maggie's fierce whisper followed her down the back stairs. Grace kept going. She carried her boots into the dark corridor leading to the kitchen. Guilt tugged at her for ignoring her catalyst, but Maggie would only try to talk her out of investigating what was going on in the carriage house. It probably was just some boring meeting.

At midnight?

She crossed the tiled floor of the kitchen, then eased open the side door. If Nan heard any sort of disturbance, she'd be out of her room swinging a giant ladle or cast-iron pan. Closing the door again just as silently, Grace paused on the small stone porch to slip on her boots. Without her coat, the dampness in the air chilled her, though not enough to thwart her decision to investigate.

You mean snoop.

She kept her ears open for sounds of discovery as her eyes adjusted to the moonlit night. So far, no one seemed to have been disturbed by her movements. Only Maggie.

A stronger pang of guilt washed through Grace. She hated to defy Maggie, but she was just too curious about the activity in the carriage house. Besides, if she got caught snooping, Grace was inured to Thomasina's wrath.

Grace kept to the shadows as she made her way across the lawn to the carriage house, frozen brown grass crunching beneath her boots. The windows of the second story, a storage loft as far as Grace knew, were dark, but the lower floor was lit behind thin curtains. If all the curtains were drawn, she'd never be able to see inside. Her gaze went to the loft windows as she came closer. At least one looked down on the lower level, and none were curtained.

Circling the small house, Grace tried to see within. As she suspected, the curtains were drawn and too opaque to allow for more than a hint of the occupants. Four or five people, she surmised, maybe two women and a couple of men from the tones of the muffled voices. She stopped at the back of the house, beside a tall trellis that supported Thomasina's beloved rose bushes. The leaves were shriveled and brown in the daylight, washed out and gray under the winter moon. Above the trellis, one of the windows of the loft glowed faintly from the interior light.

Grace set her foot on the lowest rail of the trellis, carefully grasped the vertical supports on either side, and stepped up, testing the structure. She was satisfied that the trellis, though cold and slick, would hold her weight. Grace climbed, stopping at the next-to-last crosspiece, the top of her head at the window-sill. Cautiously, she held the window frame and hoisted herself onto the uppermost rail of the trellis. It wobbled beneath her. Grace's fingertips dug into the wood frame. She leaned against the window. The wavering stopped.

Releasing a slow, relieved breath, Grace peered through the frost-rimmed glass. The floor of the loft blocked much of the main room, but she saw a man and another's arm and what may have been Thomasina's shoulder at one end of the table. The rest of the table and its occupants were obscured. Ear to the cold window, Grace could hear talking. Not actual words, but their tenor. And none seemed happy.

The man she could see was tall and broad, sitting up straight at the end of the oak table, but appearing to be uncomfortable. Or perhaps just irritated that he was there. His mostly bald head was shiny and red, as if scarred from a burn. Looking down at him, Grace noticed that his thick black brows met over a hatchet of a nose. When he turned to address a speaker at the table, she was able to see much of his face. He spoke with a low, rumbling voice, calm even as his companions' excitement grew.

Whatever the group was discussing, it was important, evoking emotional responses on the part of some of the participants. But she still couldn't tell what they were disturbed about. Cupping her ear against the window didn't do much to clarify the conversation.

Grace wracked her brain for ideas. There had been an incantation in one of the tomes she and Maggie studied that translated demon languages; there were a surprising number of dialects. They'd laughed about it, wondering why a hunter would bother to take the time to understand when a demon spoke. Their job was to eradicate demons, not negotiate with them. The spell, in essence, clarified the language. Could it clear up the muffled voices in the carriage house?

Only one way to find out.

Grace cupped her ear to the cold glass again, leaning into it and holding onto the trellis. She closed her eyes and recalled the incantation. Whispering it to herself, she drew on her power, just enough to penetrate the glass, to clear up the inaudible words.

"—you came here," Thomasina was saying.

"It's highly unusual," a woman remarked. Grace opened her eyes and noticed the man had his slash of a mouth pressed tight, looking intently at the speaker. "There's still almost a year."

"Preparations have already begun." That was the balding man, his voice deceptively soft. "If there's a problem, we'd best deal with it now."

There was a moment of silence before Thomasina spoke again.

"This is a serious matter, or I wouldn't have contacted you." She paused. The man looked at her expectantly. "One of the

Legion was killed last week. Before it died, it tried to convince the hunters to let it go, saying it had important information to share about the awakening."

No one in the cottage spoke as they digested what she had said. But what did it mean? The awakening of what, or who?

"The hunters who killed it weren't—"

"No," Thomasina said. "A different pair. They came to me, uncertain what to make of it. I told them the vile creatures were constantly performing some rite or another, and that they should never allow their quarry to live long enough to plant doubt and falsehoods in their minds."

"And if this pair spoke of their encounter with the two?" the bald man asked.

"They didn't. At least as far as I could ascertain."

He slammed his fist onto the table. Everyone jumped, including Grace.

Her foot slipped from the trellis rail. Attempting to catch herself, she grasped the windowsill, and her head cracked against the glass.

For a split second, Grace and the man locked gazes. Then his face contorted with rage. "Outside," he yelled.

Alarm tore through Grace. This was no ordinary meeting she had spied on. There would be no ordinary penance of time in the armory.

Go! Get Away! Get Maggie!

She half fell, half climbed down the trellis, vegetation slickening the rails while thorns raked the skin on her hands and cheek. Grace jumped the last few feet, leaves littering the grass around her. She bolted toward the main house as the first person out of the cottage rounded the corner, running at her.

The bald man.

Others shouted. Thomasina shouted back to be quiet or they'd wake everyone.

They didn't want others alerted, but Grace did.

"Help," she called while running. The house seemed so far away.

A familiar figure came out the kitchen door. "Grace, what's going on?"

Maggie's power joined hers. They were strong, but would be stronger if they could touch, if only for a moment.

"Maggie—"

Something slammed into Grace's back, sent her sprawling into the frozen grass. She rolled, catching a glimpse of the four people coming toward her. Toward Maggie.

"Run," she yelled to her catalyst.

Maggie ran. To her, not away, her hands glowing purple, her nightgown billowing out behind her. She sent a bolt over Grace, hitting one of the pursuers. A shriek of pain followed.

Grace lifted herself to her hands and knees. Flickering cold, orange fire surrounded her, paralyzing her. All she could do was watch a ball of green slam into Maggie, making her stumble. Then a blue one. Then a red coil wrapped itself around Grace while another ensnared Maggie. Nausea churned her stomach; dizziness tilted the ground beneath her.

No! She silently screamed in fear for her catalyst.

Then there was nothing.

Awareness slowly returned to Maggie, oozing through the thick, gray residual fog from the magic that had taken her down. Her head throbbed in time with her heartbeat; it hurt too much to open her eyes. She lay on rough, scratchy material over a hard surface. A rug on the floor. Her arms were behind her, secured with something cold. The aroma of burning wood. A fireplace. Nearby, the creak of a rocking chair. Slowly, back and forth, patiently marking time.

Mundane sensations returned. Maggie reached out with her magic to find her source.

Grace!

Grace's magic stirred nearby. But something was preventing

Maggie from achieving more than that minor contact.

"She's fine, pigeon," a man said from the direction of the rocking. His deep voice was soft, perhaps meant to reassure. Maggie felt nothing close to reassured. "You and I need to have a little chat."

Maggie opened her eyes. They were on the rag rug in front of the stone fireplace of the carriage house. An arm's length away—if she could have reached out, that is—Grace lay on her side, facing Maggie, unconscious. A dark cloth covered her eyes, and another her mouth. Her arms were angled behind her back, as Maggie's were.

Awkwardly, Maggie sat up, her legs bent under her and her head swimming. Dressed in her flannel nightgown, a chill shimmered through her. She tried to inch toward Grace. A strong hand clamped to her shoulder, holding her in place.

"She's fine," the man repeated. "I know you sense that."

She could, just as she could now sense the magic infusing her bindings. Likely Grace's as well. Could she break them? Maybe not alone, but perhaps if Grace were to wake up.

Maggie shifted, loath to allow the man to help keep her upright as she faced him. He sat on the edge of Sister Thomasina's oak rocking chair. His large body, in a rumpled expensive suit, was barely contained by the bent wood. The crackling fire lit the right side of his face. The left side was partially in shadow.

No one else was in the carriage house. The small cooking area was dark, as was the loft. A clock ticked over the mantel, though she couldn't see the face. Through the pale blue curtains, Maggie saw it was still night, or early morning. They had left this one man alone with her and Grace.

"What's going on?' she asked, the words low and coarse from her raw throat.

The man sat back in the rocker, his gaze never leaving her. "It's complicated, pigeon."

"I have a name."

He grinned. It was not a pleasant expression. "I know. I know a great deal about you and your . . . partner."

180

She wouldn't give him the satisfaction of being startled by his subtle acknowledgment of her relationship with Grace. "What do you want? Who are you?"

"You can call me Mr. March."

Whether that was his name or not—and his tone suggested perhaps it wasn't—at least she had something to call him other than the epithets in her head. "What have we done to merit this treatment, Mr. March? Grace was curious about your meeting. That shouldn't result in such a brutal attack."

The way March, Thomasina, and the others had used their power to subdue her and Grace was beyond troubling. They had meant to stop Grace, and to stop Maggie from helping her, with as much force as they could short of killing the two of them.

He reached down to retrieve a pipe from a glass ashtray beside the rocker. Leaning forward, he scratched a match against the stone fireplace and sucked the flame into the bowl. A sweet and pungent cloud puffed from his thick lips. "It's a long story."

Maggie made a show of indicating her bound hands. "I'm a captive audience, Mr. March."

He smiled again through the blue-gray haze. "Yes, you are. You and Miss Carter have made things exceedingly more complicated for us and for yourselves."

"You can't fault us for defending ourselves."

"I don't," he said. "In fact, I was quite impressed with your abilities. We knew you were powerful, but taking on four of us after a night of hunting, without any preparation or contact?" March shook his head in admiration. "Though I dare say, Mrs. Lassiter will bear a few scars from you in particular."

"But what did we do?" Maggie demanded. "Grace shouldn't have spied on you. I admit that, and so would she, I'd imagine, were she given the opportunity and not trussed like a holiday turkey."

Concern for her source sat like a cold stone in Maggie's gut. Not since they met had there been so weak a connection with Grace. Whatever magic March used to keep them subdued was terrifying in its effectiveness.

March leaned forward, elbows on knees, his face half in shadow. "My job is to ensure the Order is being maintained. I take that responsibility very seriously and use everything within my power to achieve it."

"Don't we all?" Every member of the Order was committed to the same tenets. They risked their lives to protect mankind. What had she and Grace done to threaten that?

"You don't know the half of what's required," March said. He sat back again. "But you will, pigeon. Sooner than we were prepared for, but so be it."

A chill ran down Maggie's spine. Beside her, Grace mumbled around the cloth covering her mouth. Her distress trickled through, perhaps a response to Maggie hearing the underlying threat in March's words. She and Grace had stumbled upon something, but she had no idea what.

"We don't know anything," she insisted. "And even if we did, we're loyal to the Order. We're committed to doing whatever it takes to defeat the Horde."

"I believe you are committed to the cause," March said, "but loyal?" He gave Grace a skeptical look. "Your partner has repeatedly defied Sister Thomasina and others in authority. We've been able to overlook that thus far, but no more. It's too dangerous."

"For whom?" Anger burned through Maggie. What did he want from them?

He turned his attention back to her. "Not just those in the Order, Miss Mulvaney. For mankind. For all of us."

"Which is exactly what we've been trying to do, keep people safe." Maggie shook her head. There was something she was missing, something important they weren't being told. "We may not always agree with Sister, or the Order, but we will always do whatever is in our power to stop the demons."

March cocked his head slightly. "Would you, truly?"

Maggie stared at him, her head throbbing. "Every time we go on a hunt, we're risking our lives, so yes, truly."

"Would you risk more than that? I wonder. You and Miss Carter are too inexperienced, too full of yourselves, as young people are, to grasp what's at stake."

"More than what?" What could be more of a sacrifice than life itself? Her partnership with Grace? Their love?

The possibility of what March meant seized her like a giant fist closing around her chest. Her voice was a rough whisper as it emerged from her throat. "What are you going to do to us?"

He shook his head slowly. "It's not for me to explain. As much as I'd love to see your reaction, we'll both have to wait a bit longer."

Anger and fear consumed her. Maggie shook, tears springing to her eyes. "You accuse us of being unable to understand, yet you give us no choice or opportunity to do so. You—all of you—have underestimated us from the beginning."

"I assure you, Miss Mulvaney, you have never been underestimated." He leaned forward and reached out to brush at the tears that trailed down her cheek. Maggie flinched from his cold touch, her stomach roiling. Rubbing his fingers together, as if interpreting the salt of her tears, he sat back again. "Separately, you and Miss Carter are impressive. Together, you are a formidable pair with great influence over each other. We need you both to be strong for what's to come. Strong and as one."

Cor unum, et fortissimi.

The credo of the Order that was betraying them.

Frustration joined anger and fear coursing through her.

"Tell me what you want!" she screamed, too tired and too scared to maintain her composure any longer.

On the floor, Grace moaned as if in pain. Was she waking?

March focused on Grace, his body tense, nostrils flared.

He was afraid. Afraid of Grace, of the two of them being together. If she could get to Grace, Maggie was sure they would be able to fight, to escape.

"Grace, wake up!" Maggie lurched forward, awkwardly landing on her side, inches from her source. If they could touch, just for a moment, she was sure they could break the magic that bound them.

"You stupid little—" March growled as strong, rough hands

grabbed her by the shoulders and hauled her away from Grace. He threw her down on the far side of the rug.

Maggie barely managed to keep her head from hitting the floor. Her shoulder burned. Her magic flared in her chest, radiated into her limbs.

March came closer. She kicked out, sweeping her legs across the back of his. His eyes widened with shock as his feet came up, and he landed hard on his back. His head slammed into the hardwood floor.

Using what little magic she could muster to lift herself, Maggie rolled to her feet. "Grace, wake up!"

She dodged March's attempt to grab her from where he lay, putting her farther from her source.

"Grace!" Maggie felt the stirring of the other woman's power. Her heart soared. "Help me!"

Grace moved her head and mumbled around her gag.
Maggie?

March was on his feet. He jumped in front of Maggie, cutting off her path to Grace. Maggie gathered her power and "pushed" hard at his chest. March winced, but nothing else happened. Damn! The bonds that held her wrists suppressed her magic. If she could touch Grace, perhaps together they could stop March.

March seemed to have that same thought. He kept himself between her and Grace, constantly moving to block her, yet out of reach so she couldn't make physical contact. Maggie couldn't deliver a magical blow, but her body hummed with power. It was painful for him when she made contact. Good. She wanted to hurt him in a way she had never wanted to hurt anything but the demons they hunted.

"You can't win this, pigeon," he said. Any pretense of amusement was gone from his expression. He was serious now, deadly serious.

"Just leave us be." Maggie steadied her breathing as she drew on her magic. Her body trembled from the effort, but she was surprisingly calm now. "Grace and I just want to be left alone."

"Maggie . . ." Grace's groggy voice sent a startled thrill through Maggie, but she didn't dare take her eyes from March.

"I'm here, love. Wake up."

March shook his head in what looked like resignation. The atmosphere in the carriage house altered, charged as if lightning was about to strike. Was he drawing up his power as well? "I wish there was an easier way."

Feeling the buzz of an impending spell, knowing she couldn't mount a counterattack in time, Maggie opted for one of Rémy's favorite lessons: Hit low and hard.

She launched herself into March, her shoulder connecting with his gut as she caught him by surprise. March fell over Grace's outstretched legs and landed on his back. Maggie fell across her source, who grunted and lifted her head.

"Maggie?" Grace's eyes were still covered.

"*Cor unum!*" Maggie called out.

Grace gasped. Maggie's power strained toward Grace. They were touching, but the magicked bindings held.

"*Cor unum*," she repeated. "Say it, Grace, say it!"

"*Cor unum*." Grace's voice was shaky the first time. "*Cor unum*," she said again, louder and stronger.

Where their bodies touched, her skin tingled with their joined power. She strained against the bonds at her wrists. The magic-infused rope chafed her skin, heating as she fought it.

"Break, damn you," she growled.

The hemp loosened, as if several strands unraveled. Maggie sent another surge of power into the bindings. Her wrists moved more freely. One hand slid out of the loop. The thrill of success made her heart jump. Almost there.

Rough hands grabbed her shoulders. March threw Maggie off of Grace and across the room. She slammed into the floor, tumbling. Her head bounced against the wood. A burst of white flashed behind her eyes. Her connection with Grace broke.

No!

She heard Grace's confusion and pain as she thudded against the cabinet on the other side of the room. Head spinning,

Maggie looked up. March stood over Grace, hands fisted, his face scarlet, contorted in rage as he glared at Maggie.

"This is your own fault," he said to her and kicked Grace's prone form in the small of her back. Maggie gasped in shock, both from his brutal action and the pain she experienced through her source. Grace's body jerked under his assault, but she was unconscious again. What had he done to her?

"Stop it," she cried. "You've no reason to hurt her."

March stepped over Grace and strode to Maggie. Before she could gather her power or get up to defend herself, he grabbed her half-bound wrists together in one hand; the other he fisted in her hair. Maggie yelped as he hauled her to her feet. Magic burned into her skin as he infused the rope with power, and once again she was held fast. The bindings were tighter this time. Any tighter and they would tear through flesh and scrape her bones.

"This is why you couldn't be trusted to know your fate yet," he growled in her ear. "You think of none but yourselves." March turned her to face him. His eyes blazed. His fingers dug into her shoulders as he brought her face close to his. "But you will know it in time."

Maggie couldn't help the sob that escaped her throat. Fear, anger, frustration, guilt. She couldn't save them. *Grace, love, I'm sorry.*

CHAPTER TWENTY-EIGHT

Outside Denver, CO, October 1903

Grace came back to herself at the sound of Maggie's pained sobs. Before she was fully out of the shared memory, she had her arms around Maggie, rocking her.

"It's all right," she crooned in her catalyst's ear. "It's all right."

Maggie's arms went around Grace's waist, her head on Grace's shoulder. "My fault," she said. "Everything is my fault."

"No, if I hadn't spied on them, we wouldn't have gotten caught by March and the others."

The cold, damp grass and the paralyzing burn of magic were still the last things she recalled before waking up in bed without Maggie. Had she awakened between those occasions? What had happened? Her own memory in the carriage house with March was nothing more than fleeting impressions of Maggie needing her. Somehow, she had experienced what had transpired through Maggie's memories.

She hugged Maggie tighter. "I'm sorry I couldn't help you."

"Neither of you is to blame." Mrs. Wallace sat with her arm around Beatrix's shoulders. The young demon had her face pressed to the side of Mrs. Wallace's neck, hands clenched in her lap. "March is a powerful man, and you were likely weakened by the attack of the combined magic of so many."

"If we hadn't just come from a hunt, we could have defeated

187

them," Grace said.

Mrs. Wallace smiled warmly at her. "Of that, I have no doubt."

Maggie lifted her head. She sniffed back the last of her tears and wiped her eyes. "We still don't know what they want from us, why they took our memories, or tried to."

"We do," Grace said, drying the last of Maggie's tears from her cheek with the pad of her thumb. "At least I think we do." She spoke to Mrs. Wallace. "Thomasina mentioned an awakening. *The* Awakening. What is it and what does it have to do with the Horde?"

The older woman shook her head. "I don't know, but if it has to do with demons, Ham will know."

"Ham?" Grace asked.

"Hamilton Gallagher," she said. "He's a demonologist. His family has worked with the Order of Saint Teresa practically since its inception. If there's anything to know about demons or their lore, he'll know it."

The name sounded vaguely familiar to Grace. "Does he write books?"

Mrs. Wallace nodded. "Indeed, he does. I'm sure you studied several of his volumes, or those penned by his ancestors, during your training."

"He's nice," Beatrix said, her head still on her mistress's shoulder. "He gave me chocolate when we were there."

Grace quirked an eyebrow at Mrs. Wallace.

"Ham aided us with getting Beatrix prepared to join our family," she said.

Maggie stiffened beneath Grace's arm. She still didn't trust the young demon, not that Grace could blame her.

"We should go talk to him," Grace suggested. "Is he near here?"

"No," Mrs. Wallace said. "He's back in New York. It might be a good idea for us to accompany you. Ham isn't fond of strangers."

"But he likes demons well enough," Maggie said, giving

Beatrix a significant look.

The older woman's lips pressed together, obviously irritated by Maggie's statement. "He understands them better than anyone alive, I'd imagine. And yes, he was fascinated by the idea of Beatrix's situation. He's helped us a great deal over the years, though we haven't exchanged letters in a number of months."

Grace felt Maggie's wariness, but they needed Mrs. Wallace's help. Setting the woman against them would put them back at square one. "Then he's the person we want to see. Can you give us his address? It would be faster and draw less attention if Maggie and I went on our own."

"As you wish," Mrs. Wallace said. "I can cable him to let him know you're coming."

"I don't know if that's a good idea. What if someone knows we've been here and manages to get hold of the cable?" Such a scenario was unlikely to happen, but Grace had learned long ago not to trust anything to chance.

"I'll wait until you are on your way and word it so he'll understand while sounding innocuous to anyone else." She gave them a sly smile. "Don't worry, this isn't my first go at surreptitious activity."

"What about March?" Maggie asked. From their shared memories, Grace knew she wasn't merely afraid of the man, but angry about what he'd done to them. "Does he know about this Gallagher?"

Mrs. Wallace's good humor faltered. "He does, and it may be that he's in close contact with Ham for the same reason. You'd best be on the lookout for him. Another reason to have more eyes and ears with you."

"We'll be careful," Grace assured her.

"But why are they after us?" Maggie asked. "What did we do? There's nothing we remembered between the two of us that would merit the Order siccing their damn dog on us."

"Nothing you've remembered so far," Mrs. Wallace said.

Grace shrugged and shook her head. "I don't know. They must think I heard more through the window than I did."

"They'll likely never believe otherwise, especially after these past months of you on the run," Mrs. Wallace added. "Escaping the Long Island house probably made you look even more guilty of knowing something damning."

Grace narrowed her eyes. "I wasn't about to stay there. And I wasn't going to leave Maggie after what they'd done to her."

"I'm not saying you would or should have, dear." Mrs. Wallace's reassuring tone allowed Grace to relax some. "There's something fishy happening, and I don't like it any more than you do. Go to New York and talk to Ham, but promise you'll let me know what's going on. You aren't alone in this." A fire seemed to light behind her eyes. "Whatever they're doing, it needs to stop."

CHAPTER TWENTY-NINE

Brooklyn, NY, November 1903

A cold, damp wind whistled down the cobbled Brooklyn street, funneling between the facing rows of brownstones. Skeletal trees along the walk rattled in response, their fallen leaves dancing and whirling across the ground while a few hearty individuals fluttered on branches. Winter had come early to the city.

Maggie hunched her shoulders against the cold as she and Grace walked toward the home of Hamilton Gallagher. There were few others on the street, it being late Sunday afternoon. They were exposed, vulnerable. She couldn't detect anyone watching or following them, but the Order and the Horde were quite good at keeping themselves hidden. The journey from Denver had included four days of doubling back in case they were being followed.

"There. A few houses up ahead," Grace said, taking Maggie's arm and patting it reassuringly.

Ascending the stairs, Maggie's stomach quivered, like something she'd eaten had gone off. Beside her, Grace's step faltered. She grabbed the wrought iron railing, her brow furrowed.

"You feel it?" Maggie whispered. Now that she knew what to look for, she could detect certain differences between "normal" and something being off.

Grace nodded.

With each step closer to the door, the feeling of wishing to turn away increased.

"Another ward," Grace said. "Ignore it. Knock on the door."

The Gallaghers had a magical ward on their home, as had the Wallaces. As he was a man who dealt with demonic forces and the Order, that didn't surprise Maggie.

She took a steadying breath and lifted the ornate cast-iron knocker. Three raps and a minute later, a bespectacled woman in all-black garb answered. "May I help you?"

Before either Maggie or Grace could respond, a large, wiry-haired Irish wolfhound pushed his way between the woman and the door frame. His shaggy brows furrowed as he studied them, his shoulder brushing the woman's hip.

She touched the back of the dog's neck.

The animal lifted his grizzled muzzle, sniffing them. His long tail wagged, tentatively at first, then with more enthusiasm. The woman, about Maggie's and Grace's age, seemed startled by his reaction.

Maggie smiled, maintaining a cushion of distance so as not to alarm the young woman or her canine companion. "Good afternoon. We're looking for Doctor Hamilton Gallagher. This is the address we were given by a mutual friend. Are we at the right place?"

The woman's expression briefly changed from curious wariness to sadness, but she quickly recovered. Her fingers gripped the coarse fur on the dog's neck. "This is the correct address, but I'm afraid Doctor Gallagher isn't—. He—he passed away a month ago."

Maggie took in the woman's garb. Mourning attire. This wasn't Hamilton Gallagher's servant; she was a relative.

"We're so sorry," Maggie said, feeling a pang of sadness for her. "Our friend hadn't known, of course. She lives quite a distance away."

Above her spectacles, the woman's eyebrows rose with recognition. "A cable arrived the day before yesterday, but I hadn't made the connection. I let her know about his passing."

Again Maggie and Grace exchanged looks. How much could they afford to share with this unknown woman? The Order was after the two of them. Gallagher was supposedly neutral as far as the happenings within the Order, but was she, whoever she was? And how safe was the quiet street?

You're being paranoid.

Perhaps, but after the attack on the train to Denver, she and Grace had decided there was no such thing as being overly cautious.

"I don't think this is a good place to discuss the matter at hand," Grace said.

The young woman glanced up and down the street.

The dog's tail thumped softly against her leg.

She released his scruff and offered her hand. "I'm Emmaline Gallagher. Hamilton Gallagher was my father. This is Conrad. Please, come inside." She opened the door wider. "The odd feeling will pass."

They followed Emmaline and Conrad into the house, waiting until then to share their names. The foyer was spacious, with a few upholstered straight-back chairs, and an occasional table. The chandelier overhead was unlit, though two sconce lamps flanking the arch leading into the house gave off soft light. Emmaline offered to take their coats. Maggie and Grace hesitated, exchanging looks as they set their respective bags down. Both wore the pistols they'd acquired in Laramie in holsters at their hips. How would the young woman react?

Grace shrugged and peeled off her coat. Maggie followed suit, watching their hostess.

Emmaline glanced at the weapons, but other than a brief rise of her eyebrows, she gathered the garments and hung them in one of the closets. Conrad waited at the archway.

"Let's sit in the library." Emmaline gestured down the corridor. "Marie has the afternoon off. I'll bring us some tea."

"That would be lovely, thank you," Maggie said. She touched Grace's arm and the two of them followed the loping dog into a room on the left while Emmaline hurried down a few stairs that likely led to a kitchen at the back of the house.

The warmly decorated and comfortably furnished library held floor-to-ceiling shelves of books, pedestals with sculptures of great historical figures, a massive oak desk, and a worn but plush seating arrangement of brocade-covered chairs and a love-seat. Conrad headed directly for a large cushion on the floor near the fireplace. Flames danced in the blackened box, as if tended in anticipation of the arrival of guests.

"Do you think we're wasting our time?" Grace asked, taking in the room.

Maggie shook her head and shrugged. "Who's to say? Perhaps Doctor Gallagher shared his work with his daughter."

"Maybe."

Grace wandered over to the desk. She lifted a few papers, perusing the text. Maggie glanced out toward the hall. It would be socially scandalous should Emmaline catch them snooping. The soft scrape of wood on wood spun her to face her source.

"Grace!" she hissed out. Grace had one of the drawers open and was moving papers and things aside. Curiosity getting the better of her, Maggie hurried over to join Grace. They quickly searched the contents of the top drawer, closed it, and then Grace hooked a finger around the intricately wrought handle of another. "She'll be back any moment."

"Under the circumstances, I don't feel the need to explain myself," Grace said.

Maggie glanced toward the door just in time to see Emmaline walk in.

"Under the circumstances," the young woman said, "I don't blame you."

Maggie's cheeks flamed. No, they were in no position to be subtle or polite, but you caught more flies with honey, as her mam always said. "Miss Gallagher, I'm sure this appears to be quite unusual and inappropriate."

Emmaline entered the library, her dark eyes wary and her lips pursed. "Not particularly. I know who and what you are."

Beside her, Grace stiffened, and the bubble of their power

formed. Grew, really, as it never quite went away, even when they weren't calling upon it.

"Aside from Mrs. Wallace's cryptic cable, the Order contacted my father some months ago. About you, Miss Carter." She nodded toward Grace. "They were sure you'd find Miss Mulvaney eventually."

"Why weren't they waiting for me in Harrington?" Grace asked.

Emmaline crossed the room, gesturing toward the seating area near the fireplace. Conrad watched from his cushion, his bushy eyebrows moving with interest. "I believe they were, but wanted to see—"

She cut herself off, brow furrowed.

"They wanted to see what happened when we met again," Maggie said. She turned to Grace. "It was a test. They've known all along where we've been, what we've been doing."

Grace grabbed Maggie's hand. "We need to go. Now."

Conrad grumbled, lifting his head and letting out a deep growl-bark.

"Please, wait," Emmaline said, holding her hands palm out. "I-I need to tell you something before you leave." Her gaze darted between Grace and Maggie. "It's terribly important."

Grace's hand tightened around Maggie's. "What?"

"Papa has some journals in his desk. Not this one, the desk upstairs, in his private office." She gestured toward the upper floor. "He told me almost a year ago that he didn't like the way things were going with the Order, and if two women around my age should come calling, I should make sure to let them in and give them the journals if he wasn't around."

"He told you this a year ago?" Maggie shook her head. "What's in the journals?"

"I don't know," Emmaline said. "He locked them away, and I haven't been able to open the drawer. It's warded."

"Like the house." Grace released Maggie's hand. "Show us."

"This way." Emmaline lifted her skirts to her shins and spun on her heel, heading back toward the staircase. Conrad launched himself off the cushion, following his mistress. Grace and Maggie came up behind the dog. Emmaline went to the closet for their coats, then led them to the stairs. She turned to the wolfhound. "Hold fast, Conrad."

The dog hesitated, whining.

"No, stay down here. Guard."

Conrad grumbled, but turned toward the front door, hackles raised.

"They're coming, aren't they?" Grace said as she and Maggie shrugged into their coats then grabbed their bags. They followed Emmaline up the narrow staircase.

An icicle of dread lanced Maggie's chest and stomach. The Order.

"They followed us here."

"Or were waiting for you to arrive," Emmaline replied, turning left at the top of the stairs. She reached down the neck of her dress and withdrew a ribbon. A brass key dangled from the faded blue fabric. Pulling it over her head, mindless of her upswept hair style, she unlocked the thick oak door. "The Order was the one who put the ward on the house, though Papa had his desk magicked by a trusted friend. They always seemed to know when he was home, or I wasn't."

The icy streak in Maggie's gut became a heavy ball. "They know who comes in or goes out."

Grace took Emmaline's arm and spun the woman around. "Then why the hell did you have us come inside? You knew they'd detect us."

Emmaline's eyes flashed behind her spectacles. "Because speaking of this outside, where someone might hear us, would have been worse. I know the Order can't hear what goes on within the walls of the house, because I've heard them demand answers to certain questions in meetings with Papa. I took a chance I could get you what you needed before they arrived. I thought we'd have more time."

Grace released her, but Maggie felt her source's anger along-side her own. They had been betrayed so often by those they knew and thought they could trust. Now, they had to trust this woman, this complete stranger. Perhaps they'd have better luck.

Emmaline slid the key into the lock and opened the door. Inside the late Hamilton Gallagher's private study there was no pretense of orderliness. Books, papers, figurines, scrolls in leather or bone protective tubes, were scattered around the room. Dust particles floated in the shaft of cold afternoon light coming from the window.

"Excuse the mess," Emmaline said as they all hurried across the room to the rolltop desk. Towers of books and papers beside it threatened to topple. "Organized chaos. Papa always seemed to know where to find whatever he was looking for. I haven't been able to bring myself to clean it up."

Maggie's heart went out to the young woman. Here she had lost her father a mere month ago and they were asking Emmaline to go through his things. "I'm sorry."

Emmaline offered a sad smile. "Thank you. He would want to help, I know that. Understanding the Horde was a way of life for him that he learned at his parents' sides. I'm proud to continue his work and legacy."

"We appreciate all the help we can get," Grace said. She caught Maggie's eye. "Let's see what we have to deal with here."

Maggie took a breath and held her right palm to the slatted front along with Grace's. Her skin itched, then burned. She pulled her hand away, shaking it. "Strong magic."

"I told him I needed to know how to get into the desk, but he kept putting me off, saying it was too dangerous for me to know some things. Then he got sick."

What would the head of a demonologist family deem too dangerous?

Grace took Maggie's other hand. Her palm was warm and slightly damp. "We can open it."

Within seconds, Grace's power met hers. Their magic curled together, filling her. Reaching forward, they each placed a palm on either side of the brass lock. Ignoring the burning sensation, Maggie concentrated on the power flowing through her. The heat from the ward on the desk held momentarily, then began to diminish.

The lock glowed violet, wavering toward indigo. The hue spread over the dark wood, and the power within Maggie and Grace surged. The magic ward cracked. The fissure started as a hairline fracture, the thinnest of weaknesses, but it was enough. They slid their power into the fault, like a trickle of water into a crack in the bedrock. Once water, or magic, gained access it was difficult to stop.

Grace gave a grunt of triumph as the crack widened and lines of weakness spread across the ward. The purple haze shimmered, and the ward shattered like glass.

Behind them, Emmaline gasped. Had she been able to see their magic? Feel it? Maggie didn't know what the young woman's abilities might be, or if she were merely sensitive to the presence of power.

She would have liked to chat with Emmaline, but there was no time. The Order was on their way.

Together Grace and Maggie raised the slatted rolltop. All manner of papers, an ink pot, pens, and other paraphernalia littered the surface and stuck out of pigeonholes. Nothing that looked like a journal. Each taking a side, they opened the drawers.

"There," Emmaline said from beside Maggie. "Those blue books in the bottom drawer."

Five identical books, not much larger than a spread hand and elegantly bound in dyed leather, with "H. Gallagher" stamped in gold on their spines. Each was marked in number order.

"Is this all of them?" Grace snatched one up. "Doesn't seem to be much for the number of years he worked for the Order."

"No, there should be six." A quick search of the desk didn't turn up the missing volume. "No time. You'll have to take these."

Emmaline ran to the smaller room off the study and opened a closet door. "Papa kept journals for years, from the very beginning of his research." Her voice was slightly muffled as she searched the closet. "Those are on the shelves behind the desk, in red." Something thudded on the floor. "But the blue ones are the books he specifically said to give to you."

She emerged from the closet with a leather satchel.

Maggie put the blue books inside. They didn't have time to read them here.

Conrad's deep bark came from below.

Damn it.

"You have to go," Emmaline said, ushering them out of the room. "Now."

Conrad's barking became frantic, a warning to them as well as to the intruders.

Emmaline grabbed their sleeves. "They're coming in the front. Come on." She tugged them back into the room to a window facing the rear of the house. "It's clear for the moment. Follow me."

Skirt raised to keep herself from tripping, Emmaline hurried out into the hall. Grace and Maggie followed as she went up the stairs rather than down. Grace carried their personal bags. Maggie slung the long strap of the satchel over her head, securing the bag against the opposite hip. At the top-floor landing, Emmaline turned left, through the open door of a tidy bedroom.

Maggie couldn't hear Conrad any longer, and she hoped the dog was all right.

"Out here," Emmaline said, pushing open a door leading to a rooftop terrace. The low-walled, rectangular space jutted out from the back of the house. Wood benches and potted plants covered with burlap for the winter lined the walls. An arbor of scrolled cast iron arched over half the terrace.

Emmaline stopped at the far corner near a solid, carved wood bench. She lifted the lid, revealing storage within. Grace and Maggie helped her lift out the rope-and-wood slat ladder hidden inside. They attached their bags to a couple of spare pieces of line, then dropped the ladder over the low wall. One end had been bolted into the floor of the terrace in the bottom of the box. The ladder just about reached the garden four stories below.

"Fire escape," Grace said as the last of the ladder came out.

"Brilliant."

"There's a hidden gate in the rear wall of the garden." Emmaline gestured in that direction. "The iron sconce in the right-hand corner releases the mechanism. Just pull it down. You'll feel a tingle of power, but don't let that concern you."

"Convenient," Maggie said as Grace helped her sit on the wall.

Emmaline smiled and shrugged. "Papa had it warded by the same friend who magicked the desk. I was always tempted to use it when I missed curfew, but he forbade such frivolity, of course." A sad, wistful expression came over her. "I'm sorry you didn't get to meet him."

"So are we." Grace grasped the other woman's hand. "Thank you for your help."

Something crashed within the house.

"I'll try to slow them down. Good luck." Emmaline lifted her skirt again and ran inside.

Grace held the rope steady while Maggie got a good grip and set her feet on the first rung. An underlying sense of urgency loomed, but if she slipped now, she'd be done for.

"Careful," Grace said as if reading her thoughts.

Maggie climbed down as quickly as she could. It had been some time since she'd partaken in physical training, and had never used such a thing as a rope ladder, but desperation inspired her. Once she was halfway down, Grace began her descent. The ladder swayed with the two of them on it, but there was no time to lose. As she passed one of the lower-floor windows, Maggie heard Conrad barking and shouts from within.

Please let them be all right, she prayed as her boots hit the browning grass of the garden.

Grace dropped to the ground from a few feet up. She untied the bags and slung them over her shoulders. Quickly and quietly, they stayed in the shadows along the garden wall on their way to the sconce at the back. Grace took hold of it with both hands, unaffected by whatever presence of magic there may have been, and pulled. Something clicked within the wall to their left and a three-foot-by-three-foot section of the wall separated from the rest.

Pushing it open, they slipped through as they heard shouts from the house. "There!"

"Go." Grace shoved Maggie along the wall, toward the street, as she pushed the hidden gate closed.

They ran down the alley between the rows of elegant homes. The satchel of books thudded against Maggie's side. More shouts sounded as they reached the street. Grace grabbed Maggie's upper arm and tugged her to the right.

They rounded the building and something hit the bricks just above their heads. A flash of light and the tingling sensation of magic washed over Maggie as dust and bits of stone rained down on them.

"Run," Grace said, accelerating down the walk before the word was out.

Maggie ran, the implication of the attack swirling in her brain. Magic, in broad daylight? According to Grace, the Order had always been reluctant to engage where regular people might see, might question. That they were willing to risk observation spoke volumes about how desperately the Order wanted her and Grace. The thought made Maggie go cold all over despite the fact that running was making her sweat.

They dodged the few pedestrians on the walk and crossed the cobbled street to a park, heading to a small copse of evergreen and deciduous species, which created patchy shadows in the waning light of the day.

"Grace, I need to catch my breath," Maggie said, slowing down as they entered the woods.

Her source matched Maggie's pace, glancing over her shoulder. "We may have lost them, but we can't stop."

"No." They had to keep moving, but Maggie couldn't sustain an all-out run with the satchel of books banging against her side.

They hurried through the trees. Golden, orange, and red leaves covered the ground, brown ones crunching underfoot. Shadows concealed them as they made their way across the park to what sounded like a busy thoroughfare. Maggie heard the clatter of iron horseshoes on cobbles, the shouts of men, the occasional rumble of a motorcar. It wasn't the most active street in New York, but there would be enough going on to help them blend in.

Where could they go next?

A tree beside them sparked and crackled as it was pelted with magic. Grace and Maggie ducked to the left, behind the wide trunk of an old maple. The attack had come from in front of them.

"Damn it to hell." Grace called up her power, triggering Maggie to do the same.

"Did they circle around, or are there two teams?" Maggie's body, arms, and hands warmed as she brought her magic to the ready.

"I don't know." Grace gave her a quick once-over. "Ready?"

Their power infused her, giving Maggie a rush of adrenaline that made her almost light-headed. She smiled and leaned forward, kissing Grace with a heated fierceness that should have been reserved for a more private location. Grace returned the kiss, her fingers digging into Maggie's upper arm.

Maggie broke the kiss and smiled at Grace's somewhat dazed expression. "Ready."

They stepped out from behind the tree, back to back, magic spilling out of them. In sync, as if a year apart had never occurred, they coordinated offensive attacks, drawing from each other, feeding each other. Maggie's heart raced as the exhilaration of power coursed through her, yet she was as calm and serene as a summer lake.

At the first sign of someone coming through the trees, Maggie released a purple-blue flame. Behind her—inside her—Grace's grim satisfaction was her own as she cast the same spell at the foes she faced.

Magic flared as defensive spells met offensive. Flashes of purple and green illuminated scurrying bodies and cast long shadows against the trees. Women, judging by a glimpse of fluttering skirts as they ran for cover.

Without giving the members of the Order the opportunity to regroup, Maggie let off another barrage of bolts that popped like fireworks, but were much more than pretty lights. Hopefully, that was all the locals thought they might be seeing and hearing.

"We need to get out of here," Grace said.

A ball of orange hurtled at Maggie. She took a split second to funnel power into a shield. The fireball sparked and sputtered, dispersing around her and Grace.

"How?" she asked. "Where?"

Grace threw another series of bolts. "We'll cast a God's Hammer."

Maggie didn't hide her surprise, not that she could truly hide anything from Grace when they were connected. A God's Hammer would be draining, and having already spent energy in the last several minutes it would deplete their magic reserves, if not knock them unconscious. Could they do such a thing after only a few days back together?

"We don't have many options," Grace said, as if reading her thoughts.

True enough.

Maggie drew on the depths of her power. Grace did the same. Their chanting began at the exact same moment, and a complex incantation they had learned, internalized, years ago came back to her. For the briefest of moments, Maggie couldn't remember the next segment of the spell, but then her connection to Grace filled in the blank space in her memory.

Power flowed out of her, met Grace's, and flowed back in, entwined and growing. Maggie felt as if she was being lifted off her feet, encased in a bubble of pure energy.

The air around them shimmered like heat waves across a desert. From the cover of trees, the attackers let out stunned cries as they recognized what Grace and Maggie were doing. They turned and fled.

Not this time.

Their combined magic boiled and expanded until Maggie

thought her skin would split; then the God's Hammer burst out of them like a rocket. Waves of power smashed through the trees, the blinding, bright white incandescence slamming into the backs of the retreating hunters.

CHAPTER THIRTY

Brooklyn, NY, November 1903

The area filled with deafening noise and dazzling light. The concussion of the backwash as the Hammer hit the trees made Grace and Maggie stumble. They fell into each other, kept each other on their feet. Even braced for the result, Grace had a hard time staying upright. Her ears popped, and it felt as if someone had filled her head with bricks.

Maggie grabbed her arm and shook it. Blinking to clear her vision, Grace faced her partner. Maggie spoke—yelled was more like it—but the words were muffled by the ringing in Grace's ears. Reading her lips, Grace managed to suss out what Maggie was saying. "We have to go."

Grace nodded, grabbing Maggie's hand, and they ran toward the more populated area of the neighborhood. Someone would be on their way to investigate the explosion that had occurred. What would they chalk it up to? Gas leak? Anarchists? Chances were someone in the Order would find a way to explain it to the unenlightened public.

As expected, many people were running toward the park as Grace and Maggie kept to side streets to avoid being seen coming from the center of the commotion. When they were far enough from the stream of curious civilians and responding policemen, Grace nudged Maggie toward the main walk. By this time, her hearing had returned to normal, for the most part.

"That was . . ." Maggie's voice trailed off as she shook her head and shivered. From the cold or from the thrill of power?

Grace thought both. Her body was still vibrating from the creation and release of so much magic at once. Never before had she experienced such a sense of completeness.

"Yeah," she said, understanding exactly what Maggie meant, but not having the words for it.

Maggie stumbled, reaching out for Grace. Grace grabbed her arm, but a sudden feeling of utter weakness overcame her. Her knees threatened to buckle as she and Maggie barely managed to keep each other on their feet.

"Grace."

"Are you all right?" In the yellowish light of the gas lamp, Maggie looked pale. Grace searched her partner for any sign of wounds or illness.

"I-I think so. You?" She looked over Grace in the same way. "What happened?"

Grace blinked away spots that danced before her eyes. "I guess the drain of power caught up with us. I'm exhausted."

Maggie nodded as she glanced up and down the street. "We need to find a place to hide. To sleep. And to look over the books."

And quickly. Between their fatigue and the Order being hot on their trail, they needed to get off the street. Grace joined Maggie's search for any indication of a hotel or rooming house. Nothing. Many of the shops were closed. Perhaps someone could direct them to the nearest lodging where they'd be all right, at least for a little while.

"Come on," Grace said, taking Maggie's arm as much to help Maggie as to keep herself upright. "We'll ask."

They passed several dark storefronts for a block or two until they came upon a man locking the door of a candy store. He gave the two of them a curious look—they were assuredly bedraggled and of questionable reputation—but provided the address of a boardinghouse around the corner.

Grace and Maggie thanked the man and headed in the direction he indicated.

A small sign in a window indicated Mrs. Ludlow's Boarding House: Rooms for Women. Though Grace would have preferred a hotel, they couldn't be particular at this point. The more time they spent on the street, the more likely the Order would spot them. They climbed the three steps to the front door and knocked firmly.

After a minute, a tall, thin woman who reminded Grace of Sister Thomasina, but who offered a genuinely friendly smile, greeted them. "Yes? May I help you?"

"Good evening," Grace said, bowing her head slightly. "We were wondering if you had a room available?"

The woman, presumably Mrs. Ludlow, looked them over, her smile tightening. "I rent rooms for a minimum of a week at seven dollars a week. Do you have that much?"

Grace's heart fell into her stomach. Of course, they didn't appear to have so much as a dime to their names, coming in off the street, disheveled and weary. Grace had some money in the pouch under her shirt, but the room fee would put a dent in that and she didn't know when they'd have the chance to get more.

Just as she was about to ask the woman if there was a less expensive hotel nearby, Maggie patted her arm.

"Here, just a moment," Maggie said. She handed Grace the satchel and hiked up her skirt to expose her lower right leg.

Grace and the landlady exchanged looks. Mrs. Ludlow's dark brows were raised, and Grace merely shrugged, as if her companion revealed herself like this every day. Maggie fiddled with something near her thigh, straightened her skirt, and turned to them once again. She held up several bills and a large coin, the gold glinting in the light streaming onto the porch.

"This'll do, won't it?"

"Yes, I suppose it will," the woman said with a slight stammer. "Come in, and we'll get you settled."

While Maggie spoke to Mrs. Ludlow about the rules and meal schedules that they would need for less than a third of the time they paid for, Grace had quietly set a ward on the front door. She did the same at the rear entrance when she asked Mrs. Ludlow about a garden. Neither spell would do anything but alert her and Maggie should anyone with magic ability cross the thresholds, but they would have to suffice, as even such simple wards made Grace dizzy with exhaustion.

Up in their shared room, after supper, they sat on one of the two narrow beds covered with matching green floral bedspreads and surrounded by pale green walls. Grace tried her damnedest to stay awake while Maggie pulled out the Gallagher books.

"Let's see what Hamilton Gallagher has to say." Maggie found the first blue volume and opened the cover. Or tried to. She snatched her hand back as if burned.

Grace held her hand above the cover. It prickled with warning. "Another ward."

"If Gallagher wanted us to read these, he wouldn't have put an unbreakable ward on them." Maggie shook her hand, eyeing the book. Cautiously, she laid her palm on the dyed leather. "I feel like it wants me to let it be, yet it's inviting me to read."

Grace mimicked Maggie's gesture. "He has it calibrated so anyone but us would pass it by. Can you open it? I'm bushed."

Maggie made a tight fist, her doubt clear on her face. "Do you think I can?"

"You just unleashed a God's Hammer. I think you can pick a little ward like this. Give it a try."

Maggie slowly opened her hand and placed it flat on the cover. Her brow furrowed. A tickle of power fluttered in her chest.

After a few moments, Maggie's eyes widened in shock. "I did it."

Grace chuckled. "Of course you did."

Smiling, Maggie opened the book.

The first leaf was blank. The second was a full page of hand-written text dated nearly twenty years before. The spidery script was not easy to read.

"March fifteenth, eighteen-eighty-eight—the child is just as Thomasina reported. Her power radiates from her like the sun. How the Horde has managed to miss her, to eliminate her, is a mystery and a great boon to the Order. Thankfully, Thomasina and Gretchen were able to set a protective ward, but we need her under the care of the Order and at the house as soon as possible. Convincing her parents to release her into the Order's care without revealing what she is and what malignant forces could be after her will take a deft touch. Perhaps Gretchen should be the one to speak to them."

"Gretchen Reynolds," Grace said, closing her eyes. "I wonder what her part in all this is."

"He's writing about you."

"Four years before I went to Saint Teresa's." She opened her eyes and met Maggie's curious gaze. "I don't remember meeting Thomasina or anyone else before that. Thomasina and Mrs. Reynolds came for me when I was eleven and brought me to the Long Island house."

The day ran through Grace's mind, though she felt distanced from it, as if it were a dream. Her mother had packed her few things in a small cardboard-sided case. Thomasina handed her father a folded leather wallet. He slid it into his back pocket and wouldn't make eye contact with Grace. He worked hard, she knew, but barely said more than a few words to Grace or her mother or her brother. A grim man, he often sat sullenly in the main room of their apartment, staring out the window, tea growing cold in the cup resting on his knee.

Mrs. Reynolds had smiled reassuringly as they descended the narrow stairs to the street, telling Grace she was so very lucky to be selected to attend a special school for special girls.

"Have you seen your parents since?" Maggie asked.

Her question pulled Grace out of the memory. "Once. When my brother was sick in the hospital with a fever. Mrs. Reynolds brought me into the city. She gave my parents another wallet."

That the Order of Saint Teresa's had essentially bought her parents' silence about what had become of their eleven-year-old hadn't eluded Grace. She knew she was different, from the time she'd nearly killed Billy Delaney with a mental shove in front of a horse and carriage when he'd tried to take her doll. Any time her dander was up, especially if someone was doing something wrong, she'd been almost dizzy and out of control. Then, she'd been terrified, wondering what evil could have possessed her when she was angry, as the priests used to warn against. Now she recognized it as her magic making itself known.

Maggie's warm hand rested on Grace's arm. "I'm sorry."

Grace shrugged off the memory and the consolation. "Long time ago. What else is in the book?"

Much of the volume followed the Order's "acquisition" of Grace and the concern of matching her with an appropriate catalyst.

"I guess I was too far away for consideration," Maggie said.

"No, here." Grace ran her finger along the lines of text. "Missive from Dublin. They may have found a candidate to match G.C. She may take a few years to develop, but very promising."

Maggie stared at the page. "The Order had been watching me too?"

That didn't surprise Grace. Maggie was as powerful as a source in her way. The Order was always on the lookout for talent like theirs.

"We're powerful," Grace said simply. "Separately, we're powerful enough to have the Order take notice. Together, we've created some of the most potent magic they've ever known."

"Is that why they want us back? Because they don't want to lose that power?"

Grace thought about it for a moment before shaking her head. "I don't know if it's that, or if we know something we shouldn't, or if I made Sister Thomasina so damn mad she'd risk blowing up a park in order to get us back to her."

"Or some combination thereof," Maggie suggested.

"Let's see if Gallagher has something useful for us."

They skimmed the rest of that volume, then others in search of some indication of what the Order had planned. Much of Gallagher's writings followed Grace and Maggie as they were prepared to come together at the Long Island house and after they met.

For at least seven years, Thomasina and the Order knew Grace would eventually be paired with Maggie. Every time Thomasina put her off as being too unstable to have a catalyst yet, each testing with the young women who were "capable" and bore the brunt of not being her match, was a ruse. None were meant to be her catalyst, but Thomasina couldn't—or wouldn't— tell Grace the truth.

"She lied. All those years, she lied to me." *That* shouldn't have surprised Grace. From the time she had arrived at Saint Teresa's, Thomasina had kept secrets. They all had, and were still trying to.

"We were always meant to be paired, weren't we?" Maggie asked quietly.

Grace raised her head, breaking from the words swimming in front of her. "Yes. Not that I'm complaining," she said, smiling to let Maggie know she was thankful, no matter how they were brought together. "But it would have been nice to know the truth."

"Whatever that is. Listen to this." Maggie read a date less than a year after they'd met in the courtyard. "G and M have exceeded the Order's expectations. Their combined power is unlike anything seen in generations. I dare say, anything since Saint Teresa herself. But they are playing a dangerous game. Should the agreement fall through, there will be literal Hell to pay."

"What dangerous game were we playing? What agreement?" Grace wondered.

"I don't think he meant us. Maybe he's talking about Thomasina and the Order." Maggie reached the last page of that volume and tossed it aside. She reached into the satchel for the final book and hesitated.

"What is it?" Grace asked.

She met Grace's questioning gaze. "This isn't going to be good, is it?"

Grace's throat closed at the anguish on her catalyst's face. Maggie may have had most of her memory returned, and she may have regained her ability to wield magic, but she was still unsure of so much. As was Grace. Too many whys and questions about who they could trust.

"Probably not," Grace managed. "But at least we'll be closer to the truth."

Maggie pulled out the final book.

The text started with an apology.

"If there was any other way to go about this," Maggie read, "I pray we'd pursue it rather than the path we're about to embark upon. Alas, I see no other alternative. I'm sorry, *G* and *M*. May God have mercy on all our souls."

"What in the world is he talking about?"

Maggie shook her head, indicating she wasn't sure either, and kept reading. "Never in my years of association with the Order have I considered myself swayable in matters of the novitiates' duties and obligations. My task—*my obligation*—is to study the Horde and provide information to assist those who engage directly. While I make the effort to defeat the demons, I never question how that information is utilized. It is the novitiates' choice to join the Order, and the risks they take are appreciated, but they should go in with open eyes. What to do when those choices are taken away? When one is coerced or the truth obfuscated?"

"They lied to us," Grace said. "They didn't just withhold information. They lied."

"About what, though?" Maggie frowned down at the book. "What's this?"

"What?" Grace tried to see what she was studying. There was a full page of writing on one side that ended without any

212

punctuation and a blank page on the other.

Maggie ran her finger down the crease between the two leaves. "Someone cut out some pages after this."

Of course there was information missing. That was the main theme of their lives, wasn't it? Bits and pieces, crucial parts, removed or covered up? Grace's head throbbed with the disgust and anger that welled up from her chest.

"Must have been Gallagher," Maggie said. "He was the only other person who could access the drawer and open these journals."

Despite her bone-weariness, Grace rose from the bed, her emotions too consuming to remain prone, and started pacing. "Everything, from the very beginning, has been withheld or lied about. They wanted us for . . . something, but did they ever tell us the truth? They didn't even tell us the truth about being matched."

"Could they have told us and we were made to forget?" Maggie's question turned Grace around before she crossed the room. "It's possible, isn't it?"

Grace hadn't lost as much of her memory as Maggie had, and she was fuzzy on a few things. It was possible they knew everything in Gallagher's books. But her gut told her it was just as possible they hadn't ever been aware of what Thomasina and the Order were doing.

"We need to find out what the hell's going on."

Maggie closed the book and slid it into the satchel. "We need to get Thomasina to talk."

CHAPTER THIRTY-ONE

Freetown, Long Island, NY, November 1903

The hansom cab slowed to a stop in front of the gate of Saint Teresa's, the driver clicking his tongue as he gently drew back on the reins. Rain dulled the clop of restless hooves, and thunder grumbled in the distance. The gas flame of the street lamp flickered within its glass housing.

Grace descended from the cab and held out her hand for Maggie. Two days at the boardinghouse had done them both a world of good. She felt ready to take on Thomasina or anyone else the Order threw at them.

When Maggie was securely on the slick cobbles, bags at their feet, Grace handed the driver his fee. The driver snapped the reins, and the horse and carriage moved on.

Before them stood the solid iron gate with *Cor unum, et fortissimi* arcing across the top in cold, black script. One heart, many strong. Did that still apply to how Sister Thomasina and Silas March and the others saw her and Grace? Were they all still of one heart?

Beyond the gate, few lights glowed from the upper stories of the house; otherwise, the grounds were dark and quiet.

"Gate's probably locked," Grace said softly, as if anyone in the house could hear them from fifty yards away. "There's a side entrance over here."

She led Maggie around the corner of the stone wall to a dark section. Maggie tried to turn the iron ring, but the person-sized gate was rusted shut.

"Here." Grace grasped the ring and slid her booted foot under the lower rail. With a grunt, she lifted the gate and turned the ring.

"And you knew to do this, how?"

Grace dusted her palms across her thighs. "When I used to go out after curfew. Come to think of it, we might have been wise to stop at the Black Briar first. Could have used a pint. Come on."

They stayed in the shadows as they crossed the yard. Maggie glanced at the darkened carriage house as they passed. Things had happened in there that she didn't want to remember. Fear and betrayal, the beginning of a path she half remembered but knew was dangerous for them both.

Without a word, they continued along to the back of the main house. Another stone wall enclosed the garden. Grace led them to a second gate, and without hesitation drew a circle around the face of the keyhole of the iron lock, clockwise as if to mimic using a key. A faint *click-click* indicated success.

"Lovely," Maggie said. "Another skill acquired for curfew violations?"

Grace pushed the wrought-iron gate open. The faint squeak sounded loud against the night. "I learned a few things not in the Order's curriculum."

Maggie suppressed a chuckle as she passed through the opening. Within the walls, a row of hedges created a second wall with a path running parallel to the ivy-covered stone, disappearing into shadows. The aroma of rich earth and greenery had been intensified by the rain, rather than muted.

"This way," Grace said, taking Maggie's hand. "The hedge makes a maze leading to the center courtyard and the house."

Another breath brought Maggie more intense aromas and a flash of memories: running the paths with Grace or Rémy hot on her heels as they trained. Or her pursuing one of them. Then a brief image of her and Grace in a secluded dead-end, far from the eyes and ears of the house, touching, kissing.

"I remember," Maggie said, tucking that particular memory away for now. "This way."

Still holding Grace's hand, she led her source down the path, taking the first right. Their feet crunched lightly on the wet gravel. After a few wrong turns, they entered the center court-yard at the rear of the house. No lights were visible from within.

Another image floated into Maggie's mind. Grace and Rémy sparring with swords. A surge of power unlike anything she'd ever known. Her heart swelling with both longing for that power and fear of it. Pain in her left hand as she watched Rémy's sword strike Grace's left hand. Thomasina's anger. The thrill traveling through her as she looked into the sea-green gaze of the woman destined to be her source and so much more.

"This is where we met," she said, her throat suddenly dry.

"You remember." Grace had promised to not push Maggie, to not insist she return to her past self, but Maggie shared her relief that what they were and what had happened to them was coming back.

"More and more as we move closer to what's going on." Maggie looked up at the other woman. Her face was partially in shadow, but Maggie didn't need to see her expression. Grace's tumble of emotions—hope, concern, and something deeper she kept behind a mental wall—came through their connection, swirling deep in her chest. "Not just our training together."

"Maggie . . ." Her voice was thick with that unidentified impression.

Maggie grasped her coat lapel and drew her down for a kiss. Nothing more than a light touch of lips, but Grace trembled with what Maggie could tell was fear of scaring her off. Maggie broke the kiss and grinned at her source, her partner. "For luck. Let's go inside."

Grace took them across the stone patio to the French doors that led to the parlor. Another circle around the lock and the door clicked open.

"I need to learn that trick," Maggie whispered.

"With your power, it'll be as easy as if you had a key. Come on."

They entered the parlor. The only sound was the ticking of the mantel clock. A light scent of polish, late-season flowers, and tobacco smoke lingered in the air.

"Unless Thomasina has taken up a new habit," Grace said, "I'd wager March is here somewhere."

A cold ball of anger mixed with fear churned in Maggie's belly. March and Thomasina were likely directing the others in their pursuit. Even without a clear recollection of either of them, Maggie wanted nothing more than to make them pay for the terrible things they'd done.

"Easy," Grace said, laying a gentle hand on her arm. "They might be able to sense us."

Maggie made an effort to calm herself, then laughed quietly. "Funny. That was always something you had to struggle with, I believe."

"Was. Is." Grace kept moving through the parlor to the doorway to their right. A short hall took them to the darkened kitchen. "Thomasina said on more than one occasion that I was a bad influence on you."

"Were you?"

"As bad as you were on me, I reckon."

Though she didn't see it, Maggie could swear she heard a smile in Grace's words.

They exited the kitchen, crossed a small dining room, and entered the main hall. A few lamps glowed softly, showing the large front door, several interior doors, and an open staircase. A thin bar of light glowed from beneath the double doors of what Maggie remembered to be the library. She and Grace walked carefully to them, mindful of creaking floorboards. The raised voices coming through the narrow crack were indistinguishable, other than a decidedly deep masculine one that seemed to growl more than speak.

March and Thomasina, most likely.

"Who else might be in there?" Maggie wondered.

She wasn't scared exactly, but something must have come through in her voice because Grace cupped her cheek and stared into her eyes. "Gallagher said we were the strongest catalyst and source he'd seen or heard of in generations. I'm done with being hunted."

Maggie couldn't agree more. She smiled and nodded.

Grace faced the dark wood before them.

A flicker of blue surrounded Grace's hands as she held them to the panel of the door. Maggie brought up her power as well. How easily it came to her now, just days after rediscovering who she was. Standing there, beside her source, her partner, like it was the most natural thing in the world. Because it was.

"Let's get some answers," Grace said, blowing open the library doors.

CHAPTER THIRTY-TWO

Freetown, Long Island, NY, November 1903

The heavy oak banged against the walls, sending tremors through the floorboards. The three people within turned, mouths agape. March, Thomasina, and Emmaline Gallagher.

March recovered first, stepping toward them with his hand clenched and arm cocked as if about to throw something, but he was too slow.

Before he could get off a spell, Grace flicked her hand and white bolts flew from her palm. They hit March's chest, sending him flying backward over a bulky chair and a side table. A small lamp crashed to the floor. He hit a shelf of books with a solid thud and dropped onto the carpet.

"No one move," Grace said as they entered the room.

Thomasina stood behind her desk, her hands raised in a familiar offensive position.

Maggie caught the sister's eye. "Don't."

Thomasina lowered her hands.

"What are you doing here, Emmaline?" Grace asked.

Emmaline remained sitting, perfectly still, with her palms flat on her thighs. Maggie didn't think she had any magic ability, but she did have the brains to not show herself as any sort of threat. "They brought me here after coming to the house the other day."

Maggie glanced around the room. "Where's Conrad?"

"Upstairs." Emmaline cast a quick glance at the prone figure of Silas March. "He doesn't like certain people."

"Smart dog," Grace said.

March stirred, lifting his head.

Maggie stepped closer to the dazed man. "I've got him."

"We're trying to come up with a solution to the . . . situation," Emmaline said.

"I have an easy solution." Grace made a pushing motion toward Thomasina. The nun stumbled back, sitting hard on the chair behind her. "Leave us alone."

"It's not that simple." Emmaline shifted on her chair. "The Awakening is almost upon us."

"I don't give a rat's ass about any Awakening. Leave. Us. Alone."

Grace's anger flared, heating Maggie's hands and filling her head. She understood and shared her source's reaction, but she still made the effort to temper the rage flowing between them.

"You don't know," Thomasina said with a quiver in her voice. "You need to understand."

"What I understand," Grace said with a low, menacing growl, "is that you didn't want us to know what you were doing, and then came after us because we learned something about it."

Slowly, March gained his feet. Seeing Maggie focused on him, he raised his hands in supplication, not attack. "You don't remember."

"And whose fault is that?" Grace snapped.

She threw a second handful of bolts. They struck March, flinging him backward once again. Books rained down from the shelves on top of him.

As she drew her hand back for another volley, a memory assaulted Maggie, making her flinch.

"Wait," she said, stopping Grace. Her source looked over at her. Grace's face was a mask of rage. She wanted to kill March. Though Maggie couldn't blame her, they needed to get things straight. "I remember."

Freetown, Long Island, NY, December 1902

Maggie wished with all her heart she could speak with Grace, but March insisted Grace remain unconscious as he silently rocked in the old oak rocking chair nearby. After Maggie had tried to escape and free her source, March had secured her bonds with cruel deliberation.

Now, they seemed to be waiting, but for what or whom?

If only Grace were awake.

Please hear me, Grace. I need you.

Something tickled Maggie's awareness of her partner. Was she waking, or was it wishful thinking?

I'm here! Wake up!

The door to the carriage house opened. Sister Thomasina came in, shutting the cold December out. She stood still for several moments, staring down at Maggie and Grace, rubbing her chapped hands together.

Anger, confusion, and disappointment raged through Maggie. This woman was supposed to be their guardian, their leader. Instead, she'd betrayed them. Why?

"Silas, untie them," Thomasina said in her maddeningly self-possessed way.

March continued rocking. "I don't think that's a good idea."

It took every bit of energy Maggie had not to laugh and say he was damn right. Given the opportunity, she'd do everything and anything to get herself and Grace free.

Thomasina sighed. "At least release Margaret. We can't have a civilized conversation like this."

Now Maggie did laugh. "Civilized? Go to hell."

The sister's lips pursed, and March chuckled, a low, menacing sound.

"I like her," he said.

"Silas."

He rose slowly, shaking his head, and stepped behind Maggie where she sat on the carpet in front of the fireplace. He placed one large hand on her shoulder, the other under the opposite arm. Thick fingers dug into her flesh, and his hot breath seemed to scorch her ear.

"You will behave. Try anything, and *she* suffers."

March nudged Maggie to indicate she should look at Grace. She did, then felt-heard the buzz like angry wasps of his magic. In her sleep—or whatever state it was—Grace winced and whimpered.

Fear and anger balled in Maggie's gut. "Stop. I understand."

The buzzing subsided. Grace's pained expression eased, though she still seemed uncomfortable.

"Smart girl."

March brought her to her feet. Her body protested, stiff and aching from the position she'd been forced to endure that evening.

He guided her to the small dining area, and had her sit on a wood slat chair on the opposite side of the table. She could see Grace, but would need to get past March and Thomasina to reach her.

March touched the bindings around her wrists. More buzzing, and a sharp, hot flare of pain. Her arms were released and, for a fleeting moment, she considered attacking. But could she take down both March and Thomasina alone? Before March hurt Grace?

She brought her hands up to the table. There were still lengths of rope around them, like bracelets. Bracelets that prickled. Magic. She was magically bound. It was a spell she vaguely recalled, something that required energy one didn't usually waste when killing demons was the goal. Drawing on her own power, Maggie mentally attempted to untie them, but was met with a vise-like crushing of her wrists, and and she immediately stopped. She was still too tired to break such a strong spell on her own.

"I told you we can't trust her," March said.

Thomasina took the seat on the opposite side of the table and folded her hands in front of her. Ignoring March's comment, she spoke to Maggie. "I'm sorry it's come to this."

"Somehow I don't believe you." She'd put her trust in this woman. Being bound before her made Maggie question everything the sister had done, everything she had said for the past five years.

"Tell me," Thomasina said in a conversational tone that belied their positions as captor and captive, "why did you join the Order of Saint Teresa?"

The question caught her off guard, but Maggie didn't hesitate in her reply. "Once I'd learned what I could do, how I could help combat evil in the world, I felt obligated."

Hers was not an unusual answer. Many a young woman heeded the calling, some more dedicated to the religious aspect than others, but all dedicated.

Thomasina nodded. "You understood that we all risk much in battle, including our lives."

"Of course."

The scars on her body, the number of times she and Grace had saved themselves and others from what would have been fatal demon attacks, proved that.

"Do you recall the origin of Saint Teresa? What she did?"

A silly question, as all hunters, whether they took the sacred vows or not, were required to learn the history of their patron saint. The library held several volumes of theological and biographical accounts of what had occurred.

"Teresa was visited by the Magdalene. She was instructed to utilize her power to defeat Ammemnion."

Sister Thomasina nodded, then quoted one of the accounts. "'The Blessed One was drained of her very essence. Not a modicum of her power remained.' That's how she did it. She poured her magic, her very life, into the incantation she used."

"Teresa sacrificed herself to thwart the demon lord Ammemnion." That was basic Order catechism. "In doing so, she was canonized."

223

"Teresa didn't kill Ammemnion."

Maggie stared at the sister. Everything in the teachings of the Order said the hellacious demon was defeated. "Of course she did."

Thomasina shook her head. "She used her power and faith to put him into a deep, expanded state of suspension. It was all she could do. Unfortunately, that condition is deteriorating, and the Horde intends to take advantage of that fact to bring him back."

Not dead? Not only not dead, but returning? The Order of Saint Teresa had perpetuated a half-truth for years, centuries.

"Why did they lie to us?" Maggie couldn't fathom the reason. "What did they think they'd accomplish by letting us think he was dead, only to have him come back one day?"

"It wasn't a lie, exactly," March said. "Just a . . . misinterpretation."

Thomasina shot him a glare that might have been admonishment for interrupting as Maggie processed one simple, impossible statement: The demon lord was returning.

"For years, scholars assumed she had eliminated him." Thomasina clasped her hands together atop the table. "It's only been in the last half-century or so that we've realized that wasn't the case, that the Horde was preparing to take advantage of the weakening bond."

"The Awakening," March interjected, but this time Thomasina didn't acknowledge the interruption.

"You've known for half a century?" Maggie couldn't hide her shock at the incredible revelation. "And you didn't tell us? Any of us?"

"We couldn't risk a panic within the Order," the sister said. "We had no way to stop them at the time, and we thought it best to try to find a solution. It took our scholars decades to develop a counter ritual. Then we needed the right people to enact it."

"That's where you two come in, pigeon." March winked at her, and Maggie sneered.

Thomasina ignored him.

"You and Grace have the power to prevent his return." A strange look came over Thomasina's narrow face. She seemed genuinely regretful. "There would be a need for you to make a great sacrifice, as Saint Teresa did. You would have to suffuse your power into the very fabric of the incantation."

"We'd lose our magic." There was a deeper undercurrent of dread in Thomasina's words. "Our lives."

The sister took a slow breath, as if girding herself for what was to come. "Since Saint Teresa, scholars from the Order have examined her writings and those who were with her. They determined how she did what she did. In her own words, she prayed to the Magdalene and was told she needed to make the ultimate sacrifice. She died as Ammemnion was defeated and returned to his plane."

The idea of sacrifice shouldn't have surprised Maggie; they risked their lives on every hunt. But with death came a greater question.

"If this doesn't work, and Ammemnion takes our lives, what happens to our souls?"

Sister Thomasina paled. "I-I don't know."

"My guess is Ammemnion gets them," March said flatly.

"Silas."

Maggie barely registered the sister's admonishing tone.

Their souls. The very thing Maggie's upbringing had held sacred. The church had instilled in her the absolute need for her to safeguard the state of her soul. Loving Grace was already supposed to be a stain on it, though she couldn't fathom how love was wrong. She hadn't been overly concerned about what would become of her soul for that, but giving it up to a demon was never a consideration.

"Are you sure?" Her voice sounded small to her own ears. She glanced over to where Grace lay. Her source moaned, frowning, perhaps in response to the dread seeping through Maggie.

"There has been some debate. We've been studying the Horde for nearly a millennium, and have determined what would be most effective." Thomasina shifted on the hard chair.

225

"They are preparing to rouse Ammemnion. We must be ready to neutralize him in any way, by any means possible."

That way was her and Grace.

"When?"

"Not for a number of months," Thomasina said. "Even the Horde can't rush into such serious activities."

"Why didn't you tell us from the beginning? Why keep it from us when we're supposed to be so integral to the plan?"

"We had hoped you'd be more of an influence on Grace's faith." The sister turned her head to look at Grace. When she faced Maggie again, her expression said it all. She was disappointed that Grace hadn't fallen into line. "Taking vows isn't a necessity, but it certainly wouldn't have hurt for her to be more dedicated."

Maggie couldn't decide if she was more angry or confused by the implication. "You don't believe she'd do it? When has Grace ever given you reason to doubt her dedication, even if she didn't want to take the vows?"

"It's not her dedication to fighting demons that's in question." Thomasina quirked a severe eyebrow. "It's her feelings for you that we thought might make her balk. She wouldn't want anything to happen to you, especially since you *have* agreed to take your vows. She wants you to fulfill your aspirations."

Agreed to take her vows, but hadn't done so yet. Maggie seemed to always find some reason not to declare her readiness. Did Sister Thomasina think Grace was influencing her?

Wasn't she?

"Her adversarial nature was also taken into consideration," March said. "Giving you both too much time to think about it increased the risk of you talking yourselves out of participation. We can't afford that."

Maggie nearly laughed at the irony. In part, it was their love for each other that made them such a formidable pair, yet it was those feelings that would, essentially, see them lose their souls to Ammemnion.

Maggie . . .

Grace!

The voice of her source—her love—buoyed her. But Grace sounded tired, weakened by their earlier battles and March's bindings.

Don't—something smothered their connection.

Maggie looked up at March. His expression was unreadable. "We need to keep you from doing something rash, and at the same time protect you should the Horde get wind of who you are. We need to keep you safe."

"Safe? Safe how? We are who and what we are. Nothing will change that."

"Protective custody, so to speak." He shrugged. "You'll get used to it."

Turning back to Thomasina, Maggie asked, "What do you want from us? From me? Am I supposed to convince Grace our sacrifice is more important than our freedom and our feelings for each other?"

"She'll listen to you," the nun said. "If you both truly believe in the Order and our cause, you'll have no trouble."

Maggie couldn't help her wry smile. This was Grace they were talking about. Of course there would be trouble. "Because if *you* were to talk to her, she'd flat out say no. I'm supposed to be the reasonable one, is that it?"

Thomasina's thin face pinkened. "I haven't been particularly patient with her."

"No, you haven't, and now you need someone to get her to go along with this, because you're afraid she'd resist saving humanity from literal Hell if it came at *your* request." Maggie shook her head. "You did this to her, you know that. Your fear of her."

The color deepened on Thomasina's cheeks. "She needed discipline. Her loss of control was damaging to more than a few people. Including herself."

"So you've told her. Repeatedly." Maggie gazed at her source again, but heard nothing in her head from Grace. "I can't talk to her when she's like that." She looked at March and spoke with more confidence than she actually had. "Release her."

March and Thomasina exchanged some sort of silent conversation. A glimmer of hope sparked in Maggie's breast. Would they allow Grace to gain consciousness? In their weakened state, with the bindings, would they be capable of escape without physical contact? There was only one way to find out.

"You want to put us under lock and key for months. I cannot—will not—speak for Grace. We're partners. A team. We both have to agree. That's why you wanted to talk to me first, isn't it? So I can convince her. Because you need *both* of us to do this willingly."

There was something a little heady about having even so small a sense of control.

After a moment, Thomasina rose. "Release her."

March frowned and didn't move. "Bad idea. I don't trust them."

"Without their complete cooperation, we will all pay the price." Thomasina's eyes hardened. "All of us."

The corner of March's mouth twitched into a brief snarl. He stalked over to Grace with fists clenched. "Fine. I'll wake her up, but I won't untie her."

That meant the magical bindings would remain, probably stronger than what Maggie had with her separated "bracelets."

Thomasina motioned for her to come around the table, but made sure Maggie didn't get too close to Grace. She knew, perhaps better than March, that to have them touch would likely be a tremendous mistake on their part.

March knelt down near Grace's head. He ran his palm over her eyes, murmuring words of power that buzzed in Maggie's brain. What sort of magic did he possess? Was he a source? Men, if blessed with power at all, were typically catalysts.

The moment March moved his hand from Grace's face, her eyes flew open. Grace's magic tried to intertwine with her own, but something prevented the connection from being complete. Grace sat up suddenly, sweeping her legs toward March. He stumbled back, avoiding the worst of the blow.

"Bitch," he growled as he gained his feet.

Maggie couldn't make out what Grace called March, her voice too low and rough, but she'd heard enough of Grace's vocabulary under less strained circumstances to hazard a good guess.

Grace looked around until her gaze fell on Maggie. "Mags . . ."

Maggie started forward, but Thomasina held out her gray-clad arm, blocking her.

There would be no physical contact. They hadn't needed one to join their power in forever, but they were drained and fighting magicked bindings. Touching Grace now might overcome even those obstacles. Thomasina and March knew it.

Maggie tried a mental connection, pouring as much love and assurance into it as she could. "I'm all right. We have to talk about what's going on."

Grace glared up at March and Thomasina. "To hell with talking. People who want to talk don't tie you up."

"It was for your safety as well as ours." Thomasina's hands were clasped in front of her waist, but Maggie saw they were clenched tight. She was afraid. "We need—"

"I don't give a damn what you need," Grace growled.

March waved his hand, and Grace flinched. Not from physical danger, as he was well out of reach, but he had done something to her. "Be nice, girl."

Pain lining her face, Grace let off a string of profanity.

March frowned and raised his hand again.

"Enough!" The word shot out of Maggie's mouth, anger lodging in her chest. "Stop hurting her."

Their weakened and bound state gave him the advantage, but she and Grace didn't have to completely give in. The Order needed them.

Slowly, March lowered his hand. He seemed to realize that as well.

"What's going on, Maggie?" Grace's voice sounded stronger despite March's treatment.

Maggie took a couple of breaths, then explained the need for them to stop Ammemnion's Awakening. She left nothing out that March and Thomasina had told her, including the idea of being kept in a sort of protective custody until the time they would be called upon to sacrifice themselves. To her credit, Grace listened with only the furrowing of her brow to indicate any reaction to what she was being told.

When she finished, Thomasina asked, "Do you understand what needs to be done?"

Grace glanced at Thomasina, then March. When her eyes found Maggie again, they shone with barely repressed rage. "Yes."

"And you'll agree to do it, without reservation?" Thomasina had caught the loophole Maggie realized she'd inadvertently left open. Without complete consent, the ritual would not, could not happen.

Grace narrowed her eyes. "Without reservation? You're asking us to die, to probably forfeit our souls. I'm not a martyr. We won't be canonized for this."

Thomasina pressed her lips together for a moment. "Is that what you need? Sainthood? Recognition for your achievements? Fine. We'll write your names in the annals of our history. Will that make you happy? Will that make you agree to help humanity survive?"

The two women's innate stubbornness and more than a decade of their battle of wills hung between them like a hornet's nest.

"Please," Maggie said. Her usual role as peacemaker, as soother to her volatile source's emotions, was no match for the tensions here.

She took a step forward, intending to help Grace calm down. March immediately aimed his palm at Grace. Grace gasped, her eyes going wide with sudden pain.

"No!"

"Stay put," March said. "I won't warn you again."

"What are you?" Grace stared at him, confusion clear on

230

her pale face. When March didn't reply, she turned to Thomasina. "You want us to stop fighting demons so we can be used to prevent a larger threat. We'll hide away rather than do the very thing we've been trained for."

"You cannot be risked," Thomasina said. "To lose either of you will allow the unthinkable to happen. No one else has the capability. The rest of us can maintain the fight for now."

Grace barked out a humorless laugh. "Apparently having us die isn't so unthinkable."

Thomasina's fists and jaws clenched. "Do you think we considered this path lightly, Grace Carter? Do you truly believe we'd be so cavalier with your lives? That we didn't explore every option? Ammemnion is the most powerful force of evil known. Allowing him to awaken will be devastating. Humankind will become enslaved and consumed like so much cattle. Having you and Margaret perform that ritual isn't for the sake of myself or even the Order. If he isn't stopped, the world as we know it will end."

The vehemence in her voice surprised them all. Never had the sister spoken with such passion on any subject Maggie could recall. The deadly seriousness of their task was unquestionable as her words reverberated within the room.

Still, Grace held her glare on Thomasina. "You should have told us from the beginning."

"Maybe so," the sister admitted. She looked tired all of a sudden.

"Grace." Her name caught in Maggie's throat. Grace looked at her. No longer was there defiance in her eyes, but anger still lingered. "It's what we were put on this Earth to do. It's our calling. Our destiny. We'll have almost a year."

Grace's jaw muscles bunched as she fought for control of her emotions. Maggie knew that expression well. "Only for you, Mags. Only for you."

CHAPTER THIRTY-THREE

Freetown, Long Island, NY, November 1903

Grace remembered now.

How March and Thomasina had explained what was required of her and Maggie. How they'd cautiously removed the magicked bindings and allowed the two of them to return to their rooms in the house. There had been soothing baths and grand meals, and then laying out of plans to increase their skills in scope and sharpness for the ritual.

But not long after they'd arrived at March's small farmhouse at the far end of Long Island, something had gone awry.

"We were cooperating, as you wanted. Why did you wipe our memories?" Grace asked. She glanced at Maggie. "You didn't say anything about doing that."

Thomasina's brow creased beneath her wimple. "What are they talking about, Silas?"

Grace narrowed her gaze at the sister. "You were there. I remember waking up in this house with you testing me to see if I remembered Maggie."

Shock widened the sharp gray eyes. "I certainly was not. I will admit to withholding information from you prior to the events in the carriage house, for the sake of keeping you two and our plans secure. But I was never at the farm, and you never returned here. As for tampering with your minds? Never.

Absolutely not."

Never returned? Grace had been sure she'd escaped *this* house and Thomasina.

Much to her chagrin, Grace believed the woman. Anger renewed itself, heating her gut and chest as she looked at Silas March. "You made me think I was here when I wasn't. I escaped your farm in a haze and thought I'd run from Thomasina, not you and what you'd done."

"You all agreed to protective custody," he said. His face held no sort of emotion Grace could read. "You are who you are. I had to try to make you *not* who you are, at least temporarily. It was for your own good."

"Somehow I doubt that," Grace said.

Thomasina's face paled. "Silas, what did you do? You were charged with taking them to a more secure facility and training them, teaching them, nothing more. You told us they had run off. We enacted a monthlong search for them on your word, saying they had balked."

"Their preparation for the Awakening is critical, but they grew restless and contentious." March's lips curled into a sneer. "Had we been able to perform the ritual six months ago, I would have gladly sent them to their fate then."

Watching March, Grace's head was suddenly filled with flashes of memories, images too fleeting to completely understand. Training while March looked on, arguing with him, flares of rage and power, a . . . wrongness. She knew in her gut that these things told one truth: Silas March had significant power, but he wasn't who—or what—he claimed to be.

Grace wove a finger of magic around March, seeking a way past his defenses. A mental pulse against her power proved he was, indeed, hiding something.

March twitched, then glared at her. "Stop."

Grace redoubled her efforts, sliding a tendril of power through a small weakness she found in the ward he'd placed around himself. Why would he need a ward? "What don't you want us to see?"

March snarled, his hands coming up. The distinct impression of bees buzzing irritated Grace. He flicked his wrist as if shooing a fly. A zap of electric pain shot up her arm. Grace's probing tendril retreated.

"Silas!" Thomasina seemed to sense something as well and raised her hands, palms facing the man. Was she going to help? Not only had March gone behind her back on what they'd planned, he'd crossed the line by tampering with their memories.

He gestured toward the prioress. Thomasina spun and slammed into the wall. Artwork fell, and glass trinkets shattered.

Emmaline dove behind the desk.

March swept his hand before him. Books and papers flew around Grace and Maggie in a cyclone like a flock of possessed birds. Through the rising din and the frantic flutter of pages, Grace saw him dash toward the door.

"Stop him, Maggie!"

They hit him with a binding spell, freezing him in place.

"Hold him," she said to Maggie. She walked up to March. "What's the rush?"

"Don't," he said, more angry than afraid, but there was definitely fear there.

Grace spread open the edges of his defenses, peeling them back like old wallpaper to expose what damage awaited beneath. A familiar bitter spice aroma assaulted her. She mentally stumbled. Not from the strength of his magic, as she and Maggie could handle that, but from what it revealed.

"Demon!"

March struggled, but to no avail. His face and the bare skin on his head turned crimson with effort, and rage contorted his features.

"You bitch," he growled. "You'll ruin everything."

"Good." Grace glared at Thomasina, who was just coming to her feet.

The sister shook her head. "I didn't know. I swear. I thought he was a particularly strong male. Rare, but not unheard of. He's been with the Order for at least two decades. His ward was never detected."

"Legion." Maggie flicked her wrist, and Grace's magic pulsed, though she was not the aggressor in the attack. March winced. "There may be more of them."

The possibility chilled Grace. Demons within the ranks of the Order. It was a terrifying thought.

She turned her gaze to Emmaline. The young woman was out from behind the desk, standing with her back against the wall, hands clasping something that hung from a thin chain around her neck. "Papa worried that there were spies in the Order, but I don't think he suspected them among the higher levels of trust and responsibility. No wonder Conrad growls at him."

"Always trust a dog," Maggie said, then addressed March. "It was you who did this to us. You who put me under the guard of that . . . thing in Wyoming."

Her words were even in tone, but Maggie's hatred and disgust, both toward March and toward herself, came through loud and clear. Grace's heart cracked for her catalyst. It wasn't Maggie's fault, none of it, especially not how March had treated them and what he'd put her through. Would Maggie ever recover from that?

Grace's anger flared, white-hot, desperate for revenge for what he did to her catalyst. "I'll kill you, you bastard."

With barely a thought, her magic came up, and she plunged a knife of power into March's chest. The demon screamed in pain. Satisfaction flooded her being. It wasn't meant to be a mortal blow, but she'd succeeded in the desired result. She twisted the knife. March dropped to his knees, his back arched and his mouth open in silent agony.

"Don't kill him," Maggie admonished, and her gentle "hand" of power stilled the knife. "Not yet. We need answers."

A sob escaped Grace's throat. "After what he did to you? To us?"

Maggie's dark eyes were nearly black. No, she was just as enraged as Grace, but as always, more levelheaded than her source. "I know. But first things first." She narrowed her gaze on March. "He's not going anywhere."

CHAPTER THIRTY-FOUR

Freetown, Long Island, NY, November 1903

Between Grace, Thomasina, and herself, along with Emmaline commanding Conrad, they bound March with ropes of magic and brought him to the warded testing room in the cellar. He resisted going deeper into the house, flinching as if in pain, though he had no choice but to comply. Maggie suspected now that his protective ward was gone, the Order's wards were taking their toll. Good.

Lashed to one of the straight-backed chairs, he was as secured as they could make him, but Maggie kept watch while the others laid out tea that had been brewed and brought down. It was going to be a long night.

"Here." Grace set a cup and saucer by Maggie's elbow. "Nice and strong, with a bit of milk."

"Thanks, love." The sentiment came out automatically. Heat flared in her cheeks as her gaze met Grace's green eyes.

Grace smiled, hopeful yet cautious. "You're welcome."

It was oh so easy to see herself with Grace. The memories of their life together, before that night months ago, were as real as the chair beneath her. So why couldn't she allow herself to embrace what she knew was hers to reclaim?

John Dalton's face surfaced in her mind's eye.

Demon-touched echoed in her head. A shudder ran up her

spine. A cold, slimy lump churned in her stomach. *Unclean.*

Maggie closed her eyes, her jaw clenched against the bile that rose at the back of her throat.

"Maggie?" Grace's voice was soft, full of concern.

She opened her eyes and nearly wept. Grace knelt before her, warm, rough hands grasping Maggie's. Maggie attempted to smile, to reassure her source, though she was just as sure Grace could feel what she was going through.

Grace's brow furrowed. "I can tell what you're thinking about yourself," she whispered, her words cracking with emotion. "You aren't damaged or ruined or anything of the sort. Far from it. Please believe that."

A sob nearly escaped her. "I wish I could."

Grace's desire for her to heal filled her, but it wasn't as easy as that. Her love and concern enveloped Maggie. Would she ever be able to feel it for herself?

Grace stood suddenly, rage tinting the gentler emotions coming from her. Not rage at Maggie, she knew, rage at who was responsible.

Her source strode to where March was secured. She kicked the seat of the chair, nearly knocking it backward. "You bastard."

March's eyes went wild as he tilted, then was righted once again. Falling wouldn't have hurt the demon, unfortunately. When he realized he wasn't going to topple, he schooled his features into a more neutral mask that bordered on unconcerned.

"We're on the same side."

Grace brought her face close to his. Her eyes blazed. Maggie's power sparked half a second before Grace's hands took on a blue tint. "Never."

March grinned. "But it's true. We want the same thing, you and I."

Grace laid her palm on his chest. His clothing smoldered. His face contorted, his lips pulled back in a grimace of pain. She pulled her hand away, leaving a perfect black handprint burned into him.

"We will never want the same thing," she said with quiet

238

rage. "You know how I know this? Because *I* want you dead."

March breathed heavily through clenched teeth. "Kill me—I know you can—and you'll have no help in stopping Ammemnion, no chance to keep your people safe."

"Grace." Sister Thomasina stood near Maggie. She didn't dare get any closer to Grace and March. "He has a valid point. We need his insights."

"Then we can kill him," Maggie heard herself say. A sharp look from Thomasina did nothing but fortify her resolve. She shrugged. "I see no problem with it."

"Nor do I," Grace said. She raised her hand again, the blue surrounding them becoming brighter.

To March's credit, he allowed nothing to show on his face, though he swallowed hard and moistened his lips. "If you're going to kill me anyway, I have no reason to cooperate with you."

"Tell you what." Grace touched a single finger to his cheek. March's jaws clenched. "You'll get to decide how quickly it goes, how's that?"

"Grace." The sister's tone was sharper. "We need him," she repeated with deliberation.

March had the gall to grin, even as his face burned.

Her source's frustration mirrored Maggie's. He was responsible for so much pain they had suffered, but Thomasina was right. Grace moved her hand away and stepped back. Crossing the room, she sat beside Maggie.

"I'll tell you what you want to know," March said. "But I want a promise of clemency from you."

Grace laughed. "No."

March shrugged. "Then you get nothing. You go into this battle ignorant and without useful resources at your disposal. I can tolerate a lot more pain than you might realize. A lot more."

Grace narrowed her gaze at him, her disgust and anger rolling off her as she started to rise again. "We'll see about that."

Maggie laid her hand on Grace's arm, stopping her from outright killing him.

It was her turn.

Grace lowered herself back onto the wooden chair. She nodded once, a mix of concern and pride in her eyes.

Maggie sipped her tea, set the cup and saucer on the chair on her other side, and stood. She needed to confront him for what he'd done to her, to both of them. She smoothed her skirt and moved to stand in front of him.

March smiled up at her. "Going to play the opposite and try to sweet-talk me, pigeon?"

"No." Maggie let her power accumulate. She held up her glowing hand.

His brow furrowed for a split second, and then his eyes bulged as she closed her fist, imagining her fingers around his thick neck. A gurgling sound bubbled from his lips.

"You set your watchdog on me. You put us through nearly a year of fear, not understanding what was going on." She squeezed her fist tighter, her knuckles white beneath the purple aura. "At this point, I don't give a tinker's damn if we never hear another word from your filthy mouth."

"Margaret, you must stop." Sister Thomasina spoke with more urgency in her voice than she had with Grace. Maggie was supposed to be the calm one, the one who reined in Grace's more volatile reactions. Thomasina knew they were at the end of their rope.

Still holding her fist in front of March's face, Maggie half turned toward the sister. "I don't have to do any such thing. He has information. We need it. I lived with his damn demon."

Her voice was rising and her chest quivering, remembering what she had done while in Wyoming, while living with what she'd known as her husband. "He deserves every bit of pain he can feel now. It won't come close to making up for what he did."

Thomasina started toward her, but Grace rose and blocked the nun. "No. We're done with bargaining. If he wants to play more games, we're done."

"I'll not condone torture," Thomasina said. Her voice shook with outrage.

Grace smiled grimly. "You're not in charge of this little

scenario. Have a seat." The sister started to argue, but Grace's mouth curled into a snarl. "I said, sit down."

Whatever Thomasina saw in her former charge put fear and anger in her eyes. But she did as she was told.

Maggie turned back to March, whose face was crimson, his eyes bulging from his head. Sweat poured off his scalp. She opened her clenched fist.

The demon fell forward as far as his bindings would allow, gasping for air. After catching his breath, he looked up at her. "Don't expect an apology from me, pigeon." His voice was rough from the near-strangulation. "I did what I had to do."

"Oh, I understand that." Maggie bent down, making sure their gazes were level. "And I know you won't break easily. That's fine. Whatever you did, it's because *you* will benefit." Acknowledgment of that fact lit his bloodshot eyes. "You have to understand that Grace and I don't care what others want of us anymore. If we let the entire world collapse, you're going with us, aren't you?"

Thomasina gasped, then began whispering a prayer to Saint Teresa. Good. She believed. Now Maggie needed March to.

"This is exactly what I was afraid of," he growled. "You two are so damn selfish. We couldn't possibly trust you."

"No, you can't." Maggie crossed her arms, holding herself together against the pretense of calm. "Instead of hiding us away, you tampered with our memories so we'd do as you bid."

"Tried to," Grace said.

March glared at Grace. "You proved to be a challenge. That was actually a good thing, in retrospect."

"How so?" Maggie hoped he couldn't detect how she was shaking with still-unappeased rage. But he was talking, and she had to keep that going.

He met her gaze again. "Resisting the memory block is unheard of. You were difficult enough." Maggie's jaw tightened at so casual a reference to his manipulating her mind. "I had to have your 'wedding ring' infused with spells to make sure the block held."

241

The gold band she'd thrown into the fetid pit along with the body of the demon. No wonder it had irritated her so.

"Miss Carter lost little, relatively speaking," he continued. "Her mind was foggy for a time, and she was disoriented, but she still managed to get off the farm and to a train station. It proved we had the right pair for the job."

"You wanted to make sure we were strong enough to take on Ammemnion." Grace's frustration was palpable. "What was your plan, March?"

"I still want a deal," he said. "We do need each other for this, no matter what you say or think."

He smiled, knowing they had no choice but to agree.

Out of nowhere the saucer Maggie had used with her tea spun past her and caught March above his left eye. The demon yelped, more from surprise than pain, she guessed. The china disk crashed to the floor and broke into half a dozen pieces.

He glared at Grace. Dark blood dribbled along the corner of his eye. "You are such a bitch."

"Like I care what you think of me," Grace said.

Maggie picked up one of the shards. March watched with narrowed eyes as she imbued it with her magic. The delicate piece glowed purple with threads of silver running through it.

"I know you can withstand a lot of pain," she said stepping closer. "Still, this will hurt, and I will feel better having done it."

"Margaret, no!" A chair scraped against the floor.

Conrad barked sharply.

"Sit down," Grace commanded.

There was a solid thud and the scrape of chair legs as Thomasina sat hard, either of her own volition or not. Maggie didn't care.

"This isn't right," Thomasina said.

"He's a demon," Grace said. "He deserves no consideration."

"It isn't who we are," the sister responded.

Maggie hesitated for a moment, still watching March keep his unaffected expression. She had so much rage and disgust, within herself and with him, and he cared not a whit.

"It's who he's made me into," she said, and pressed the shard point into the side of his neck.

The veins on March's neck and forehead stood out as he grimaced. Maggie twisted the shard, sending the thread of power slicing into his body. Had the silver been actual metal, it might have hurt more, but this would suffice. March shook. She shoved the piece deeper, and he closed his eyes, his face a rictus of pain.

"This will make up for only a fraction of the terrible things you did to us," she whispered. "We'll make your deal, not kill you, but know that we could, and we'd enjoy it."

Leaving the shard in place, Maggie turned to bring a chair closer. Thomasina stared at her as she muttered prayers. Not for March, Maggie was sure. Maybe for what they'd done, or what March had done to her and Grace, or what they'd become. Maybe for her soul, which was likely damned anyway, no matter how this ended.

She looked at Grace. Her source was stone-faced, her green eyes dark as she kept them on the demon, a hint of satisfaction glinting in them. She met Maggie's gaze briefly and nodded. Of course she understood. Who else on Earth could?

Maggie set the chair before March. She sat and straightened her skirts, taking her time, collecting herself, calming the rush and turmoil within. Grace was right there, right alongside her, as Maggie knew she'd be.

"Now," she said, folding her hands primly in her lap. "Talk."

243

CHAPTER THIRTY-FIVE

Freetown, Long Island, NY, November 1903

March breathed through his nose like an angry, wounded bull at the mercy of a matador. "You agreed to go into hiding, for the sake of keeping you both safe from the Horde and for specialized training."

"Yes, we know." Maggie resisted the urge to twist the shard still in his neck or send a burst of magic through it. "Get to the part where you thought it was a good idea to wipe our memories."

"Not wiped," he corrected. "Just masked. Couldn't risk you losing everything."

"How thoughtful," Grace said from behind her.

"What did Thomasina know?" Though the sister had insisted she was ignorant of March's memory spell, they needed to be sure.

He glanced at Thomasina. Maggie couldn't tell what was passing between them, but she assumed it wasn't a pleasant exchange. He brought his gaze back to her. "Only that I was taking you away. For training. She didn't know about the memory thing. She only knew the arrangement went off when Miss Carter disappeared and another Order member said something to her."

"I can only imagine the lies you would have spun if you had been there to intercept Christina when she went to look in on them." There was no mistaking the anger in Thomasina's voice. "You implicated me in your foul doings with Grace."

March grinned. "Convincing her you were part of it all along was both necessary and a pleasure."

Grace's emotions spiked inside Maggie, but she quickly gained control of them.

"You are a vile bastard, aren't you?" Thomasina muttered.

"Comes with the territory," the demon replied with a shrug.

Maggie could imagine Thomasina's pinched face going pale, then red.

"Why mask our memories to begin with?" she asked to get them back on topic. "You said something about us balking at the mission."

"I did, didn't I?" March rolled his shoulders and stretched his neck muscles, wincing when the china shard moved within his flesh. "You had reason to balk, I suppose."

"We had committed to the mission," Grace said. "Something must have happened for us to consider backing out."

"It did."

They waited for March to continue. He sighed, glancing beyond Thomasina. Maggie turned her head. Emmaline came closer, with Conrad beside her. The wolfhound growled at March.

"Hamilton Gallagher came to the farm," March said. "He'd learned what I was. You two, with your knack for putting your noses and ears where they don't belong, overheard. If I didn't stop you, you'd have told Thomasina and everyone, ruining decades of planning. The farm is a Legion stronghold, the power imbued in it strong enough to subdue you, if only temporarily."

Emmaline blanched. Conrad leaned against her, giving a whine-growl of indecision. He wanted to protect his mistress, but the desire to tear March to shreds was clear in his eyes.

Maggie could relate.

"What did you do to my father?" Emmaline asked in a horrified whisper.

"Nothing." March had the decency to look somewhat

embarrassed. "Nothing intentional anyway. I liked Gallagher, even fed him some good information to help with the counter ritual, but he was getting nervous. I laid a small mind control on him so he wouldn't reveal my identity in a fit of guilt and honesty. Had him forget what I was and made him destroy any written details of the Awakening. He was quite the note taker."

That explained the missing pages of the blue journal Emmaline had given them. Gallagher must have cut them out under the direction of March's control. Emmaline had sworn there was another volume. Chances were Gallagher had destroyed it as well.

"He took ill not long after he'd gone to visit you." Emmaline's voice was sharp and rightfully accusatory. "Your fault?"

Conrad growled louder.

"Not directly. I swear." Surprisingly, the demon seemed remorseful. "Once he left the farm, the residual magic could have caused physical problems. Humans without power can be delicate things."

"After we overheard you," Maggie said, "you did the same to us. But humans *with* power can be difficult to control, is that right?"

March nodded. "You weren't easy, but I managed with the ring and guard. But you," he nodded toward Grace. "You were downright obstinate."

"So I've been told."

Maggie heard the wryness in Grace's voice and smiled. Her amusement didn't last long as memories of living with John Dalton over the last nine months crashed into her head. How he'd touched her, or tried to if she hadn't claimed a headache or "woman troubles" to get him to leave her be. But the times he had managed to defeat her efforts . . .

Her gut cramped, and the tea threatened to come up.

"Why did you use that thing to guard me?" she blurted.

March shrugged, his indifference doubling her disgust and anger. "He was available. Cheap. Willing. I have to use my resources wisely. Wyoming seemed out of the way enough. After

246

Miss Carter flew the coop, things got a bit hairy, but we took it as an opportunity to learn more about you as well."

"Us?" Grace asked. She was standing by Maggie now, her hand warm and reassuring on Maggie's shoulder. "How many of the Horde are you working with?"

The demon gave her a crooked grin. "More than you care to think about, I'm sure. But no worries, Miss Carter. As I said, we're all on the same side. More or less."

"And what side is that?" Maggie asked. "Why are demons helping the Order?"

March tilted his head. "Isn't it obvious, Miss Mulvaney? I told you, we want the same thing: to keep Ammemnion imprisoned." He took on a thoughtful expression. "Admittedly, killing him would be preferable, but that's a tall order when it comes to a demon lord. So, cooperation in countering the Awakening will have to suffice."

Maggie let his words sink in. Cooperation between the Order and demons. She realized she was shaking her head. "No. Impossible." She turned to Sister Thomasina. "Did you know about this?"

Thomasina glanced at all of them before responding. "I knew Doctor Gallagher was working on some sort of intelligence gathering, that we needed cooperation from within their ranks." She nodded toward March. "I had no idea what he was, I swear it. I feel sick that a demon has been among us for so long."

March curled his lip at the sister. "It was no picnic for me either, but we all do what we have to do, eh?"

"And what you had to do was tamper with our memories so the truth wouldn't get out," Grace said.

Maggie felt the tension running through her, with both the sense of her magic and the grip Grace had on her shoulder.

"As I said, a necessary action meant to be a temporary condition. Things didn't go as planned." He shrugged. "It happens."

Maggie raised her hand and made a shoving motion. Flaring violet and silver, the magicked shard in the demon's neck sank deeper.

March gave a roar of pain. Panting, he glared at her. "You asked. I answered. Don't blame me if you don't like what you heard."

"What was this plan of yours involving the Horde and us?" Maggie asked.

He sighed, rolled his shoulders, and cracked the vertebrae in his neck before responding.

"Sequestering you was a legitimate concern," he said with less bravado. "My associates and I are a relatively small faction. Had any of the Horde who support the return of Ammemnion learned who or where you were, they would have torn you to shreds. And not quickly."

"You and your associates as well, I'd wager."

"Without a doubt," March said.

There were demons trying to prevent the rise of Ammemnion? Why?

Grace's fingers dug into her shoulder for a moment, relaxing when she realized what Maggie was doing. "Your 'small faction' is a rebellion."

"Not quite." March thought about it for a moment. "Well, not technically."

Maggie twisted the shard again.

"Ouch! Stop that!" The demon snarled, his eyes going black.

There wasn't a lick of sympathy in Maggie for him.

"Then tell us what you're talking about."

"The Legion. We like things the way they are, the power that we've accrued these last few centuries," March said. "Should Ammemnion awaken, he will demand fealty, demand we give the choice pick of humans over to him. He'd feed first, and greatly, while we'd be left with scraps."

The Legion. Those higher-echelon demons who used cunning for long-term, sustained assaults on victims. How many had worked their way into human society in order to slowly feed? How deep did their vileness penetrate? If March could infiltrate the Order, where else had the Legion sunk its fangs?

There was silence in the room while they digested what he'd

said, discussing humankind as if they were selections of meat at a butcher shop.

Grace was the first to break, barking a laugh that held nothing but stunned disbelief. "You're so afraid of being denied your share of human misery that you decided to work with the Order? Why?"

"To maintain the status quo." March grinned. "With Ammemnion in stasis, the human race continues on its miserable, ignorant way, and the Legion and Horde can still feed. The Horde in favor of Ammemnion returning would need to be dealt with, and we'll still have to battle you now and again, but ..."

He shrugged, willing to make that concession for the benefit of himself and his fellows.

"My God," Grace whispered, incredulous.

The demon frowned at her. "It's a win-win. Or at least not an absolute loss for either of us." His gaze went to Thomasina. "Count your blessings as you can, eh, Sister?"

"I thought you were perhaps a go-between, nothing so foul as, as ..." The horror was clear in Thomasina's voice.

"Are you sure it would have mattered had you known?" he asked with a smirk. "The devil you know, and all that."

The silent rage from Sister Thomasina filled the room; Maggie didn't need magic to recognize it.

What March revealed was at once horrific and understandable, from his point of view at least. It took Maggie a few moments to find her voice. "Who else in the Order knew of this arrangement? Knew what you are?"

He flicked a glance toward Emmaline. "Only Gallagher knew what I was. Several others understood, albeit mistakenly due to deliberate misinformation, that I was meeting with one of the Legion. You saw them the night we met here."

"And none of them know the truth?"

March looked at Maggie. "No. Keeping my identity a secret was paramount, obviously."

"How long do we have?" Grace asked.

The demon shifted on the chair, clearly uncomfortable. "Twelve days, fifteen hours, and thirty-seven minutes. You have a bit of catching up to do."

The sharp hiss of Grace's breath mirrored Maggie's own feelings. Not much time to learn how to thwart a demon lord.

"We would have brought you together again and restored your memories," March said. "The masking was designed not to eliminate your power, but to keep you under control. We planned to bring you back together, oh, a month or two before the Awakening. With your abilities, we realized that would have been plenty of time to prepare. I was going to plant false memories to keep you in the dark about my identity. Then Miss Carter fled. It was troublesome at first, but it gave us an opportunity to gauge first her, then both of you once you reunited."

"You knew what I was doing the whole time?"

"More or less," he admitted. "We had to make sure the rest of the Horde didn't know what was happening or who you were. Your stops in Denver were an interesting turn."

He meant Mrs. Wallace and Beatrix. Were they working with him? Or had she and Grace revealed Mrs. Wallace and her ward as a danger to March and his associates? Maggie couldn't stomach the idea of asking, let alone learning the answer, though she now knew the older woman was a true ally. She hoped Mrs. Wallace and, yes, even Beatrix were safe.

"From those observations of how quickly your partnership rekindled," March continued, "we determined you could be ready in time. With a little effort, at any rate."

Maggie stood and turned to face Thomasina and Emmaline. The sister was as white-faced and disturbed as expected, yet perhaps unwilling to concede that the overall idea of dealing with the demons was wrong. Emmaline seemed pained, and Maggie's heart went out to her. She would never be sure that her father's dealings hadn't directly led to his death. Not unless she took the word of a demon.

"I suppose now we do what we were tasked to do all along." Maggie walked over to March and slowly drew the piece of china from his neck. Nearly black blood oozed from the wound. She dropped the stained shard onto the floor.

"We can't let him run loose," Grace said, coming up beside her. Grace's hatred for the demon rivaled her own. "We have to make sure we're fully prepared. He'll be useful for that."

Thomasina joined them. "I have a more secure binding spell, but I'll need Gretchen."

"In the meantime," Maggie said, wiping the demon's blood on her skirt, "we get some rest, hone our training, learn the ritual, then use Mr. March and his friends to defeat the demon lord."

"Piece of cake."

Grace's sarcasm actually made Maggie smile, but they grew quiet with contemplation.

Could they learn all they needed to learn in time to defeat Ammemnion?

Did they have much choice?

CHAPTER THIRTY-SIX

Freetown, Long Island, NY, November 1903

After securing March in the basement, Grace and Maggie climbed the stairs to their old bedrooms. A single lamp lit the way along the corridor. All six doors were closed.

There were no other junior members of the Order in the house, at the moment. Those who had tried to capture them at the Gallagher residence had stayed elsewhere. Thomasina shooed the few others living there out of the house for the duration, claiming they needed to fumigate the premises. Only Mrs. Reynolds and Rémy had been permitted to return after ensuring the others were safely away. Emmaline and Conrad occupied one of the unused rooms.

Grace paused with Maggie when she stopped to study the portraits hanging on the walls of the hallway. Did she remember the names of those who came before them? Mary. Camilla. Lupe. Antoin. Bernadette. All the others. Would they have offered their souls to stop the rise of the Horde?

The window and alcove where Grace and Maggie had watched carriages arrive that fateful night was a dark nook. What would have happened if she hadn't gotten the bee in her bonnet and run out to investigate? March and Thomasina claimed she and Maggie had been told everything that night, but they hadn't. Thomasina had known years before they'd met that she and Maggie would likely become partners. The sister had tormented her, pushed her, punished her, for what? In order to make Grace stronger, or for her own need to control?

Did it matter now?

"This one is mine," Maggie said, stopping at the door to her old room.

Grace glanced at the next room over. Funny, despite the familiarity of seeing the scars and spots of worn varnish, she didn't think of it as hers any longer. Something had shifted. They belonged here, yet they didn't.

"Get some rest," she said. "Good night."

"Grace." Maggie said her name as she gently grasped Grace's arm.

Grace looked down at her catalyst's hand on her sleeve, resisting the urge to fall into her arms. She was so weary, so physically and emotionally done with it all. Yet there was so much more that had to be accomplished.

"Grace," Maggie repeated, tugging her coat. Grace looked up. "Will you come stay with me tonight? Just . . ." Her cheeks pinkened. "Be with me."

Grace's heart soared at the prospect of spending a quiet night together. When was the last time that had happened? They'd been on the run since reuniting in Wyoming. She needed this. They both did. "Of course, whatever you want."

Maggie offered a tentative smile and, slipping her hand into Grace's, opened the door.

The room was dark and chilly, a little musty from being closed off for several months. Maggie ran her hand along the wall, twisted the light switch. The stained-glass fixture in the ceiling slowly glowed to life. The bed was made, the room neat. Most of Maggie's belongings had probably gone to the farm with them, but a few remnants of her had been left behind. A bottle of perfume on the vanity. A forgotten shawl draped on the chair. The room no longer carried Maggie's scent or sense of her other than those few items and Grace's lingering memory.

Grace closed the door behind them. Maggie released her

hand and walked to the dresser. She opened and closed the top two drawers.

"I don't have anything like nightclothes here. I don't feel like going downstairs for our bags."

"I don't either. We'll just have to make do."

Maggie smiled as she sat on the bed and worked the laces of her boots. "I suppose we will. Come get comfortable."

Grace circled around to the other side. She removed her boots while watching Maggie from the corner of her eye. Maggie kept her head down as she unbuttoned her blouse and skirt. She hesitated, casting a shy glance at Grace.

"I'll turn out the light when you're ready," Grace said. She rose, crossed the room, and touched the switch.

After a few moments, she heard the rustling of covers.

"Ready."

Grace turned out the light and made her way to her own side of the bed again. She turned down the covers. The sheets beneath the blanket and comforter weren't as crisp as a freshly made bed, but they were clean and soft. She loosened her trousers and let them drop to the floor. Her shirt came next. Only her short shift and undergarments remained. Grace slid between the sheets and adjusted the covers.

It wasn't the first time they had slept side-by-side since Grace had found Maggie in Wyoming, but there was something different now. There was no need for them to be together out of necessity or protection. Maggie had *asked* her to stay.

It didn't mean anything, yet it meant everything.

"Thank you," Maggie said softly.

Under the shared covers, Grace felt the heat of her body, though they weren't touching. She inhaled Maggie's lilac scent.

"Yeah, sure. It's—" Grace stopped herself from saying "nothing" because it wasn't nothing. It was definitely something. But what?

She just needs company right now, after confronting March.

So did Grace, truth be told.

In the dim light of the room, with only the vague glow of

the window allowing her to see, Grace watched Maggie roll onto her side, facing Grace but not touching her.

"I'm exhausted, but my mind is running like a locomotive," Maggie murmured.

"Think of something pleasant," Grace offered. "A field of flowers maybe. Or count sheep jumping over a wall."

Maggie gave a small grunt of frustration. "I keep seeing Sister Thomasina and March and—"

Grace knew who else kept intruding on Maggie's thoughts. She wished they could forget about him for the night at least.

"Count Sister Thomasinas jumping over a wall."

The image of the nun leaping over a stone wall, habit flying, must have hit Maggie the way it hit Grace, and they both burst out laughing. The lateness of the night and their old practice of self-restraint to not disturb others around them—despite the fact that no others were asleep nearby now—prompted them to try to quell their amusement. But the harder they tried, the more determined the exhaustion- and stress-fueled laughter became.

"Shhhhh," Maggie gently pressed her fingertips to Grace's lips. "We'll get into trouble."

Getting her giggles under control, Grace grasped Maggie's fingers. "We're adults. What can they do to us?"

Instead of pulling out of Grace's grip, Maggie squeezed her hand. "Nothing, I suppose. It's strange to be back in this room, in this bed, and feeling . . ."

"Older. Like a lifetime has passed since we were last here."

"It sort of has, hasn't it?" Maggie turned her hand so their palms met and laced their fingers together. "We aren't the same people we were even a few months ago."

She had said as much when Grace had hoped Maggie would remember who they were back at Mrs. Wallace's, but she wasn't angry now. There was acceptance in her tone. There could be nothing else, for either of them.

"I guess we aren't."

Grace stilled. Though unable to see her catalyst's face clearly enough to read her expression, a tumble of emotions came through from Maggie. Worry. Desire. Need. Confusion. Uncertainty. Love.

That last one simultaneously made Grace ecstatic and heartbroken. It was there. She knew it. Maggie knew it. What could they do about it?

Her own emotions ran a similar course, but she tried not to let Maggie feel them. Her catalyst was dealing with more than enough without pressure from Grace, even if it wasn't intentional.

Grace brought the back of Maggie's hand closer and pressed her lips to the soft skin. "Go to sleep."

She started to move their hands lower, to rest on her stomach, thrilled there was even that much intimacy between them after so long. Then Maggie loosened her grip. A small pang shimmered through Grace's gut as she spread her fingers to let her go.

Instead of rolling away, Maggie touched her palm to Grace's cheek. Her breath feathered across Grace's lips a moment before Maggie unerringly brought their mouths together. It was a soft, tentative kiss, testing their reconstructed relationship.

When Maggie hesitated, her hand warm against Grace's skin, Grace swallowed a threatening sob. She had been encouraged by the impulsive kisses in the Wyoming woodland, in the city park before their defensive attack, and just outside the doors of the house earlier that evening, but this felt different, more deliberate. Grace had waited so long for Maggie to come back to her. She was afraid to move, afraid to breathe for fear of putting her off.

"I can feel you," Maggie said quietly, "inside. Your power. You. Your mind is racing and your heart is pounding."

Grace moistened her lips. "I don't want to scare you. I don't want to lose you."

Not again. She could manage there not being a physical aspect to their relationship—had managed it before—but to lose Maggie to her own recriminations and fears would break Grace as surely as it would break her catalyst.

256

Maggie kissed her again, and Grace swore the other woman was smiling. "I'm not scared, not when you're with me. And as for losing me ..."

She pressed her tongue against Grace's lips. With a hitch in her breath, Grace let her in, let her set the tone and pace of their first real kiss in what seemed like forever. Their tongues met and gently slid along each other.

Grace drew her hand along Maggie's shoulder, to the back of her neck. She threaded her fingers through Maggie's thick red hair, holding her close, but ready to let her pull away if she wished, praying she wouldn't.

Maggie traced the curve of Grace's jaw and neck with her fingertips. She sketched a line across her collarbone. Her thumb brushed the top of Grace's breast. Desire for more danced along her skin. Grace moaned, letting Maggie feel her hunger.

Maggie broke the kiss. "Grace, I need you."

Grace captured her lower lip. "I need you too."

"I need you to show me."

Grace hesitated. Show her? Show her what?

"I need you to show me," Maggie continued, "that I'm not tainted by that ... thing."

Grace's heart clenched. Maggie still believed her time with John Dalton had been a stain on her soul. She drew Maggie down against her, holding her close, wishing she could wipe that memory from her catalyst's mind.

"You are nothing of the sort," Grace whispered fiercely into her ear. "I wish I knew how to make you believe that."

Maggie trembled in her arms. Grace kissed her hair. She rubbed her palm up and down Maggie's back as if to warm her, to bring life back into her.

"You are beautiful and perfect and pure." She maneuvered her arm out from under Maggie and framed her face with her palms. The dampness of tears trickled along her fingers, and Grace brushed them away with the pads of her thumbs. She held Maggie's gaze in the dimness of the room. "Anyone who says otherwise will have to answer to me. Even if it's you."

257

Maggie gave a laugh-sob. "I wouldn't dare cross you."

"Good." She drew Maggie down for another kiss, gentle and accompanied by all the love she could pour into it. Maggie gasped. She felt it. All of it.

Maggie tugged on Grace's shift, on her drawers, at the same time a rush of desire from Maggie coiled around her own.

She slid her tongue between Maggie's lips, and levered herself onto her side. Maggie rolled to her back, her palm hot even through Grace's shift. Grace hooked the shoulder strap of Maggie's shift and drew it down. She kissed her catalyst's throat, tasting the delicate skin, taking in her lilac scent. Maggie's heartbeat gently thrummed beneath her mouth as well as within her.

"I feel you," Maggie said again, her voice full of awe and wonder. "More, please."

More, yes, Grace wanted more as well, but they had agreed to *not* doing more.

"Your vow," she said. "You never made it official, but it had been important to you."

Much had changed in the last year. Had that as well? She had to be sure. They both did.

Maggie said nothing for a few long moments, and despite their closeness, their connection, Grace tensed in anticipation of her renewed dedication to a life within the Order's monastic calling.

"No, I never made it official. I didn't know why, until now. In my heart, I knew I would be lying to myself and the Order, and I didn't want to break the promise I'd made. But better to break a false promise than to live a lie." Maggie brushed a loose tendril of hair from Grace's face, then cradled her jaw in her hand. "I want to make a different promise, one I will keep until my last breath. My vow is to you, Grace Carter. In the name of God, Saint Teresa, and the Magdalene, I forsake all others and dedicate myself to you. Do you accept this pledge?"

Love for Maggie filled Grace and tightened her throat. It took her a moment to swallow it down and respond. "I do. And you, Margaret Mulvaney, do you accept my complete and

258

unwavering dedication to you until I breathe my last?"

Maggie drew her close and whispered against her mouth before their lips touched, "I do."

Grace kissed her back, then made her way down Maggie's throat to the hollow between her collarbones. Lips and tongue marked a light trail to the swell of Maggie's breast. Grace found the firm peak of her nipple, covered by the cotton shift, and circled it with her tongue.

Maggie's back arched. Her fingers dug into Grace's side, drew her closer. "Please."

Grace pulled the material down, exposing her nipple, and took it in her mouth. Maggie sucked in a breath. The hand at Grace's hip moved to the back of her head, fingers tight in her hair, holding Grace there.

Grace rolled so she was over Maggie, her knees on either side of her partner's hips. She tugged the shift up, breaking her kiss to Maggie's breast only long enough to lift the garment over her head. Maggie pulled at Grace's shift as well, disposing of it over the side of the bed.

Maggie captured Grace's mouth with hers again, her—their—desire growing. Her hands found the drawstring of Grace's bottoms as Grace found Maggie's. They fumbled and yanked on material until both were naked, skin to skin.

Grace leaned back, hands braced on either side of Maggie's shoulders, the curls of their sexes brushing together, their magic flowing between them. "You're sure?"

Maggie cupped Grace's cheek with one hand. The other skimmed down her breast, her ribs, traced a thin scar along her side. She stopped at Grace's hip, thumb caressing the jutting bone. She lifted her head up from the bed and pressed her lips to the V of Grace's collarbones. Her tongue flicked against Grace's skin and she moaned softly. Grace trembled.

"Love me," Maggie whispered, lying back again.

"I do. I will," Grace said. "Always."

Grace kissed her, long and deep, gentle at first, then with a hunger that swelled into need.

They moved their hips together. Grace pressed into Maggie, but it wasn't enough. She leaned on one elbow and caressed Maggie's breast, pinching the nipple between her fingers. Maggie gasped into her mouth, and her hips jerked.

Grace smiled at the flash of desire that went through them both. She slid her hand down Maggie's ribs and belly. Her fingers twirled the curls of her mons.

Maggie moaned, one hand digging into Grace's hip, the other grasping her hair again, holding her in place as they kissed.

Grace slipped a finger between the curls. She found the bud of flesh at the apex, firm and slick. Further down, the heat and wetness at her fingertips made Grace shiver. The scent of lilacs filled the air.

Maggie shifted, nudging Grace to her side so they faced each other again. She kissed Grace's throat, then the scar on her left shoulder. Maggie brought her mouth back to Grace's, and her fingers feathered across Grace's chest to her belly, to her mons.

Sparks of need danced through Grace as Maggie found her objective. Grace arched her back, adding the bliss of skin on skin to the symphony of sensation.

Kissing and stroking, their anticipation built as they shared touches and memories. They relived the thrill of their magic coming together for the first time, of finding the person who completed them. Training and hunting, laughing and crying, but always trusting each other.

Their bodies moved together, in sync, questioning and answering each other's needs. As one, they fell then soared.

CHAPTER THIRTY-SEVEN

South Shore of Long Island, NY, near Shinnecock Bay,
November 1903

The proper alignment of stars, planets, and moons, or whatever demons used to gauge the best time to perform the Awakening, occurred on a perfectly lovely, cloudless November day. According to Silas March, however, this was a high holy day for the Horde. Or unholy, as Maggie thought of it. They didn't have many, so they had to strike at Saint Teresa's bindings on Ammemnion when they were strongest, accelerating his return.

Maggie, Grace, Thomasina, Mrs. Reynolds, March, and Rémy arrived at the site just before two o'clock in the afternoon. No "stroke of midnight" cliché for the Horde. The absurdity of it would have had Maggie laughing were it not for the absolute dread eating its way through her gut.

Rémy stopped the carriage along the road that paralleled the long stretch of the empty South Shore beach. This late in the season, summer visitors had long ago returned to their regular lives, leaving memories and sand behind. No one was within miles of them, something Thomasina wanted to be sure of during the counter ritual. It didn't necessarily matter where they performed the ritual. The veil between their world and the demon realm would open wherever Ammemnion was being roused.

According to historical texts, the first battle between Saint Teresa and Ammemnion created flashes of "heavenly light" and the booming of thunder "like the voice of God." That was fine justification for tenth-century Europeans, but residents of twentieth century Long Island, New York, might demand a more relatable explanation. Staying far from the population would save lives and unwanted attention.

Grace pushed open the carriage door and stepped out. She offered a hand up to Maggie. The cool salty air blew in from the Atlantic, and waves rolled onto the beach some fifty yards away. Gulls called overhead, their plaintive cries more raucous with each pass.

"Are you warm enough?" Grace asked.

Maggie adjusted her great coat, reassuring herself by patting the pockets that her revolver and bullets were still there. They wore similar outfits of long coats, trousers, and sturdy boots, though Grace also had her silvered knife in a boot sheath. "Fine. Just . . ."

She didn't quite know how to finish the sentence. Fine, just hoping our souls aren't destroyed by Ammemnion after we die, or worse, subjected to eternal torture? Fine, just wishing we had one more day together? Fine, just wishing we'd gone to Oregon or Alaska instead? All were true. None made it past her lips.

Grace seemed to read her mind, her emotions, because she smiled grimly and bent to peck Maggie on the cheek. Her breath warmed Maggie's skin. Grace took her hand and gave it a gentle squeeze. "I know."

No false reassurances. Grace wasn't like that. Hopeful, but realistic too.

"Down closer to the water would be best," Thomasina said coming up to them. She was bundled in a heavy wool coat, a thick green scarf around her neck, and oddly cheery matching mittens on her hands. Her pale face was dotted with blotches of red from the chill wind.

Rémy, Mrs. Reynolds and March joined them, grim expressions on their wind-chapped faces.

They had essentially said their good-byes the night before at a gathering in the library. It was at once sad and cheering, with memories and stories told, along with several bottles of port and whiskey consumed. Afterward, Maggie and Grace had retired to Maggie's room. They talked for a little longer, then, as they had for the last twelve days, made love in a way that surely branded their souls.

At least we'll have that, Maggie thought.

March scanned the road and beach. Having anticipated interference from the Horde, he'd posted his allies around the area. Other members of the Order of Saint Teresa had been dispatched along the road in preparation of keeping Ammemnion's loyal demons away from the battle site. They all contributed to additional layers of protection for Grace and Maggie, as well as creating a buffer zone to keep any stray people away. Even Virginia Delacroix and her catalyst, Jane, had joined them, nodding solemnly to Maggie and Grace as they left the house.

Holding their skirts up just above the ankles, Thomasina and Mrs. Reynolds led the way down to the beach along a dirt path through scrubby brown grass. Maggie and Grace followed, with March behind them and Rémy bringing up the rear. Maggie didn't like having March anywhere within sight, but he was deeply involved and committed to the ritual's success. Ironically, if it hadn't been for that, Maggie was sure most of the last year wouldn't have happened.

It also didn't hurt that Thomasina and Mrs. Reynolds had March "leashed." Should he go back on his word to help, or sic any of his friends on them, the older women would take care of him. The threat of turning him over to Ammemnion's loyal demons had put a glint of fear in his eyes. Maggie still wanted him dead, and couldn't deny the satisfaction she took in seeing him terrified.

The onshore breeze picked up, blowing sand around them as they plodded across the beach. Gulls dipped and called. Thomasina and Mrs. Reynolds stopped roughly halfway between the road and the breaking waves to survey the spot.

"Far enough from anything that might get hurt or damaged," Mrs. Reynolds said, tugging off her gloves, "but close enough to the water's edge."

"Demons don't particularly care for oceans," Thomasina added, her voice barely heard over the rolling waves. "They won't approach from that side, even through their portals. At least that's what Doctor Gallagher concluded."

Maggie noticed March absently nodding agreement as he scanned the road and beach.

Grace quirked an eyebrow. "Let's hope he was right."

"Are you two ready?" Thomasina rubbed her now bare hands together. The lines around her eyes had deepened over the last few days. Maggie saw the same weariness and worry in the mirror every morning.

"As we'll ever be." Grace squeezed Maggie's hand.

Rémy stepped up to them. He placed a gloved hand on each of their shoulders. "This is what you were meant to do. What you trained for. May God, Saint Teresa, and the Magdalene be with you both."

He bussed them each on their cheeks, then moved back to stand beside March.

Maggie took in the chilled beauty of the sandy beach, the calling gulls, the crash of waves, the salted air. The caring face of her source, her partner, her lover, the woman with whom she'd spent her last nights on this Earth. All the sights and sounds and smells and memories washed through her in a rush of joy and sadness. Grace's emotions mirrored her own.

Maggie cupped Grace's cheeks and drew her forward for a kiss. No mere peck, but a deep, searing kiss that none would ever mistake as a wish for luck or the indication of a platonic relationship. Let them know. Let them all know what drove her and Grace, what made them who they were together.

"I love you," she said, breathless, her forehead against Grace's.

"I—" Grace's voice caught. "I love you too."

The fear that had been twisting Maggie's gut subsided as her love and magic mixed with Grace's, giving her strength, shoring up her certainty. They were the most powerful source and cata-lyst pair in generations. They would bring Ammemnion to his knees, remind the Horde what they were dealing with when it came to the Order of Saint Teresa.

And likely die in the process. So be it. At least they'd die together.

Rémy and March stepped aside as the four women stood at the cardinal points, Thomasina at the east, Mrs. Reynolds at the west, Grace to the north, and Maggie to the south. Maggie smiled at Grace across the ten feet of sand. Grace's blonde hair blew across her face, and she smiled back. Deep in Maggie's chest, her source's power joined her own.

"Let's begin."

Maggie began the breathing exercises she and Grace had recently learned. With so much at stake, they needed to be clear of mind. Calmness and clarity. Faith and dedication. She and Grace inhaled and exhaled in sync, as did Thomasina and Mrs. Reynolds.

Thomasina held her arms out from her sides, signaling the start of preparations. Maggie and the others followed suit. Together, they recited the words of the ward they would estab-lish for Maggie and Grace to fight from. Slowly, chanting the mix of Latin and English, they walked in a circle, first clockwise, then counterclockwise. The tips of her fingers tingled where her magic reached out to touch Thomasina's and Mrs. Reynold's power. The air around them crackled like paper being crumpled in a fist.

The nape of Maggie's neck tightened, the hairs standing up as when a lightning storm passed overhead.

A warm feeling of protectiveness surrounded her and Grace.

"There," Thomasina said. "That should help."

"Grace and Margaret, move to the center," Mrs. Reynolds directed them as she and Thomasina gave them space. "Rémy, take March back to the carriage." She stared hard at March. "You'd best behave."

March sketched a bow. "Your success is my success, my

dear Mrs. Reynolds."

Mrs. Reynolds threw him a withering glare. March flinched, then grimaced at whatever she had done to him.

"No need to be heavy-handed," he said. "I'm well aware of my situation."

Rémy looked at Maggie and Grace in turn. "Remember to have faith in each other's abilities."

"Not a problem," Grace said with a smile.

"Good luck," the weapons master said. "And . . . thank you."

He nudged March on the shoulder and the two returned to the carriage.

Thomasina and Mrs. Reynolds watched them leave, then faced Maggie and Grace.

"We'll be here helping as we can," Mrs. Reynolds said. Her hands glowed a soft blue.

Thomasina's palms also became tinted. "May God, the Magdalene, and Saint Teresa bless and keep you."

Maggie and Grace thanked them. Then they stared into each other's eyes and held hands. Their magic whirled together within Maggie, like the convergence of rivers, or smoke from two sources of fire. Fear tickled the back of her throat, but it wasn't nearly as strong as the love and strength she felt for and from Grace. Their combined power filled her with each breath.

Together, they began the spell.

The first part opened the veil between their world and that of the Horde. Emmaline and March had instructed them in how to gain access. There only needed to be a small fissure, just enough to slip their magic through. Once they were in, their power would find Ammemnion on that plane.

Something shifted around them. The ward held, but the heaviness in the air thinned.

Their grip on each other's hands tightened. Every word they spoke was lined with their magic. Every syllable locked their power into place.

They called on Saint Teresa to guide them.

They beseeched the Magdalene to protect them.

266

They demanded that Ammemnion be rendered inert.

Maggie and Grace repeated the spell without pausing, their voices growing louder and stronger. The sea breeze became a steady wind whipping around them. From the corner of her vision, Maggie saw Thomasina's skirt and scarf flapping like the wings of an angry bird. Mrs. Reynolds held her hat to her head with one hand as the other shielded her face from the stinging sand. Their lips moved, but Maggie couldn't hear the words.

"They're coming," March called out over the wind from near the road.

The very air crackled and hummed like a nest of hornets.

Ammemnion's loyal Horde were on the way.

A figure materialized behind Mrs. Reynolds. Tall and broad, it appeared to be hairless, with mottled white skin covered in reddish brown blotches the color of old blood. Clawed hands reached for the woman. Before they could touch her, Mrs. Reynolds turned and gestured. The demon's chest caught fire and it flew back, landing hard in the sand. Mrs. Reynolds returned her attention to Maggie and Grace as the creature burned.

Several more demons entered the human realm. Thomasina, Mrs. Reynolds, and March employed their magic to dispatch them. In the distance, flares of power roared and flashed as other members of the Order engaged the Horde.

Dark clouds gathered overhead, boiling and churning, yet the rest of the November sky remained clear blue.

"The veil is weakening." Grace stared at a spot in the air over the wind-swept beach. Thunder crashed. "He's here."

CHAPTER THIRTY-EIGHT

South Shore of Long Island, NY, near Shinnecock Bay,
November 1903

The fabric between worlds split like a knife slowly drawn along silk.

Maggie swore she felt as well as heard the barrier part. A large hand with razor-sharp claws thrust through the gap, a sudden blast of heat and a roar of rage erupting from the fissure.

The hand grasped the edge of the tear, and another appeared, taking the other side. An arm, thick with muscle and sinew, pushed through. Then a bulging shoulder, a leg the diameter of an ancient oak, a hip and lower torso covered in pale blue, translucent, moist skin.

All at once, the beast that was Ammemnion stepped onto the beach, a hurricane of sand whirling around his muscular body. Eyeless, earless, he had the snout of a pig, or perhaps a deformed dog. He opened his mouth, exposing double rows of dagger-like teeth, and roared again. The vibration rattled through her chest, down to the soles of Maggie's feet.

Twice the height of a man, the demon lord swung his head back and forth as if searching for something. He faced Grace and Maggie and opened his jaws. Saliva dripped from the points of his teeth.

"*Now!*" Grace cried.

In perfect unison, they began reciting the words that would funnel their magic and their very lives into Ammemnion. Maggie tightened her grip on Grace's hands.

Waves came up higher on the beach as the sea roiled. Maggie squinted against the pelting sand, and water soaked her boots. The air above them shimmered.

Ammemnion took a step toward them with fists clenched, his roar piercing her ears.

"Keep going!"

Maggie wasn't sure who had shouted the order. Their magic streamed toward the demon in a swirl of purple, red, and blue.

The creature bellowed as it struck him. A sick yellow-green cloud oozed out of the ragged wound. The edges of the veil flickered.

A wave of hate and despair, fear and anger, struck the protective ward around Grace and Maggie. This was what Ammemnion was made of, what he fed upon. What their souls could be subjected to for eternity should they succeed or fail.

Maggie stopped herself from giving any credence to doubt. Doubt in their abilities could jeopardize the spell.

We'll have none of that.

Ammemnion slashed at the air. An invisible force slammed into the shield. They staggered, hitting the sand and rolling. Grace scrambled to her feet, grabbed Maggie's arm, and hauled her up.

"Again!" Grace yelled.

Their magic combined, and Grace gestured.

The demon lurched backward toward the opening, slashes in his skin streaming black ichor. He shook his massive head like a dazed prizefighter and focused on them once again. Ammemnion brought his fists down like giant twin sledgehammers.

The protective shield surrounding Grace and Maggie rippled. The thousand-bee buzz of his power shot up and down Maggie's spine. She countered it before it broke her back, but the effort left her breathless for a moment.

At the edge of her vision, she saw Sister Thomasina and

Mrs. Reynolds clinging to each other, sprawled in the sand. Were they injured? Dead?

"Damn it!" Grace shouted over the wind and sea. "Again!"

Maggie took a deep breath and squeezed Grace's hand. Repeating the ritual words, she opened herself up and Grace did the same. Their magic, their lives, would bolster the spell and bind Ammemnion for another thousand years.

Their power built, seeking a pathway directly to the demon's weakest point.

It was working. They were doing it!

Elation and sadness warred within her. Yes, they would stop the Awakening, but their time together on this Earth was over.

"Saint Teresa, I beseech you!" Grace shouted.

The dark blue fireball she launched exploded against Ammemnion's chest. Grace froze in position, her palm toward the beast, her face in a grimace of rage. A stream of blue flowed from her hand. Her stance faltered, and Maggie felt Grace's power—her life—ebb.

Maggie pushed her magic, directing it toward the demon, encouraging him to take her as well.

Choke on it, you bastard.

Then, with a *snap*, Maggie lost her connection to Grace. Her magic recoiled, hitting her in the chest hard enough to make her stumble back.

What . . . ?

She immediately concentrated on Grace, desperate to reconnect with her source.

It was like being covered with a blanket, her power smothered, prevented from flowing from her. Like the night March had them in the carriage house.

"No!" Shaking with frustration, she tried again.

Nothing. There was nothing of Grace's magic. The loss made her sick to her stomach.

Ammemnion pulsed, growing for a moment, like an abscess about to burst, then fell back onto the sand, shaking the ground beneath them. He howled his outrage, his bellow weaker, but he was not defeated.

Grace stood absolutely still, love and acceptance in her eyes.

Maggie . . . Finish him. I know you can do it. I love you.

Grace!

She crumpled.

Maggie fell to her knees.

She didn't feel Grace inside her. Grace's magic was gone. Her life, gone.

"Grace!"

Maggie's world collapsed. The bottom fell out of all she knew, all she was. Her mind was a complete blank except for keening devastation. Her chest ached as if it had been torn open.

This wasn't how it was supposed to happen. They were supposed to be together, in life and in death. If they didn't die at the same time, would they *be* together in that other world? She couldn't lose her love. Not like this.

Ammemnion lifted his piggish dog head and rose, swaying on his feet.

"Margaret!" Thomasina yelled over the roaring wind and waves. "You have to finish the ritual. You have to finish him."

Maggie looked up at the sister. Thomasina was on her knees. Her wimple had blown off, and her gray-brown hair whipped around her head. Blood ran from a cut on her cheek.

"She's . . ." Maggie's throat closed around the lump of a sob.

"Finish. It." Thomasina ordered. "Or we all die."

"I—" The word "can't" half formed in her brain, then was abruptly cut off. She could. She had to. If humanity was to have any chance—minuscule as it might be—she had to.

The account of Saint Teresa's battle came back to her in a rush. The Blessed Saint had used every bit of her power to directly assault the demon lord.

What if she didn't? What if she found some other way?

Yes. She could retain a guiding force. With that modicum of power in reserve, she would do more than end Ammemnion.

She would get Grace back.

Maggie took a breath, drawing all but a scant handful of

her magic into her fist. Her arm buzzed as if she were holding a bouquet of live wires. Sweat broke out on her entire body, yet she began to shiver with cold.

The magic in her hand was linked to the power she'd hold in reserve. She needed a sink, like the shard of china she'd used on March, something to attach her magic to; then she would sever the connection without having her entire essence drained.

Like what had happened to Grace.

Maggie stifled a sob as her mind whirled. Something she could focus on and deliver directly into Ammemnion. Something fast and deadly.

She reached into her coat pocket for her pistol.

Empty.

The gun with the silvered bullets had fallen out somewhere.

No no no ... What could she use?

Her gaze fell upon the sheathed knife sticking out of Grace's boot.

Maggie slid the weapon out of the leather. The magicked silver and steel gleamed.

For you, love.

She squeezed the hilt, pouring magic into the blade. The metal glowed violet-black streaked with silver, the deepest of night filled with shooting stars.

Maggie got to her feet and faced Ammemnion. Rage and grief boiled up from her gut and chest, tinting her vision red and purple. Taking one, two, three steps, Maggie screamed out the last phrases of the spell, tears running down her cheeks, arm cocked back.

"Blessed Magdalene and Saint Teresa, I beseech you!"

As the final syllable left her lips, she hurled the magic-imbued weapon at the demon, sending a stream of power with it to guide its path. At the last moment, she severed the feed, retaining a small spark of magic.

Blade and magic struck true, directly into his chest that still glowed faintly with Grace's power. He stopped, dripping mouth agape. Purple and silver lightning crackled along his skin.

Black smoke wafted from the wound. The gash pulsed with their combined magic like an indigo heart.

A fireball as big as a carriage flared to bright white. Maggie turned away, arm raised against the blinding light. A thunderous explosion detonated. Beneath the booming, Ammemnion screamed his pain and rage.

Sparks rained down, sizzling and crackling, singeing Maggie's face and hair. She covered Grace with her body, her hand fisted in Grace's coat, protecting her from the worst of it.

After forever, the wind died, and everything was quiet.

The only thing Maggie heard was the ringing in her ears and her own ragged breath.

She lifted her head. Grace lay still—so still—sand crusting her hair and the corners of her eyes.

Maggie's breath caught in her throat as a sob of grief tried to escape.

No time for that, girl. The long-forgotten voice of the Doyenne from Dublin startled her into action.

She pulled open Grace's coat, then her shirt, sending buttons flying. Maggie placed her palm over Grace's heart. Through the thin cotton of her chemise, Grace's skin was warm against Maggie's cold hand, but just barely.

She bowed her head. "Please, Blessed Magdalene. Please, Saint Teresa. Give me strength once more. Give *us* strength."

Maggie sent the last of her magic from the center of her chest, down her arm, and into her palm, her hand tinged purple. She "pushed" into Grace's chest, wringing the last drop of her power out of herself.

"Please," she whispered. Exhaustion overtook her and she lay down with her ear against Grace's sternum.

Nothing.

It wasn't enough.

After all they'd been through, after everything Grace had done for her, *she* wasn't enough.

Maggie closed her eyes, unable to stop the tears.

Please. Don't leave me.

The ringing in her ears had faded. Her breathing slowed. Her limbs were leaden. She was cold and couldn't move. Wouldn't move.

So tired.

It didn't matter.

Nothing mattered.

Thump.

A faint sound came to her cold ear.

Thump . . . thump.

A trick of her mind, of her heart.

Thump.

Thump.

Thump-thump.

Grace's chest rose as air whooshed into her lungs beneath Maggie's cheek.

Maggie sat up. As she watched Grace's lips turn from pale blue to pink to soft red, her heart raced with hope.

"Grace?" She brushed sand away from her love's face.

Grace's eyes fluttered open. She blinked slowly at Maggie, unfocused, her brow furrowed. When she spoke, her voice was rough, as if her throat was made of grit and gravel. "Who is that?"

She didn't recognize Maggie.

Panic seized Maggie's joy and crushed it. Was this what Grace had gone through when she had found Maggie in Wyoming a month ago?

Maggie swallowed the bolus of fear and sorrow that threatened to overwhelm her.

"It's me. It's Maggie."

Grace blinked again, wincing in pain. She squinted at Maggie. Then a weary smile curved her mouth. "Mags. You did it."

Maggie touched her lips to Grace's, ignoring the dry, chapped rasp of them to delight in the fact Grace was alive. Alive!

"*We* did it," she said, cupping Grace's cheek and grinning.

"How are you feeling?"

Grace rubbed her hand over her nearly exposed chest. "Like I've been hit by a large fist. You?"

"Same. Tired. I think we both deserve a long rest."

They started to help each other up. Thomasina and Mrs. Reynolds got them to their feet, though the two of them looked as bone-weary as Maggie felt.

Rémy met them on their way back to the carriages. His face was flushed. "My God, what a sight!"

The usually restrained weapons master spoke a mile a minute about how the encounter had looked from his view, how in the distance he heard other members of the Order fighting off demons with their magic and gunfire.

He shuddered when he got to the part with Ammemnion. "Absolutely vile."

"You performed perfectly," Sister Thomasina said. "You both did. Well done."

Rémy hugged them, tears in his eyes. "I told you knife skills were important, eh, *mon minou*? Good thing Maggie also believed me."

He winked at her, and Maggie gave him a weary smile.

Rémy helped her and Grace climb into the carriage. They moved slowly. Everything ached. Maggie sat beside her and reclaimed her hand. Thomasina and Mrs. Reynolds joined them.

"Where's March?" Maggie asked. She didn't feel comfortable having the demon loose, even now.

"He's meeting with his fellows," Mrs. Reynolds said. "Don't worry. He's still under our command."

Grace rested her head on Maggie's shoulder. "March is not one to trust."

"No need to worry about him," Thomasina assured her. "He's well in hand now. And we'll figure out how many more of his ilk are within the Order."

The sister sounded tired, but also quite pleased with their acquisition of a demon of March's caliber. Hunting down the Legion among the Order would be a daunting task without him.

If they could ever really trust him. She wasn't holding her breath.

Rémy clicked his tongue and the horses started off. The carriage swayed on the packed dirt road. Gulls called again, and crisp ocean air filled the interior. A glorious autumn day.

Maggie tilted her head back, unable to keep it up.

"It's not there anymore," Grace whispered, her voice cracking with sadness.

For a moment, Maggie didn't know what she was talking about.

Their magic. The recognition of the other within. Gone.

No. Not gone. Changed.

She placed her palm on Grace's sternum. "It is. Feel."

Maggie's chest warmed. Her limbs tingled with awareness. Two hearts beat within them.

Slowly, Grace grinned. "There you are."

"Always," Maggie said, and closed her eyes.

ACKNOWLEDGMENTS

Now and again, authors wonder if what they're doing is worthwhile. Will someone, somewhere, like this story? These characters? Will they see what I was trying to do? Did it come out on the page the way it played in my head for months?

One of the first to answer these questions is a publisher. I'm so very grateful that Salem West answered "Yes." A fabulous September chat with her made me feel like she got me, got what I wanted to share, got how I wanted to tell this story. I hadn't felt that "seen" (in a good way) in a long time.

Then I was blessed with Stefani Deoul as an editor. My understanding of what a story is really about and how to wrangle it skyrocketed under her tutelage. Let's hope I can retain what I learned.

My fabulous experience at Bywater Books continued with the gorgeous Ann McMan cover that conveys the flavor of the book at a glance.

And where would any author be without copy editors and all the folks we don't see or interact with directly.

Thank you all!

ABOUT THE AUTHOR

Cathy Pegau grew up in New York State reading horror, science fiction, and fantasy novels, and playing RPGs. Writing seemed like a natural progression, adding a touch of romance to her favorite types of stories. Her science fiction romances have won Romance Writers of America Fantasy, Futuristic, and Paranormal (FF&P) Chapter Best Futuristic Romance and Best of the Best Prism Awards, and a Golden Crown Literary Award for Science Fiction/Fantasy. Cathy lives in Alaska with her spouse and critters, and can often be found counting fish for the state.

Follow Cathy here:
Twitter | @cathypegau
Facebook | www.facebook.com/cathy.pegau/

Bywater
BOOKS

At Bywater, we love good books by and about women,
just like you do. And we're committed to bringing the
best of contemporary literature to an expanding commu-
nity of readers. Our editorial team is dedicated to finding
and developing outstanding writers who create books
you won't want to put down.

For more information about Bywater Books, our authors,
and our titles, please visit our website.

www.bywaterbooks.com